GUARDIAN OF THE GIFTS

GUARDIAN OF THE GIFTS

JOAN RAYMOND

Guardian of the Gifts

ISBN: 978-1-7337915-0-2
eISBN: 978-1-733791519

Cover Design by Cathy Walker
Red Knot Logo by Todd Sturgell

Red Knot Press
P.O. Box 41745
Bakersfield, CA 93384

Created with Vellum

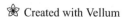

For my daughter, Michelle

1

ALLI

I thought it would be a typical Saturday morning, but I was mistaken. While poking at the last of my scrambled eggs and buttered toast, Cheryl, one of my roommates, strolled into the kitchen.

I nodded to her. "You're up early."

Wearing black polka-dotted leggings and a hot pink crepe top that clashed with her curly, red hair, she leaned on the counter. She twisted a thick curl around her finger and let it spring back against her rosy cheek. "You're looking at a gal who just published her one-thousandth blog post."

I gave a thumbs up. "Congrats. No wonder you're oozing confidence. I'll be sure to read it after I eat." Joining thousands of her other followers, I never missed her body-positive blog, *Fat-n-Sassy*.

Cheryl grabbed the coffee pot and poured herself a cup. "Along with my blog milestone, today is auction day at Uncle Dan's Store-More. I'm anticipating big finds. That is, after more caffeine." She stirred in a tablespoon of sugar, then licked the spoon. "Why don't you come? You might find some hidden treasures."

I looked over at her and feigned a frown. "I'm sorry. I planned to make chocolate chip cookies." Pointing at my phone, "Just found a new recipe online. It promises to be the best recipe ever." Hoping to hide my fib, I made finger quotes for dramatic emphasis. In reality, I didn't want to traipse through a dusty, crowded storage facility with strangers haggling over rickety furniture. Those situations exacerbated my severe panic disorder. Three years ago, I suffered a debilitating attack driving to work as curator of a museum in Balboa Park. After that experience, I couldn't go back. I told everyone I was laid off. I fibbed about that, too.

Scooting a few runny pieces of egg to the edge of my plate, I placed it on the floor next to my yellow and white tabby cat. "Here, Tippy Toes." She meowed, licked the plate clean, then placed her large, furry paw on my thigh. I shook my head and held up empty hands. "No more. You've got your own food." My mom gave Tippy Toes to me for my twentieth birthday. That was nine years ago, about a month before I lost Mom to breast cancer.

Cheryl joined me at the table and touched my hand. "Come on. It's the first weekend of September. You can make cookies anytime. Besides, Darius dreamed that me, you, and Liz found something amazing. And you know him and those dreams."

Though I didn't correct her out loud, my grammatically sensitive brain screamed, *it's you, Liz, and I.* Cheryl's boyfriend Darius worked at Hemp Friends Dispensary and smoked a lot of weed. He also experienced a lot of weird revelations.

Darius lived here, sharing Cheryl's room. Like a big brother to me, he was easy-going and protective. Meeting him for the first time, you notice two things—his big smile and his thick hair. That guy has a lot of hair. More than most. It escapes from his collar, covers his arms, neck, and even his toes. He's a bit weird, but good-weird and he and Cheryl are the sweetest couple.

As I bent over to pick up my plate, I stopped and stared as Liz, our other roommate, trudged into the kitchen. Liz has been my best friend since high school. Almost thirty, nearly six-foot-tall, and still model-thin. She wore a black silk crop top that accentuated her long blond hair along with a pair of skinny jeans embellished with rhinestones on the back pockets. Not her typical Saturday morning attire.

Cheryl jumped up and invited her to join our little auction party.

Liz's response was typical. "Heck, no. I don't want to rummage through other people's crap, much less try to buy it. Besides, I'm busy. I've got plans to meet up with some friends." Liz slapped her back pockets. "Keys. License. Money. Tampax." She marched over to the entry. "Be back later, ladies. Don't wait up." She left, slamming the front door behind her.

Cheryl turned to me and winked. "Well, looks like it's just you and me, Sweetie."

I didn't want to go, but I knew any excuse I came up with wouldn't stop her pestering. "Fine. But only on one condition."

Cheryl's eyes widened. "You name it."

"You don't get to say, 'I told you so' if I find something interesting."

She gave me a toothy grin, meaning she would give me crap if I found anything resembling "interesting."

2

CHERYL

I adore Alli. She cares about everyone—even my quirky boyfriend, Darius. I'll admit he has faults. Like leaving the toilet seat up. Eating Liz's Capt'n Crunch. Drinking milk from the carton. Farting in public. And during baseball season, his life revolves around the Padres. In spite of all those "unique" qualities, he's fun. And furry. And faithful.

Even though Alli hides it, I know about her anxiety. I've seen her hands tremble and heard her taking deep breaths. She comes up with excuses every time I want to do something. Too busy. Too tired. New cookie recipe. That's why I pushed her to come with me to the auction today, even though I knew it would be out of her comfort zone. It's also why I encouraged her to apply at *Framed* after she was laid off from the museum. She was more than qualified, and it was only a few blocks from our apartment. She got the job and has managed the store for a few years now.

Alli's so pretty. Big sea-green eyes and shoulder-length chestnut hair. She never uses makeup and doesn't wear anything flashy or sparkly like me. And she's smart. Has a grad degree. Or, is it two? Better than I ever did. I barely squeaked through high school. I got bored and wanted to start a clothing line for fat girls.

When I turned fifteen, my dad left and nothing mattered. After a while, Mom and I saw a therapist who suggested journaling. It changed my life. I'd thought Dad took off because I was fat. Turned out, he just up and left. Not because of me. Or Mom. Or anything. He was fighting his own demons.

After years of journaling, I started my blog. Writing about my body and my life. People read it and left comments. Then they started following me. It was really cool. People I didn't even know cared about me. And I cared about them. *Fat-n-Sassy*. Describes me perfectly.

A few years ago I realized I didn't hate my dad anymore. In fact, I missed him, so I hired Geoff. He's like a private detective, but not as expensive. Geoff's a friend of a friend. Doing me a favor, because the same crappy thing happened to him as a kid. Geoff understood the anguish. The secret loathing. The questions and curiosity. Then the all-out obsession with finding the truth.

When I told Alli I was looking for my dad, she gave me a big hug. Liz wasn't as supportive. "You don't need to find your effin' deadbeat dad," she said. Except she used more colorful language.

Right now, Liz is not herself. Something's off between her and Zack. They've been dating since I moved in. When they were together, Liz was always happy. But he hasn't been around for a few weeks. At first, I didn't think anything about it. But now, I'm not so sure. I heard her screaming at someone over the phone the other night. Man, it would suck if they broke up.

Alli doesn't have a guy in her life. I'm not sure if she ever has. She's never talked about anyone special. Probably hasn't met the right one yet. With any luck, we'll find something good at the auction. Maybe even a guy for Alli.

3

LIZ

Even though it's only ten o'clock on a Saturday morning, I'm headed to The Tower Bar. To get drunk. Or lucky. Or both. I really don't give a crap anymore. When I went online searching for the best dive bar around, I found it in City Heights. The actual quote from *Yelp* said: "This place smells like pee. I guess if you are into really skeevy bars and want to pick up a disease or two while you are out, this is your scene." I've just been metaphorically pissed on by my boyfriend (actually, ex-boyfriend), so smelling like pee is perfect.

Why is it when life goes well, everything gets mucked up? Zack and I have been dating since… almost three years. I thought we were special. Then he disappeared for a few weeks. Said something about visiting family. But I saw his car parked in different places in San Diego, so what the heck? I couldn't trust him, so I dumped him.

It wasn't the first time I'd been betrayed. The morning after my high school graduation I came home to cop cars lined up and down my street. They kept me outside until I showed my driver's license. Mom was hysterical. She didn't want me to see the blood. But it was hard not to notice when it was everywhere.

Mom said someone broke in and tried to swipe our TV. When Dad confronted the robber, he was shot in the face. The killer ran out the front door and got away. After what seemed like forever, the police arrested Joe Browsner, our stupid neighbor. He and my dad used to watch baseball in the den. His wife brought over chocolate frosted sugar cookies during the holidays. Joe and his wife were even in charge of our Neighborhood Watch. Then he killed my dad over a stupid TV. Browsner, our friendly neighborhood thug. It never made sense.

When Cheryl told me she was searching for her dad I gave her crap. Why put yourself through all that emotional turmoil? We've all lost someone. Cancer. Abandonment. Murder. Cheating. It all sucks.

While I might not show it, I do like Cheryl. But that boyfriend, Sasquatch. He's a hot mess. The hairiest guy I've ever met. I found hair in my cereal the other morning, and I knew it wasn't from Tippy Toes. Between him and the cat, I want to hurl. Fuzz and fur everywhere.

If he'd just remember to close the toilet lid. Falling in that black hole in the middle of the night isn't cool. And lord help us when those two slap uglies. Damn girl, turn up the music or something. No one wants to know what goes on. I'm in the middle bedroom. And to be honest, I'm pretty sure it's him making the noise. At least they could move the bed away from the wall.

Tonight, I should bring home whatever I find at this bar. Then they'd have to listen to me. Zack and I never made noises like them. I guess when you're confident about your body, you're confident about everything.

I wish I hadn't been so negative when Cheryl invited me to that auction thing. I wanted to talk to Alli, though I doubt she'd have understood. In all the years I've known her, she never said anything about a boyfriend. Plus, she's a hugger. I hate hugs. They make me cry. The last thing I wanted to do was cry.

Yesterday, I saw Zack parked down the street. The sun reflected off those neon-green framed sunglasses. With his tall, lanky frame and James Dean haircut, the guy looked spectacular. At least he used to look spectacular. Now, he just looks like a piece of crap. And I'm going to this bar. Coming out with some dude. Smelling like pee. Quite apropos for my life.

I hope Zack followed me here. Then he'll hurt like I'm hurting. *Why do I still love him?*

4

ZACK

I never meant to hurt Liz. I love her more than she'll ever know. She thought I cheated on her. I never cheated. My heart broke the other night when she yelled and cussed me out. Made me sick hearing her so upset. But I couldn't let her know what was going on. At least not yet.

I grew up in the northeast part of Flagstaff, Arizona. Mom said we moved there for her health. Little did I know, it was for her mental, emotional, and physical health. I held no memories of this until a few years ago when I heard Mom crying on the phone. Then flickers of noises and words brought back what I'd forgotten. The slapping. The screaming. The thuds hitting the wall. I remembered hiding in the closet, covering my ears.

I confronted her when she got off the phone. "Mom what happened when I was little. Why are you crying? Who hurt you?"

"Zack, Sweetie, your daddy wasn't very nice. But that's all I can say. Trust me, it's for your own safety. He can't find me. And he can't find you either." She trembled as she hugged me. I heard her crying again after I went to bed.

I waited until she was asleep, then rummaged through her desk. In the bottom drawer, I found a plain brown envelope. Inside was my birth certificate. As I read the details, my heart raced. My birth name showed Zackary Freison, mother Debora Freison, no father listed. Born in Sedona, Arizona, on March 10, 1987.

Tucked at the bottom of the envelope was a torn photograph. My half showed a lady holding a little boy's hand. They were standing at the entrance of the San Diego Zoo. My gut told me something wasn't right.

Four years ago, I told Mom I'd been accepted to Cal State Fresno and moved to California. Though I never explained, I knew she understood. I left with nothing more than my gut feeling, a copy of my birth certificate, and the torn photo. I hired a private detective, and after a year, his search took me to San Diego.

That's when I met Liz. We were sitting at the bar at Bonnie Jean's Soul Food eating LGTB 'sammiches' (lettuce, guacamole, tomatoes, sweet and spicy bacon on sourdough). I noticed her sandwich (and cornflower-blue eyes). We got to talking, discovering we shared more in common than food. Just about everything—music, movies, political views, and spiritual beliefs. She introduced me to her roommates and we all hit it off. Turns out Darius and I were both baseball addicts, although I was more of a Diamondbacks fan.

Everything was smooth. I bought a ring. *Yeah, that ring.* Liz didn't know. I planned on taking her back to Bonnie Jean's on our third anniversary to propose. Then two weeks ago everything changed. The detective located my grand-dad. I began obsessing. *Who was he? What did he look like?*

After work and on weekends I sat in my Firebird, watching a man supposedly related to me. Since he didn't know me, I didn't hide. But once, when he looked my way, our eyes locked. My head got fuzzy, and I felt weird. I don't know how to explain it.

If I'd told Liz, she'd have said I was wasting my time. Until I knew more, I couldn't tell anyone. If the guy was my grand-dad, and Mom was right, I still needed to avoid my dad.

Just when I got the chance to learn more about my past, my future with Liz was in trouble. *If we had any future left fixing.*

5

ALLI

Apparently, storage auctions were popular—more than I'd imagined. By the time Cheryl and I arrived at Uncle Dan's, all the good parking spots were taken. Walking the few blocks under the Magnolia trees didn't bother me, but my chest tightened waiting alongside the crowd of people cramped in the narrow breezeway.

Cheryl must have detected fear in my eyes because she grabbed my hand. "It's easy," she said. "Register. Figure out how much you want to spend. Find a unit that fits your price. Then bid. It's fun."

I wasn't convinced so easily. "What if I make a bad decision? What if I end up with a box of old *Playboy* magazines?"

"What if you end up with a box of old *Playgirl* magazines?" She laughed and snorted. "That wouldn't be a waste."

If only she knew how I felt about doing anything new. I didn't even change toothpaste without months of reading up on the best brands. I gulped down an anxiety pill and wiped the sweat off my forehead.

"Just a few more people ahead of us," said Cheryl. "It should go quick." As we walked into a large lot, she pointed left, then right. "Storage units are on both sides. You'll get an auction list and bid card when we register. Just don't wave your card unless you want to bid."

Reaching the table, we added our names to the list. A ruddy-faced man in an orange vest handed Cheryl bid card 72. I scrunched card 212 in my sweaty hand, along with a map and list of available units. I wanted the day to be over already.

Cheryl looked at me. "Which way we going first?"

With the medicine kicking in, my chest didn't feel so tight. "I'll think I'll head to the left," I said motioning her away. "I should be okay if you want to explore on your own."

"Cool beans. Call me if you run into trouble." Cheryl skipped off toward the east end, muttering something about a unit filled with "awesome books and antique bicycles." While navigating around a couple bickering about money, my gaze focused on an older gentleman standing alone in the shade. Wearing a three-piece grey wool suit and grey hat, he looked different than the other auction-goers.

As I approached, he smiled and nodded. "You appear to be lost."

"Is it that obvious?" I smiled and stood with him in the shade.

He chuckled and patted my shoulder giving me time to study his face. Wrinkled forehead and bushy white brows revealed his age, but his bright blue eyes sparkled with life.

I took in a deep breath. "My first auction. Do you have any advice?"

"Watch for a while, but don't bid right away. You'll get the hang of it." He focused his gaze on my eyes. "But, my most important advice is to follow your heart. When you do that, you'll never go wrong. Now, if you will excuse me." He bowed, tipped his hat, and disappeared into the crowds, leaving me surrounded with the scent of Old Spice.

That was interesting. Focusing back on my map, I headed to unit 1843 and watched an attendant sporting a handlebar mustache. His muscles flexed under his black polo shirt, and he grunted as he struggled with a pair of oversized bolt cutters. After a few attempts, the lock snapped and broke free. He pulled on the squeaky metal door, held it open with a shined boot, then secured it with a metal pin on a chain.

Standing on my tip-toes, I strained to see what was inside. About a dozen dirty boxes, two orange lamps, an exercise bike, a red bean bag chair, and several tan file cabinets. Wondering if I should bid, the gentleman's words, "follow your heart," came back to me. I stopped. And listened. My heart wasn't telling me anything.

Unit 1899 was next. After the mustached man opened it, I wasn't impressed. Bulging garbage bags stacked floor to ceiling. A ripped leather couch and love seat with missing legs. And, nine… ten… no, eleven toaster ovens. I passed on that one too.

Unit 1940. Same scenario. Different attendant. The shaggy-haired guy was more of a kid. He wore an Uncle Dan's shirt and cut the lock with smaller bolt cutters. He held the door open with a well-worn red Converse tennis shoe while he secured it with the metal pin.

Peering inside, I saw one dingy office supply box streaked with water stains and caked with dirt. A few people scanned the unit. Most kept walking. I followed them until my heart tugged at me. As I turned back and stared at the box, I felt a chill. My heart raced. Anxiety mixed with excitement. Another fellow in a black polo shirt monogrammed Lopez Auctions started talking. My stomach turned upside down—a familiar feeling, but never this intense.

"The opening bid is $50.00. Do I hear $50?" The auctioneer chattered in his lyrical voice. I waved my card. "$50. Do I hear $55?" Someone behind me upped the bid. "We have $55. Do I hear $60?" I waved mine again. Every time he called out a price, I bid, and was counter bid, over and over for what seemed like forever, but at the same time, it went so fast I could barely keep up with it all. My stomach churned. My fingers left perspiration marks on my card. Obsessed with the fear of losing, I bid again. And again. And again. My brain questioned, "What am I doing?" while my heart shouted, "Keep bidding."

The man in the black polo smacked his gavel on the table. He looked at me and pointed. "Sold to the highest bidder for $585." *Oh goodness. Did I make the right choice?*

6

CHERYL

Carrying up my second load of auction finds, I leaned against the wooden door frame to catch my breath. While living on the second floor was safer and quieter, lugging crap up the stairs, like groceries and boxes full of books and bicycle parts, made my thighs sweat and break into a rash.

Alli hopped up the stairs between my two loads. She bought one box. Lucky her. I dumped all my finds on the carpet just as her phone rang. Feeding the cat, she let it go to voicemail. I headed down the hall, my bladder was about to burst.

As I came into the front room, Alli motioned for me to come over and listen. She played the message again. A man's deep voice. Heavy smoker.

"This message is for Allison Harper. It's Ronald Garanski, manager of Uncle Dan's Store-More. Call me when you get this message. It's about today's auction."

"Geeze," I said. "Didn't even bother to say please or thank you. Kinda rude."

Alli looked at me with wide eyes.

I shrugged. "I have no idea what it's all about either. But right now,

I've got more important things on my mind." I pointed to my tummy. "Started growling hours ago." I marched into the kitchen and made myself a bologna sandwich (with extra mustard and pickles). Then I grabbed a soda, sat at the table, and ate.

Instead of making lunch, Alli brought out the vacuum. Her box was the saddest, filthiest thing I'd ever seen. I bet she got caught up in the bidding. I knew how easy that was. Once I came home with a bag full of stuffed animals, all missing their heads. Paid over $300 for it, too. Tossed the whole thing in the dumpster at midnight just to avoid Liz's "I told you so" look. Alli said this box "called to her." But paying almost six hundred dollars for a water-damaged carton is an expensive call. I'd have told her to walk away. Guess she has to learn the hard way.

The vacuum whined and sputtered as it sucked off the first three layers of dust and muck. My curiosity stirred, I walked into the living room. "What's in the box?" I asked, lifting a corner.

Alli dropped the vacuum hose on the carpet. "Hold on, I need to make lunch first."

I groaned. "Seriously? You're gonna make me wait?"

She took her time eating that peanut butter and grape jelly sandwich. No one licks each side, then chews each bite twenty-two times. But she did. I counted. The phone rang again while she ate. The same smoker, storage-dude.

"You gonna call that guy back before he has a stroke or something?"

"After I open the box," she muttered between bites.

Finally, it was time for the big reveal, but I needed to pee again. Never failed. Get excited—need to pee. After she made me wait, I made her wait. Figured it was fair. *Right?*

When I came back and sat on the couch, she raised her hands like a conductor. Smiling at me, she opened it like it was Grandma's birthday gift. One flap at a time, heightening the anticipation.

"Just open the stupid thing."

Alli laughed.

I snorted. "You're making me crazy."

Once the flaps were down, she peered in. She looked up at me and pouted. Pulling the items out, one at a time, she laid them on the coffee table. Wire-rimmed glasses missing an earpiece. A black top hat. Part of a broken quill pen. A splintered paintbrush. And a large, hand-stitched, leather journal. *Oh no. Did she make the right choice?*

7

RONALD

D*ammit, why won't that chick call me back?* I stopped pacing long enough to light another cancer stick. *That box belonged to my idiot son, Steven.* I told him to never let them open unit #1940. It'd been safe all these years since his grandpa locked it away. But Steven screwed up again, as usual. That boy don't know nothin'. It was his damned inheritance. He was gonna get it in a few months, on his thirtieth birthday. Now I got to deal with that broad and sweet talk her into giving it back.

The junk inside ain't no good to her anyway. Just a bunch of broken hand-me-downs. Stuff's been in my family too long to count. It was supposed to be mine, but Pop kept it out of my hands long enough so I couldn't claim it. That's why I live in this run-down, roach-infested apartment above the Store-More with Steven. Only way I could keep tabs on that box 'til the idiot was old enough. Then this happened.

I pushed back my glasses, grabbed a beer, and tossed my empty can toward the overflowing trash. *Why can't that kid take out the garbage when he's told?* Stupid and deaf. Only keeping him around long enough so he can claim that box. Then he'll have an accident like his no-good brother and ungrateful mom. Love, honor, and obey, my hiney.

What kind of wife takes one of your kids in the middle of the night? All I demanded was a little respect. Was that too much to ask? Worked my tail off providing for her and the boys. Sure I raised my voice, and my hand, once in a while. Wasn't that how you kept a woman in line? Too bad my other boy suffered. In the end, it simplified my life.

My mind drifted back to hazy memories of a photo Pop kept on the mantle. It was of me and Mama. I stood next to her, dressed in white pants and wooden shoes. Typical getup of our homeland. *I looked like such an idiot.* Other than that image, I don't remember anything else about her.

When I was in junior high, I was in some stupid spelling bee. Pop couldn't make it and, well, Mama was in heaven. All the other kids' parents were there, 'cept mine.

"Where're your folks?" they'd ask.

"Traveling the world," was my knee-jerk reply.

One day I finally came clean. Instead of feeling sorry for me, they mocked me. "Your Mama died 'cause you were a liar."

After school, Pop was waiting on the porch, his arms folded. "Another black eye?"

"But, Pop… They made fun of me."

"No excuse for fighting. We Garanski's don't fight."

"Pop, you don't know…"

"I know you have no self-control. How can I pass on your inheritance when you can't take some teasing. Back in the old country, we had rules…"

I tuned out his ancestor bullcrap and decided to live by my rules—my Golden Rule—"do unto others what they did to me."

Pop stomped his shoe on the wooden porch. "You listening?"

I stared at the ground.

"You leave me no choice." His face reddened; spittle flew out of his mouth. “That box will be locked away until the thirtieth birthday of your first offspring.” Folding his arms across his chest, he said, “It will go to a Garanski who deserves it. One who is kind of heart. Who will keep our family rules and traditions.”

WELL, Pop. See my middle finger? Here’s to your traditions.

Wait, she’s calling. “Hello… Yeah, I called… It’s about that box you bought today… Seems to have been a mix-up… No, not your fault… Look, I need to get this settled. Meet me in my office, tomorrow, Sunday, at two p.m. You know where we’re located. Ask for Ron Garanski. Spell it? G-A-R… Just ask for Ron. Don’t be late. And bring my box.”

Stupid broad. I’ll offer her a deal. Even double what she paid. But, if she balks or crosses me, she’d better watch out. I plan on takin’ what’s mine and do *whatever* it takes to get it back. *She better make the right choice.*

8

RUSSELL

No matter the occasion I start each day with a splash of Old Spice and don a three-piece suit, like Stefan, my Tata. Tata is Polish for father. He was also a Guardian, like most of my family before him. I come from a long line of them. Traced way back long before the 1700s in France. My ancestors immigrated to Austria, then England, back to France in 1850, and settled in Poland around 1935.

After an error in judgment in Germany in the late 30s, my papa Anton left Poland but returned to Germany to meet with Churchill in 1945. After that, he renounced our family business. All the details are recorded in the leather journal the young miss acquired. Once she opens the box, she will have many questions. While I knew choosing her would put her in danger, my heart told me she was the *opikun*, or protector, for now—maybe even forever.

As soon as I spotted the young miss, I knew she was the right one. A pure and caring heart for every creature. A Guardian's heart. She is the only one I could trust to keep the *Gifts*—my family's inheritance—safe. My son Ronald was next in line. I raised him myself, teaching him the ways of the Guardians. But he grew up heartbroken and rejected his heritage. Even though Ronald is my own potomek or descendant, I concealed the *Gifts* in the storage unit until one of his twin sons, Jason or Steven, was of the age of decision.

Many years ago the twins' mom, Jenn, came to my house around midnight. Both boys were asleep in her car. She looked at me through puffy, bruised eyes.

"I can't take it any longer," she sobbed. "I have to leave."

"Is there anything I can do to help?" I asked.

"You must keep one." She wiped her face with a swollen hand. "I cannot take them both."

My heart ached for her and the boys. I walked out to her car, and she handed me Steven, along with his blanket, pillow, and a few toys.

"Be a good boy for Grandpa. I love you." She stroked the top of his head, then gave me a quick hug. I heard her weeping as she jumped in her car. She drove away, leaving us standing on the sidewalk.

Once Ronald found out Jenn took the boy, he scoured the countryside for them. I heard he even hired men to help find them. After a few years, Ronald demanded Steven. Although I tried, the courts wouldn't let me keep my grandson. My soul ached knowing how Ronald took out his anger on the poor boy. Emotional pain goes deeper than physical pain and Ronald knew it. He never said anything kind to him or about him. I heard him threaten the boy if he did anything without permission. As far as I knew, Steven never disobeyed. Except for today. I took my only chance to get the *Gifts* out from under Ronald's control. He must never know Steven helped me.

As long as I have strength, I promise to watch out for the young miss. Getting around at my age is not as easy. Walking with a cane, I tire quickly. No matter, it is my responsibility to look after the opikun. As protector, she must decide if she will find Jason, the rightful heir, or become the next Guardian. Her decision must come soon. Before time runs out for both of them.

I'm sure Ronald's already contacted her. He will be after that box for Steven. Once he gets his hands on it, he will keep it for himself. But for the *opikun's* safety, in fact, for everyone's well-being, she cannot return the *Gifts* to Ronald. While the decision is hers, I must express my concerns before she meets with him. *I hope she will make the right choice.*

9

ALLI

Tippy Toe's throaty meows woke me Sunday morning. I slipped on my glasses. Nine-thirty. I didn't realize I'd slept in so late. "Poor little thing, you sound like you haven't eaten in weeks." I scratched behind each of her fluffy ears, then patted her silky head. "Let's get some breakfast. I'm a bit hungry myself." I pulled my jeans on under my sleep shirt and opened my bedroom door. Cheryl stood in the hall, peeking in Liz's room.

"When did she get home?" I said.

She looked back at me. "She didn't."

"Well, Liz did say not to wait up. Maybe she drank too much and stayed with friends." I checked my phone for messages. Nothing. "I'm sure she'll be home soon. You know Liz."

I fed my cat then made brunch for Cheryl and myself. Nothing like the sweet aroma of sliced bananas fried in butter, sprinkled with cinnamon and topped with maple syrup piled on fluffy pancakes to start the day, or rather mid-morning. By the time I indulged in a second cup of coffee and finished the dishes, it was past noon. Still nothing from Liz.

Cheryl kept glancing at the coffee cup wall clock. It was a roommates' present from last Christmas. Since we all loved coffee, it was the perfect gift to give ourselves. With little wisps of metal-worked steam coming out of the top and swirly second hand, it was an instant hit.

"I'm calling her again," said Cheryl.

I nodded as I walked over to open the slider door of our small, covered patio. I gazed at my miniature rose bushes, taking in their thick fragrance. During panic attacks, I forced myself to sit outside. It helped clear my head. It was also a great place to relax. Like today, when the apartment heated up.

Thanks to my spectacular cooking, it was extra warm inside. I was about to step outside when I did a double take. Glancing out the slider, I noticed someone standing among the golden leaves scattered under the neighbor's Crepe Myrtle tree across the street. I dropped to my knees and made my way over to the couch under our big picture window.

I motioned to Cheryl. "Hey come over here."

"Watcha doing?" She walked over and stood next to me. "Lose something?"

I took a deep breath. "Take a peek across the street and tell me if you see anyone weird."

Cheryl leaned in close to the glass and squinted. "I don't see anyone but that creepy dude who just walked out to his car in boxer shorts." She opened the front door and shouted. "Put on a pair of pants." She looked down at me and frowned. "Geesh, Alli. I think you've had too much caffeine today."

I reached up and grabbed her hand, bringing her nose to nose with me. "Shhhsh. Don't yell at the neighbors." I stood up again, looked out, and pointed. "There, next to that blue car. He's wearing a hat, looking this way. It's that guy I told you about from the auction."

Cheryl stared at me. "The one from the storage place?"

"I told you I felt weird about him. And he's across the street." I peeked through the glass again. "Now I don't see him." I looked at Cheryl. "That was so weird. I'm glad Darius will be here tonight. You know, just in case we need some back-up."

"That dude you described from the storage place was like ninety years old." Cheryl poked me in the ribs. "What's he gonna do—hobble up the stairs, knock on the door, and rob us at cane-point?" She stood and stared out the blinds again. "You're just paranoid. Probably some old guy visiting his grandkids. Halloween isn't for a few months, but you're seeing ghosts early."

I tried to take a deep breath, but my head only became fuzzier. Adrenaline shot through my body. I closed my eyes and begged myself to stay calm. Breathe in. Hold. Breathe out. I didn't want Cheryl to see me in full panic mode. I sat down on the carpet, leaned my head against the wall, and pulled my square, metal pill box from my jeans pocket. My hands trembled as I opened the lid. Picking out an anti-anxiety pill, I popped it in my mouth just as Cheryl looked down at me.

"You okay?" she asked.

I twisted my hair around my finger. "Maybe… I dunno. It's just…" I turned my head as several loud thwacks echoed on the wooden door. Screaming, I hopped up, ran to my room, and locked my door.

10

LIZ

I'm. Never. Drinking. Again. *Damn. My head hurts.* I opened my aching eyelids. *What did I do?*

I remembered arriving at The Tower Bar yesterday sometime before noon. I walked around for a while, then stood outside until they opened. Met a guy. His name was Rex. Or maybe Max? *Whatever.* Reminded me of a dog's name but hella cute. Dark hair with Elton John-type sunglasses. Offered to buy me a Pina Colada once we got inside.

He told me about his trip to Rome. Or was it Paris? He spoke with a British accent; I know that for sure. He said I was better looking than any women from his city and kept calling me "bird," whatever that meant. He rubbed my shoulders as Zack used to, then he played with my hair. I guess I hoped Zack was watching, so I got all cozy with the guy. Rex/Max came on to me and asked me to dance. He kissed me, and I liked it. I liked it a lot. He grabbed my butt. I think I pushed his hands away, but then we did tequila shots, and things got blurry.

I forced my eyes open again and didn't the Rex/Max guy. Though I did see a twenty-something ginger guy with multiple piercings watching TV only wearing fuzzy, purple and green-striped socks.

That was my cue to leave. I'd seen, and probably done, enough.

Now to locate my clothes. My head throbbed as stood. I spotted my jeans and top on the green carpet. Found one shoe. Where's the other one? *Damn.* Those were brand new suede pumps too. Forget it. I needed to get home before I puked. Cell phone still in my back pocket, thank goodness. Brought up my ride-sharing app and scheduled a way home. Glad I decided to leave my car at the apartment. No way was I able to drive, much less remember how to get back from… wherever I was.

I nodded off until the driver told me we were in front of my apartment. My stomach felt like crap as I crawled out of the back seat and stumbled up the sidewalk. I nodded to some old guy standing across the street and staggered over to the stairs. I gave up walking on one shoe and tossed it over the railing, along with whatever was left in my stomach.

That wasn't cool. "Sorry, old guy. Didn't mean for you to see that."

I paused at the front door but couldn't find my keys. *Damn.* I gathered the last of my strength and pounded on the front door.

Did someone just scream?

11

ALLI

I*'m such a wimp. Cheryl's out there all alone dealing with whatever's at the front door.* With a deep breath, I kicked my laundry out of the way and opened my bedroom door. Hand on my cell, I was ready to dial 911.

"Alli," Cheryl waved me over. "A little help."

I peered down the hall and saw her helping a disheveled and limping Liz.

"Hold on," I shouted.

Liz shot me a glance wishing me dead, or worse.

I moved as close as possible, but the sour odor on Liz's clothes forced me to stay just out of her reach and yell-zone. "You okay?" I whispered.

"What do you think?" she snarled. Stumbling into her room, she fell face-down on the bed.

I ran into the bathroom and soaked a washcloth in cold water. I rushed into Liz's room and placed the cloth on the back of her neck taking in the sweet scent of fabric softener. She didn't even flinch. Although she wasn't moving, I assumed she was still alive since she was breathing. I turned the washcloth over and placed the cooler side against her skin.

She moaned, and I rubbed her back. A few minutes later, I picked up the washcloth and leaned in close to her. "I'm going to get it wet again."

When she nodded, I knew it was okay to leave her for a bit. I passed Cheryl's room on the way to the bathroom.

Cheryl got up from her desk and followed me. "Is she okay?"

I shrugged, then nodded.

"Can I get you anything?" she asked.

"How about a few bottles of water?" I wrung out the washcloth and went back to Liz. She was on her back, covering her face with her arm.

"Here, hon put this over your eyes." I laid the washcloth over her face and leaned against her wall. Cheryl peeked in and handed me the waters, a bottle of ibuprofen, and my half-read literary magazine. She flashed me a thumbs-up and closed the door.

I sat on the floor and opened my magazine. This was going to be a long afternoon.

"My head… it's going to explode," groaned Liz.

I got up and helped her sip from the water bottle. "I've got pain-killers too."

She waved me away keeping the cloth over her face. This was not the Liz I knew and loved. She must have really been hurting to torture herself like this. I looked at her as she rested. One arm was bruised. A scrape on the top of her foot looked raw. Dried blood streaked down to her heel.

I decided to sit on her bed, like my mom used to do for me when I was sick. I laid my hand on hers. She held it for a moment, then let it drop back on the bed. We sat in silence until Cheryl tapped on the door.

"Hey, sorry to bother you," she said. "You left your phone in the front room and that Ronald guy called and texted. Again. Hope you don't mind, but I checked. Something about a missed appointment."

"Oh crap, I totally forgot." I glanced at Liz's alarm clock and sighed, three o'clock. "If he calls back, tell him I'll be there in the morning." Cheryl nodded, turned, and walked down the hall.

Liz pulled the towel off her face. Her voice was strained. "What Ronald guy?"

"Oh, it's nothing." I tried to laugh it off. "Some guy at the auction place. They need me to sign some paperwork."

"You should go, I'm fine." Liz attempted to sit but stopped and groaned. "Um, not ready for that yet."

"Just take it easy. I'm not going anywhere."

Liz opened one eye. "Auction stuff? How did that fun trip go?" She rolled the cold water bottle across her forehead. "Find a lot of good stuff?"

"Yeah, I guess. Got a box with a few things in it. No big deal."

"Sounds like it." Liz turned over. Soon I heard steady breathing.

I opened my lit magazine but couldn't concentrate. With Tippy Toes following me, I walked into the front room. I picked up my auction box and carried it to my room. My cat jumped up on my unmade bed and began kneading a pillow. I placed the box on the floor and reached in, taking out each item and laying them on my wrinkled sheet.

Tucking a strand of hair behind my ear, I adjusted my glasses and squinted at the scribbling in the leather journal. *German? Or with the way the z's are written, maybe Polish?* I gave up trying to decipher it and picked up the damaged paintbrush. Running my fingers down the length of it, I observed the split wooden handle and missing sable bristles. Useless to anyone in this condition. The quill pen was in no better shape. The tip was twisted. The hollow ostrich quill, broken in two. Another useless item. *Darn.*

My mood brightened as I examined the wire-rimmed eyeglasses. Although one earpiece was missing, the round lenses were in pristine shape. Upon closer inspection, they seemed familiar. Like I'd seen in pictures or a library reference book. As I set them back on the bed, my attention turned to a piece of torn cloth inside the black silk top hat. I picked it up, holding it close to the crookneck lamp on my nightstand. A label sewn into the inner lining was faded, but I could make out some of the writing: *Lieferjahr 1936. Herrn Reichskanzler A…* The rest was illegible.

Cheryl poked her head in the door. "You say something?"

"Um, no, just reading. What's up?"

"Darius just called. He's stopping to pick up a pizza. You want anything?"

"Just a small chicken salad. Probably nothing for Liz… but just in case, better bring two salads. Italian dressing. Thanks." After Cheryl walked away, I focused back on the top hat. Opening my laptop, I typed "men in top hats" in the search bar. Too many images—everything from Johnny Depp to Mr. Monopoly. That didn't help.

Wait, maybe I could search for the label. I typed in the words, but nothing came up, though it suggested the translate function. I copied and pasted the phrase. That worked. "Delivery year 1936. Lord Chancellor…" Lord Chancellor of what? I kept putting in phrases and got "Lord Stanley Baldwin, Lord Chancellor of Britain…1935 to 1937." I searched for the name but didn't see anything with Lord Stanley wearing a top hat.

I looked at Tippy Toes. "What should I do?" She responded by purring. I flipped through the leather journal but couldn't read any of the words. With my fingers hovering over the keyboard, I paused, hoping for inspiration to strike. After a moment, I typed "Lord Chancellor of Germany, 1936." Images of one man filled the screen.

My heart pounded. I couldn't catch my breath. *This couldn't be.* I scrolled through other pages of images to see if that man ever wore a top hat. *Oh. My. Gosh.* I pointed at the screen. There it was, right in those pictures.

I picked up the silky hat again and scrutinized the label. To obtain a better view, I licked my finger and wiped it across the thin cloth, forcing the words to appear. The images were correct. The Lord Chancellor of Germany in 1936 was Adolph Hitler. *What was I doing with Hitler's top hat?*

12

ALLI

My phone rang again. I ignored it and rolled over. Tippy Toes padded across the bed, kneaded the sheet, then snuggled against the back of my knees. Her purring soothed me back asleep… Until the voice mail chirp. *I've got to remember to turn my phone off at night.* I picked up my phone and squinted at the display. *That Ronald guy.* I'm supposed to meet with him today.

As I sat up, Tippy Toes jumped in my lap. She rubbed her head under my chin. "Yes, I know you're hungry, sweetie. Me, too. Let's go get some breakfast."

As I spooned wet food into Tippy Toes' dish, Liz walked into the kitchen. "Feeling any better?" I asked.

She nodded. "Yeah, thanks. And thanks for… You know…"

I walked behind her and squeezed her shoulder.

Darius sat at the table with a Pop Tart in his hand. He shoved half in his mouth, then chugged the carton of orange juice.

Liz rolled her eyes. "So friggin' gross."

He shrugged and finished the pastry.

Cheryl sliced a banana into her bowl of cereal. "Can someone pass the milk?"

Would someone pass the milk? my grammar brain silently

corrected. I pushed the carton to her as my phone buzzed with an incoming text message. "Hey, Cheryl *would* you run me over to that storage place before work. The guy isn't letting up. Calls. Texts. I wouldn't be surprised if he showed up at the front door."

"I hope not," gasped Cheryl. "He seemed kind of creepy, watching us from across the street."

"What? Where?" I cowered behind my toast. "Why didn't you tell me?"

Cheryl snorted. "The old guy from the other night, remember?"

I relaxed. "I don't think that was Ronald. He sounded different when we talked." I picked up my phone and replayed the message. "Kinda hard to tell with the scratchy voice. I don't think that's the same guy. Do you?"

"Wait," Liz waved her spoon in the air. "I thought the Ronald guy was the one from the storage place. I'm confused."

"You're not the only one." I stood and took my dishes to the sink. I turned and faced Liz. "I met the old guy at the storage place. But when I got home, I started getting messages from Ronald. I have no idea who he is or why he's calling."

"Once we get over to the Store-More," said Cheryl, "I guess we'll find out."

"Oh, how I wish I could be there to solve the big mystery… Not," chided Liz. "I have a room to clean." She got up from the table and wiped her mouth on a napkin. "But please, don't spare any details of your little adventure when you get back."

Cheryl turned to me. "She doesn't give a rip, does she?"

"Not in the least," I said.

"You want some backup?" Cheryl asked as we arrived at the Store-More.

"Naw, he's a nice old man. I'm good. Just drop me off. I'll text you when I'm done. Shouldn't be too long." I wasn't nervous—well, I'm always nervous, but not as bad this time. As I walked through the gate and grasped the office door handle a cold chill passed through my body. *That was weird.* I took a deep breath and walked through the doorway.

"I'm here to see Ron, um Ronald Garanski." I squinted through the smoky haze to the lady behind the counter working a crossword puzzle. Without looking up, she picked up a walkie-talkie and pushed a button with her thumb.

"Ron, some lady at the front desk to see you."

Static, then a harsh voice came through her walkie-talkie. "Be there in five."

The woman pointed to a folding chair with her pen. "You can take a seat or wait outside. Don't matter to me."

"Thank you," I managed to say between coughing. "I'll wait outside." I pushed the door open and filled my lungs with fresh air. *And something familiar. Old Spice?* The same sweet smell I noticed after the older gentleman walked away the day of the auction.

A voice from behind startled me.

"Hey there, sorry to keep you waiting. Was way in the back cleaning out an empty unit."

I turned as he spoke again.

"I'm Ron, nice to meet you…um…"

"Alli… Allison Harper." I peered through my sunglasses. It wasn't the older man I'd seen the other day. This guy was much younger, maybe in his late fifties, and wore glasses. Dark brown hair touched the collar of his pseudo-patriotic shirt—red and white stripes on one side, blue stars on a white background on the other side. It was unbuttoned almost to his navel, revealing an untanned beer belly and a dozen or so salt and pepper chest hairs.

He removed his shabby cowboy hat for a moment and wiped his forehead, then stomped dust from faded cowboy boots. Holding a cigarette in his left hand, he extended his right one. I reached out but jerked back as our fingers touched. It was as if a bolt of electricity passed from his fingers to mine, then through my entire body.

"So sorry, I injured my wrist a few years ago." *I didn't mean to fib, but that was just weird.*

Ron cleared his throat. "You must be wonderin' about my calls. I'm a bit embarrassed. You see my office made a mistake opening that unit you bid on the other day. The items you bought, they belonged to my son, Steven. You see… they were his inheritance. Due to a mix-up, they went to auction."

As I waited for him to continue, his right eye twitched.

"Seems you bought my boy's things by mistake… I, um, he, wants 'em back. Of course, we're willing to make it worth your time."

He must have noticed me staring at his twitchy eye because he pulled a pair of aviator sunglasses from his front pocket and put them on over his regular glasses even though we were standing in the shade.

Ron dropped his half-smoked cigarette on the ground and crushed it with the toe of his boot. "Let's go fill out some paperwork." He opened the main office door and waited for me to enter.

I followed but kept my distance. "I'm not sure I understand, Mr. Garanski."

We walked down a short hallway until he turned and motioned to a chair in a small office. As he sat, he tossed the sunglasses on a stack of papers and thumped his filthy fingers on a manila folder. "I'll pay you twice… that would be about…" He coughed from deep within his chest. "…one thousand, one hundred, seventy. How 'bout I throw in gas money? Let's make it twelve hundred even." He fixed his dark eyes on me, causing the hair on my neck to prickle.

I stared at my trembling hands and took a deep breath. "I… I'm not sure, Mr. Garanski. "I was thinking about keeping a few of the items…"

Ronald slapped the desk. His smile faded. His hands formed tight fists. "Look, Missy, my son wants what's rightfully his." His voice took on a persuasive tone. "I'm offering you a fair deal. More than twice what you paid." He stood, staring down at me. "We'd both be much happier if you'd accept my offer… if you get my drift."

I got up. "I really need to think about this. I have to go…"

Ronald jumped up and blocked the door. As he brought his face close to mine, I felt his foul cigarette breath on my cheek. "If you know what's good for you, you *will* call me back tomorrow morning and tell me you've agreed to my deal." He moved to the side, leaving little room to get past him. "And remember," Ronald hissed, "after that, my offer will drop considerably. Along with my patience."

I rushed out the door. After I passed the gate, I reached for my anxiety medicine. Popping the white pill in my mouth without water, I swallowed hard several times. As I texted Cheryl, the familiar scent of Old Spice drifted with the cool breeze. Turning the corner, I saw him again and screamed.

13

RUSSELL

I stopped walking and leaned on my cane. "I am sorry to have startled you, Miss Alli. I meant no harm."

Her eyes widened. "You're... the man from the auction... You've been following me."

"Yes." I stepped back a bit and removed my hat. "You have just been to see Ronald, am I correct?"

"Who are you?" she asked.

I offered my hand. "Please accept my apologies for my lack of manners. My name is Russell... Russell Garanski. I..."

Alli jerked her hand back. "Garanski? That's the same last name... he just threatened me. Who are you people?"

I watched her eyes and felt she had many questions. I shifted to my other leg, balanced my weight on my cane, then reached for my handkerchief. "It is a bit balmy this afternoon." I wiped my forehead and offered a smile. "Please allow me to put things into perspective. As I said, my name is Russell. Ronald is my son."

She thought for a moment. "Ronald said I bought his son's inheritance by accident. Does that mean Steven's your grandson?"

I folded my handkerchief and tucked it back into my pocket. "Yes.

But, the inheritance truly belongs to my other grandson, Jason, Steven's twin brother."

Alli folded her arms across her chest. "I don't understand. Does it really make a difference? They are twins..."

I smiled again. "That box you won from the auction was put into safekeeping for my heirs over sixty years ago. I could not pass it on to Steven, because of Ronald. That's why it was in storage for Jason."

"This makes no sense." She glared at me, then began tapping her foot. "If it's Jason's, why not give it to him?"

"If it was only that easy." I paused, choosing my words. "Jason is missing. I have not seen him since he was a young lad. He is to inherit the box on his thirtieth birthday, in a few months. I needed to find a new place to hide the *Gifts*, um... I mean items." *The heat must be getting to me to use our word with the opikun, the protector of the Gifts.*

Alli squared her shoulders. "Okay, so you have a bunch of birthday gifts for your missing grandson. And now I have them... because... wait. I have them because..." She pointed her finger at me. "You told me to follow my heart. Now you're following me. And your son is yelling at me..."

I motioned to a small tree, heavy with thick purple blossoms. "May we continue our conversation in the shade of that wisteria?"

She nodded, reached into her bag, and offered me a bottle of water.

"Thank you." I took a sip and continued. "Alli, I have been searching for someone like you for quite a while. Time is running out for Jason."

"Why? Is he dying?"

"I only have a few months to find him. Ronald cannot have the box..." I let out a long sigh. "I wish I could tell you more, but for now, please trust me. The items inside are of the utmost importance to my family. It's better for all of us that you keep..."

"Hitler's hat?" Alli clamped her hand over her mouth. Her eyes filled with tears. "I'm sorry. I did some research."

I paused and studied her. A heart full of compassion and fear. "So you have seen the *Gifts*?"

She wiped her eyes with the back of her hand and nodded. "I've screwed everything up, haven't I?"

I reached out and touched her shoulder. "You have done nothing wrong. I will explain everything. But not here. May we meet later this week?"

She nodded.

I reached into my pocket and pulled out a card and a pen. I scribbled my contact information on the card and handed it to her.

Alli's lip trembled. "Ronald wants everything back by tomorrow." She turned and watched a red Honda pull up to the curb. "My friend is here to pick me up. What should I say if your son calls me again?"

"Avoid him until I explain more." I tipped my hat showing respect, a habit from my Tata father. "Alli, follow your heart. And, call me."

The *opikun* nodded and shook my hand, then scurried to the idling car. I wished she could understand how much her patience and courage would affect our futures.

14

ALLI

I climbed into Cheryl's car, closed my eyes, and rested my head against the back of the cloth seat. A gentle breeze drifted through the window, cooling my sweaty forehead. As Cheryl pulled away from the curb, she pointed to Russell.

"So it was the old guy, after all?" she said. "He seems nice."

My eyes popped open. "No, no," I wailed. "I went to see the other guy. That older one was the man from the auction."

Cheryl tensed her shoulders. "Come again? I don't understand. Wasn't that the one you saw across the street?"

"Yes, *he's* from the auction. But Ronald was the guy who kept calling. He wants the box back for his son, Steven. But Russell wanted me to keep it for his grandson, Jason."

She looked at me. "You realize you're making no sense."

"I was there and I don't even know how to explain it." I took a deep breath. "The storage guy…"

"Ronald?" said Cheryl.

"Yes. Ronald told me to bring back the box tomorrow for his son. Or else."

"Or else what?"

"I don't know. All I know is the older gentleman…"

"Does he have a name?"

"Russell. He encouraged me to stay away from Ronald, until Russell and I could talk again in a few days. Meanwhile, I have the box, and Ronald wants it. Or else."

Cheryl merged into traffic. "You keep saying 'or else.' What's the big deal? Give the guy, Ronald, the box for his kid and be done with it. Unless…" She stared at me as we waited at a red light. "Is there something mysterious hidden in that box? Are we're all involved in some weird cover-up?"

I sighed. "Just because you're a writer doesn't mean there's a story in everything that happens. All I know is I'm supposed to avoid Ronald and call Russell to set up a time to meet." I looked at my phone. "Shoot, it's almost ten. I need to be at work. Do you mind dropping me off?"

"Not a problem," she said, pointing to the sky. "Looks like rain. I suppose you'll want a ride home too?"

"Yes, thanks. As much as I love a good downpour, I don't want to walk home in one tonight." I paused and twisted my hair behind my ear. "You know, this is all your fault."

"Pardon me? Why my fault?"

"If I'd refused to go to the auction with you and just stayed home and made cookies…"

Cheryl snorted. "Nice try, sweetie, but I won't take the blame for all this. By the way, I need to pick up a small picture frame for Darius. I'll come by early, do some shopping, and bring some cookies. We can sort this out while you close up."

CHERYL SHOWED up about five o-clock wearing a black lace camisole covered with a shimmery, crimson-striped cardigan. She stomped her black boots on the welcome mat, leaving a small puddle of water on the floor.

"Loving this weather." She walked up and down each aisle, picked up each frame, and turned them over to read each price tag. I followed close behind straightening up. Seems the more I was stressed, the more the neatness freak in me kicked in.

I tried to focus on something else. "I love your outfit, where did you find the adorable sweater?"

Cheryl ran her hand along the front of her cardigan, brushing off raindrops. "Thanks. Just happened to find the last one in my size yesterday at Chic Boutique, that little shop down the road from us. They have a ton of cute things. You really need to go with me sometime."

I held up a simple black frame. "What about this?"

"How did I miss that?" She inspected it and nodded. "This will go perfectly with Darius' new prized possession—an autographed picture of Tony Gwynn."

"Who?"

She shrugged her shoulders. "Some Hall of Fame guy with the Padres. Just don't ask him about it, or he'll talk stats for hours… Trust me."

I laughed. "Yeah, I remember how Darius and Zack would go on all night challenging each other… I miss Zack. He always made everyone laugh."

"Me too. Darius keeps asking if Liz and Zack are back together. They were best friends, yet Zack hasn't called Darius." Her voice trailed off as thunder rumbled in the distance.

"It's almost time to close, I'd better ring up your purchase." I walked over to the register and completed the transaction, handing Cheryl the receipt. As I went over to the front door to put the "closed" sign in the window, I gasped. "Oh no, it can't be."

Cheryl turned. "What is it?"

"I'm not sure," I said. "But let's get out of here as quick as possible. I think I saw someone I'm supposed to avoid." Lightning flashed, reflecting off the wet parking lot. Thunder rumbled, shaking the front window.

"The mystery continues. Who are you running from?"

"Seriously. I think I just saw Ronald."

Cheryl walked over by the large front window. "It's raining outside, I can't see anyone. You really think he's following you?"

I pointed. "Look, behind your car. See the guy with the cowboy hat smushed on his head?"

Cheryl squinted. "Hon, I think it's just some dude putting groceries in his truck."

My heart pounded. I grabbed my pillbox from my pocket and took another anxiety pill, then walked toward the back room. "Give me a second to make a phone call and close up. We should leave before this storm gets any worse." Taking out Russell's contact information, I called the number. *Darn.* I left a message, asking him to call back as soon as possible. "You about ready?" I shouted to Cheryl.

"Hold on, gotta pee." She headed to the restroom while I dropped the cash bag in the safe and turned off the store lights.

I practiced my deep breathing. The rain hitting the roof reminded me of popcorn cooking in the microwave. Fast and poppy, louder and stronger. Cheryl came from the bathroom, zipping up her pants.

"You couldn't do that in the restroom?"

"You said to hurry."

"Let's just go." I pushed a sequence of six numbers, arming the store alarm. It beeped the thirty-second warning as I locked the heavy door and pulled my jacket over my shoulders. A brisk wind sent wet, muddy leaves swirling around us.

"Hurry and open my car door," I shouted over the thunder. "Rain's dripping off my nose." Lightning flashed again. *Crap, that storm is right on top of us.* As I got in the car, my hair and clothes dripped water on the plaid fabric seat.

Cheryl shoved the key in the ignition and twisted it. "What the…?" She tried again. Nothing happened.

I gripped the dash. "What's wrong? Why won't it start?"

Cheryl removed the key and shoved it back in, twisting it with more force. She looked at the side mirror and then at me with wild eyes. Clenching her teeth, she whispered, "There. Is. Someone. Behind. My. Car." Another flash of lightning. Thunder. Rain pelted the windshield and hood.

I looked in the rear-view mirror and caught the outline of a sizable man pacing behind us. "This doesn't make sense. He said he'd give me until tomorrow." I shivered under my damp jacket. Another flash, then a crack of thunder.

"Might be a dead battery…" Cheryl placed her hand on the handle. "I can—"

"Call a tow truck. You're not getting out of this car with him back there."

Cheryl fumbled for her phone and made a call. "Tow truck'll be here in thirty minutes. We're safe for now."

Safe? This was not my idea of safe. Trapped inside with the windows closed. My fingers tingled. My head became woozy. Struggling to breathe, I hyperventilated. I squeezed my eyes tight.

"Alli, look at me." Cheryl patted my arm. "Hey, it's going to be okay. He's not going to do something in the middle of this parking lot. The tow truck will be here soon." She grabbed my hand. "Hon, it's gonna be okay… Listen, the storm is blowing over. Just rain now." Hearing her soothing voice and pattering rain on the roof helped. I opened my eyes and watched fat drops roll down the windshield.

Cheryl glanced at the side mirror while chewing on her lower lip. "That guy is kinda creepy. He just keeps pacing back and forth."

"I swear there's something up with him. When I shook his hand weird energy shot through my arm. And his eye, it twitched…" As I looked back, Ronald caught my gaze and stared at me.

Cheryl peeked into the review mirror. "Oh no, he's coming this way…"

15

RONALD

I rapped my knuckles on the hood of the fat broad's car as I passed by. "Sounds like a dead battery. Better have that checked ladies. Wouldn't want you to get stuck without a reliable car. Alone. Especially at night."

Watching them freak out was the highlight of my day. *Such wimps.* "Oh no. I'm so afraid." Laughing so hard, I barely made it across the parking lot to my truck. That broad has no idea who she's messing with. And, I'm just getting started.

Gunning the truck engine a few times, I cut across the parking lot, squealing the tires so they wouldn't forget me. *Dumb broads.*

I pulled up in the driveway of Uncle Dan's Store-More just about closing time. *Hope the annoying customers are gone.* I got a sign out front warnin' them the gates automatically lock at 6:55 pm sharp. None of this 'open til seven' crap. I got no time for stragglers.

I manage this place Friday through Tuesday. Ed and Betty Shears take over Wednesdays and Thursdays. They're in their mid-60s and don't bother me none. If they stay outta my way.

Walking upstairs, I opened the door to "home." A small, dark, plain apartment with an old Magnavox tube television set. Only worked if the antenna was bent at a right angle against the shorter wall. Two mismatched lamps in the corner came from one of the storage units, along with the kitchen table and chairs. Doubt the owners even missed them. Never did hang pictures on the walls. Don't have nothing worth showing off. I spotted Steven on the green crushed velvet couch. "You been loungin' all day?"

The springs squeaked as he jumped up. "Got dinner waitin', Pops."

"Still smells like burnt toast and stale coffee from what you called breakfast this morning. Hope you done better with supper." Stupid kid probably got his lack of smarts from his mother. Damned doctors said he was slow in the head. I never believed any of them. What do they know anyway?

"So, what happened, Pops? Did you find her?"

"I not only found her and her fat friend, but I also scared the crap outta 'em." I looked around, then turned to Steven, "Where're my smokes? You know I need my nicotine before dinner."

He pointed to the end table with the wobbly leg. "What happened, Pops? Did you tell her you wanted my stuff?"

Taking a drag, I blew smoke toward the filthy ceiling, "Did somethin' better. Disconnected their battery cable so the car wouldn't start. Then, I paced behind 'em, freaking them out. When I thought they suffered enough, I rapped on their hood and warned 'em to get the battery checked. Stupid broads."

"Yeah, stupid broads," laughed Steven.

"Don't talk like that in front of me." I left a red mark on his cheek to make sure he'd mind his manners.

"Sorry, Pops."

"You'd better be. Where's my food?"

Steven hurried over to the stove and filled two plates with overcooked spaghetti and then covered them with half a jar of store-bought sauce. He rushed back to the counter and brought back a loaf of French bread. We tore off pieces, sopping up the sauce as we ate.

"So, what are you gonna do next, Pops?"

"I got a few things up my sleeve. When I get through with Ms. Harper, she'll have wished she'd taken me up on my offer. She messed with the wrong person." I looked him in the eye. "Now, I won't let up until she begs me to take that box off her pretty little hands."

Steven twisted spaghetti around the end of his fork. "Pops, you think she knows? Maybe that's why she's keeping it."

"Don't think so…" I lit a cigarette and took a long drag, exhaling through my nose. "…Them things are powerful. I aim to get 'em back so me and you will be in control. If she really understood what she got, we'd be screwed. Lucky for us, her skinny roommate, fat-arsed friend, and that scraggy boyfriend won't be of any help to her—if they're around long enough."

"You wouldn't hurt anyone. Would you, Pops?"

"I'll do whatever I want to get that box by the end of the month… What day is it?"

"I dunno, Monday?"

I pointed toward the kitchen with my middle finger. "You too stupid to read a calendar? Pull that greasy hair out of your eyes and look—it's Tuesday, October 16th. We got the next two days off to get a few things done, including going through units before next month's auction. By the way, them roommates is going to some Halloween bash–perfect time to get into their place and take the damn box if Ms. Harper hasn't come to her senses."

Steven's eyes widened. "How'd you find out about the party? They tell you?"

I smirked. "You can find all kinds of stuff by going through people's trash. An invite, plus a few other items that could prove useful in our quest—and guess who found them?"

"Who, Pops?"

"Seriously?" I sneered. "You got mud for brains?"

"Sorry, Pops. You're a genius."

"Quit kissin' my 54-year-old backside and get me some chocolate chip cookies. And a Tallboy while you're at it. Make yourself useful for once." I fidgeted around on the couch to find the remote. "You're going to have to stop being a wimp and be my right-hand man. Once we get that box, the whole world'll be ours. Now get to your chores and let me watch my show. You know how I love my Andy Griffith reruns."

16

ALLI

Ronald's eyes went wild. He stood over me with clenched fists. "Show me where you hid my box."

Pushing against him, I tried to run. "You can't have it."

He blocked the front door.

I pulled my phone from my pocket.

Before I dialed, he snatched it and threw it against the living room wall. Pushing against me with his sweaty body, he pinned me to the wall. "Just show me where it is." His breath reeked of cigarettes.

"Please." My voice cracked. "Leave me alone."

"Give it to me…" Grabbing my arm, he dragged me to my bedroom and pushed me onto the bed. "Or how about we have a little fun first?"

I screamed. *Why can't Cheryl hear me? Where's Liz?* I kicked him in the thigh with my foot, thrusting him back against my dresser. I tried to get up, but my other leg caught in the blanket. "Get out…"

"You don't scare me, you little…" Ronald closed in. He raised his hand.

I grabbed my pillow, bracing for the blow…

A loud meow came from the floor next to my bed. I sat up and ran my fingers through my damp hair. My forehead was clammy. My hands trembled. I put on my glasses and glanced at my alarm clock. *Oh, my gosh. Two thirty-three am. A nightmare. But it was so real. I smelled his breath. I felt his nails digging into my arm.*

I turned on the nightstand light and noticed red scratches on my arm. *Meow.* Glancing over the side of my bed I saw Tippy Toes sprawled on the floor.

"Oh, poor baby. I must have kicked you off. Come back up here." I patted the spot next to me and made a little nest in my blue fleece blanket. Tippy Toes jumped up and sniffed my arm. She kneaded the blanket and purred. Soon, she fell asleep. Now, I was wide awake.

I found my pillbox and swallowed an anti-anxiety pill, then pulled on my flannel robe and made my way into the kitchen. Liz sat at the table holding a can of ginger ale.

She gave a weak wave. "You awake, too?"

I grabbed a banana from the red ceramic bowl on the table. "Bad dream."

"Want to talk about it?"

"Not really… It was terrifying, and… if we start talking about it, I'll never get back to sleep." I peeled the banana and took a small bite. "What about you? Not feeling well?"

"Just kinda bloated and icky. Probably that stupid greasy taco I ate for dinner."

"Anything I can do?"

Liz finished the last of the ginger ale. "Naw, this seems to be working. I'm headed back to bed. Hope you get some rest."

"At least I don't open in the morning. Hopefully, I can catch up on some sleep. 'Nite."

Liz trudged down the hall as I finished my banana. With the medicine kicking in, I headed back to my room. I hoped my relaxed state would be reflected in my dreams.

I HIT the snooze for a second time. Nine-fifteen. My neck ached. Maybe I did wrestle with Ronald. I still couldn't believe how real my dream was. I started dozing… until my phone rang. I grabbed it. Glancing at the caller ID, I gasped. Uncle Dan's Store-More. *Ronald.*

As I dismissed the call, I noticed two unread texts and a voice mail. *Crap.* I got up and headed to the kitchen to feed Tippy Toes. Realizing I was the only one home, I ate a muffin, then got dressed for work. Didn't even take time to brush my teeth. I patted Tippy Toes on the head, then rushed out the door, down the stairs, and didn't stop until I got to *Framed.* This day needed to be over already.

"Mr. Garanski? This is Alli. I really need you to call me. It's six-thirty. You said to call you about the box… Plus, I wanted to tell you about something. It happened a few days ago, with Ronald… I'm… I'm frightened. Please call me back."

"I couldn't help overhearing. Is everything okay?" Liz stood in the doorway to my room.

"Not really." I looked at her and sighed. "I don't know what to do. Ronald scared the crap out of Cheryl and me the other night. I need to talk to Russell, but he hasn't called me back. I've left several messages." I kicked off my shoes and searched for my slippers. *One under the bed… where's the other?*

"Maybe he doesn't pick up his messages every two minutes like Cheryl," chided Liz. "If she doesn't check her social media accounts all the time, she thinks she's missing something important. Technology is great, but for me, once or twice a day is fine. If I was that obsessed, I'd never get anything done."

I nodded as I spied the other slipper in the closet. "She's worse since she hired that investigator, Geoff. She keeps hoping for a message that he found her dad. But, it's been so long."

Liz chewed on a hangnail. "I hope she's not getting her hopes up too much."

"Me too." I walked down the hall toward the kitchen followed by Tippy Toes and Liz. "Are you hungry? Does my baby want dinner?"

Liz rolled her eyes. "What is it about animals? You cat people and that dumb baby-talk. Like she even understands."

I smiled and placed the can of cat food on the counter. Tippy Toes jumped up and sniffed the lid as I stroked her soft, furry neck. "Such a hungry kitty."

"Can we keep our friggin' cat off the counter where the rest of us humans prepare real food? Geeze, I hate seeing cat fur everywhere, especially in the kitchen." She tucked her hair behind her ear, then nudged my cat off the counter with her elbow.

"Fine, we will stay out of your way so you can make your precious human food without extra ingredients..." As I turned, my phone rang. I pulled it out from my jeans pocket and checked the caller ID. "Thank goodness. It's Russell." I walked into my bedroom and closed the door. "Mr. Garanski. I'm so glad you called..."

17

LIZ

S*tupid cat. Stupid cat hair.* If that cat weren't so special to Alli, I'd have left the front door open years ago. "But nooo, you were a gift from Alli's mom." I turned my back on the furry beast, then she friggin' purred.

"Don't go doing that. You might think that purring thing works on Alli. But, not me. I refuse to get attached to you…" She arched her back and purred even louder. *Now I'm petting her silky fur.*

Okay, fine. I do care. About a lot of stuff. I just don't know how to talk about it. Now, I'm talking to a cat—and bawling. "I remember when you were just a kitten. You were so little when Alli got you. She didn't let you out of her sight when her mom passed. She shut everyone out but you. Why am I telling you all this blubbery stuff?"

I waved my hand shooing her away, then grabbed a handful of tissues. Still purring, Tippy Toes followed me to the couch. She jumped up on my lap and nuzzled my hand. "I'm only petting you because there's nobody else to talk to. Fine, keep me company. But when they come out—this never happened. Agreed?" *Dammit.*

After Dad was killed, Mom got me a dog. I didn't want a dog. I wanted Dad. Poor Mom, she didn't know what to do. The dog got out and ran away. Mom probably thought I let it out on purpose. But, I didn't. "Really, I didn't," I said.

Tippy Toes blinked and yawned.

I stared into her eyes. "I feel like crap. And I miss Zack. He always knew when I was sad or needed a hug. He sensed my feelings. Sometimes he'd even say just what I was thinking." I blew my nose and she startled. "Sorry. My mom said I sounded like a foghorn."

As I petted Tippy Toes, she calmed down. "Zack's new girlfriend must be really special. I yelled at him the other night. And just before our anniversary too." *Sigh.*

Tippy Toes snuggled against my arm and closed her eyes.

"Do you think I should try to call him? How about this… flick your tail if you think I should call?" *Nothing.* "Seriously? I poured out my heart and you don't even respond…"

A squeal came from Cheryl's room. Her door opened and hit the wall with a thud. *Crap.* As I jumped up, the cat fell to the floor. Gathering my wadded-up tissues, I shoved them into my pocket.

Cheryl dashed into the front room followed by an out-of-breath Darius. "Glad you're here," she said. "Where's Alli?"

"In her room." I picked cat hair off my pants. "What's going on?"

Cheryl pointed down the hall. "Darius, go get Alli. I have amazing news."

18

CHERYL

Alli rushed into the front room pointing at her phone. "I have great news."

"Wait," I said. "You have to hear mine first. I'm so excited I can barely breathe."

"For goodness sakes," said Liz. "Would someone please share their enchanting news before I pass out from excitement."

I looked at Liz. "You're kidding, right?" She nodded and gave me "the look." That girl knew how to put a damper on a room faster than, well, I don't know. I just knew I was excited and no one was going to take this moment from me. Except… *Damn.* I had to pee. "No one move. I'll be right back."

I heard them mumbling about something as I ran down the hall—which wasn't easy with a full bladder. I didn't even close the door all the way. This was a quick sit and go. I wished my bladder would behave. Just. One. Time.

"Okay, I'm back. Sorry about that." I looked around the room and made sure everyone was there. Darius sat on the couch devouring a bag of chips. Liz rested on the khaki ottoman, sipping on a soda. Alli stood, holding her phone to her chest, shifting from side to side.

I held up my phone. "So, remember I told you I hired the private detective-guy, Geoff…?"

Alli gasped.

"I just got a phone call from him."

Liz rolled her eyes. "Please, don't keep us in suspense."

Ignoring Liz, I looked at everyone else and took a deep breath. "Geoff thinks he might have a lead on my dad, he, I mean Geoff, found evidence of my dad, Richard Wright, living somewhere in Reno, there was a newspaper article about a local resident who rescued some guy in the snow, the rescuer's name and age matched my dad, Geoff's researching further, should get back to me soon, he's almost positive it's my dad…" I exhaled. *Whew.*

"That's awesome, Cheryl," said Alli. "I'm so happy for you." She rushed over and gave me a big hug.

Liz stayed on the ottoman. "Congrats, Cheryl," said Liz. "That's great news. I hope it's what you wanted."

Why can't Liz just be happy for me? My heart raced, but instead of confronting her, I kept my mouth shut. It wasn't worth it.

"What's the next step?" asked Alli.

I walked over to the couch and sat next to Darius. "We wait. And hope we get some positive news."

"Well, I wish you the best," said Liz. "Sorry. I don't mean to be cranky. I'm not feeling well. Just hungry, I guess." She got up and patted me on the shoulder, then headed into the kitchen.

What a shock. Liz never shows any emotion.

"Wait," said Alli. "You haven't the news about my phone call."

"What phone call?"

"Oh, that's right," she said. "You weren't in the room. Russell Garanski finally called me back.

"That the old guy or the mean guy?" asked Darius.

"The older man," said Alli. "He said his phone was on silent and didn't know I'd called. We talked about everything—the disconnected battery and harassing calls and texts. I'm meeting him tomorrow before work. Maybe I'll finally get some answers."

19

ALLI

When I came into the kitchen the next morning, I found Liz making breakfast. She even offered to drop me off at the coffee shop for my meeting with Russell. Maybe it was her way of apologizing for her crappy attitude last night.

LIZ PULLED up in front of Starbucks. "You need me to stick around?"

"I'm good. Thanks for the ride." I cinched my sweater around my waist as I stepped out of her car. A scattering of crimson leaves swirled around my feet. Octobers in San Diego. Not too warm. Not too cool.

Russell and I had agreed to meet at the Starbucks on Washington Street in the Hillcrest area. My shop, *Framed*, was just down the road off Washington, within walking distance. I checked my phone—eight o'clock. Since I didn't need to be at work until ten, I'd have more than enough time.

The Starbucks occupied the bottom floor of a whimsical, two-story building with large stones on the pillars and façade outside. The chocolatey scent of espresso enveloped me as I walked through the door. I drew in a deep breath and glanced around. Customers crowded around tables were absorbed in books and laptops, or engaged in indistinct conversations. I spotted Russell in the far corner and nodded to him.

A thin barista with spiked aqua hair smiled as I walked up. "'Morning. What can I get you?"

"Grande Vanilla Bean Frappuccino and one of those, please." I pointed to a giant muffin with enormous blueberries and coarse sugar sprinkles. After picking up my order, I wove my way around customers holding coffee and pastries until I reached the back of the room. Russell stood and pulled a chair out for me. Wearing a dark gray suit, light pink shirt, and a matching tie, he removed his steel-gray hat with the perfect crease on top. After I was seated, he sat down across from me and placed his hat on the table. In the bright morning sunlight, I noticed deep creases in his forehead. His hands appeared frail as he gripped a ceramic mug of steaming black coffee.

Russell watched as I stirred my coffee. He took a deep breath, then exhaled. "I'm sorry Ronald frightened you and your friend."

I considered his gentle eyes and sensed he was hiding much pain. While I wanted to respond to his apology, I couldn't help blurting out my questions. "Mr. Garanski, I need to know about the items in the box —the top hat, the little round wire glasses—and especially the leather book. I tried to read it, but nothing made sense. Did that hat really belong to Hitler?" I took in a quick breath. "And why is Ronald hunting me down and harassing me?"

Russell's eyes widened. "Very astute questions. May I start at the top and work through them?"

I nodded, running my trembling finger along the rim of my coffee mug. One barista ground beans. Another called out "Jack." I sipped my scorching-hot coffee and reminded myself to stop talking so much. My gaze shifted for just a moment to a dark-haired guy in a suit picking up his order. *Must be Jack.* He passed by our table and smiled at me.

Russell leaned in close.

I took in the familiar scent of Old Spice and refocused.

He spoke in a hushed tone. "The items—the hat, paintbrush, glasses, and rest of what you acquired from the storage auction are known as *Gifts*. The well-worn, leather journal is their history. A record of who received them, written in the languages of the past Guardians from Austria, Italy, and Poland."

Russell paused for a moment and glanced around before focusing back on me. "Perhaps you might find this information hard to grasp. And, most certainly you might believe I'm just a crazy old man, but you need to know the truth. I am one of the Guardians—a Guardian of the *Gifts*. Since history has been written, men and women have been given gifts. You might recognize them as talents."

I nodded.

"Mozart was a brilliant musician. Picasso, a prolific painter. Churchill, a superb negotiator. Austen was a talented writer. And so on. Each of them was given a tangible *Gift* by one of the Guardians. Some used those *Gifts* to make the world a better place, and others, well, they made it hell on earth."

His eyes softened and filled with an inner glow. Listening to him speak, my stomach began to flutter. But, instead of anxiety, I was filled with curiosity.

"Since you mentioned the top hat, let's talk about that. Guardians gave that hat to individuals displaying a great deal of oratory talent. When Mark Twain visited London in 1897 my grandpapa, Stefan, gave the hat to him. Then, before Twain left Europe Grandpapa acquired the hat back so it would be available to the next Guardian, my papa, Anton.

"When Anton became of age, he acquired the *Gifts* to bestow them on specific individuals. During the 1930s, Anton watched a brilliant young man give speeches in Germany. Anton believed the speech-giver should receive the top hat. That man was Adolf Hitler. Although Hitler was a great orator, the influences from his evil heart transformed into an evil hatred. Hitler almost destroyed all of Europe, not to mention the six million Jews he exterminated. When Hitler invaded Poland in 1939, many of my own family were killed, including my grandpapa, Stefan."

I dropped my spoon. "Wait. Are you saying that your father Anton caused the death of your grandfather Stefan?"

"Yes, that is correct." Russell paused tracing his finger along the crease of his hat. "Not all of his choices were as tragic. Anton was also responsible for giving the glasses to different individuals throughout history. Although worn by many, one man, who preferred peace and love received them after his fast in Bombay. Mahatma Gandhi. I'm sure you've heard of him."

I nodded.

Russell paused, then continued. "I shudder when I think of mistakes my papa made, but he did not know until it was too late. After careful planning and some sleight of hand, Papa procured the top hat back from Hitler and managed to give it to another man, Winston Churchill in 1940. Churchill turned out to be extraordinary, but Papa couldn't forgive himself. After years of soul-searching, he presented the *Gifts* to me, making me the next Guardian. Haunted by his mistakes, I sealed them in a cardboard box, then secured them in the storage unit at the Store-More until one of my heirs was old enough. Before Papa died, he said errors like that could never happen again. He passed away, leaving me to find a new *opikun*, or protector of the *Gifts*."

I stared at Russell trying to make sense of his story. I wanted to respond, but it was too much to absorb on just one cup of coffee. I looked around the coffee shop, focusing on a reprint of van Gogh's Starry Night. The picture jarred my memory.

"You know," I said. "A week ago my roommates and I went to Balboa Park. At the Museum of Art, we viewed paintings by different artists. During our tour, I noticed how certain paintings evoked happy memories in me, while other paintings caused terrible, sad, even depressing memories. By the end of the morning, I was emotionally drained. And confused. As many times as I'd been to that museum, I'd never noticed anything like that before. Does that make any sense to you?"

Russell looked at me and smiled. "In one artist's hand, the paintbrush brought joy and tranquility, while another artist invoked sorrow and fear. That paintbrush, which is in your box, manifested feelings from the artist's heart. Because you are the *opikun*, or protector, you will experience intense emotions when you come across items created by those using the *Gifts*.

"Maybe now you understand I speak the truth." Russell paused, as a customer walked near our table. "If you trace the history of the paintbrush, you will see who used it and why their art made you feel joyful or sad. Each of the *Gifts* intensified the love or hatred within the one who held or wore it." He let out a long sigh. "Do you understand why Ronald wants them? And why he must never have them? He knows the Guardian controls the fate of everyone they encounter."

"But Mr. Garanski. I can't. I don't know how… This 'oh-pee-kin' that you talk about, I'm not them… or her. I'm not anyone special. I've got stuff I deal with… I…" The flutter in my stomach twisted into fear. I reached inside my pocket for my anxiety medication.

Russell placed his warm hand on my arm, and though my chest was tight, my stomach settled. "But, my dear sweet child, you are already a Guardian. Not by heredity. Not by coincidence. But by fate. As Guardian, I chose not to use the *Gifts*, or give them to Ronald. I left them in storage until I located my grandson, Jason. Ronald eyed them for over twenty years. He almost got them when the storage unit was opened the other day. Didn't you ever question who was bidding against you that day?"

"I… I vaguely remember someone else bidding. But then they stopped and I won the auction. If it was Ronald, why didn't he just take them or outbid me?" I stirred my coffee, staring at the swirling liquid as I picked bits of sugar from my muffin.

"Fate intervened when your heart told you to bid. You didn't stop or back down. Because of your inner strength, you received the box. For now, the *Gifts* are safe."

How could he know about my inner strength? My anxiety... I'm weak. I can't do anything. If he really was a Guardian why doesn't he know about my fear?

"You are stronger than you know," he whispered.

I pushed back my chair back. "Now you read minds, too?"

"Though I cannot read your mind, I sense your fear. I also sense your love. And how much you care about others. Please, don't leave." Russell opened his jacket, pulled out a frayed handkerchief, and unfolded it on the small table. His fingers traced over the initial G. "This was given to me by my papa before he passed. It was hand sewn by my grandmama representing our last name Garanski."

I ran my finger over the embroidered initial. "I think it means Guardian."

Russell smiled. "You might be correct. When I'm in doubt, I hold this. In memory of all the Guardians who came before me. We didn't start out strong. But, in time we realized we each possessed more within us than ever thought possible." He pressed the handkerchief in my hand. "Alli, please take this. It will help you find your strength."

I held the thin, linen square and caressed the embroidered monogram. My eyes prickled. My breath caught. Grinders whined. Timers buzzed. Conversations faded in and out around us. My head became fuzzy. "It's getting warm in here." I jumped up. "I need some air."

Russell stood next to me. "Let's go outside and sit," he said as he put on his hat. Then he picked up my coffee and muffin and led the way out of the coffee shop.

I grasped onto each chair as we made our way through the room. The door opened. *Air.* I took in a deep breath.

"Here?" he pointed to a table outside.

I took a seat.

Russell placed my coffee and muffin in front of me. "Will you indulge me a few more minutes?"

I forced a smile and nodded.

Russell placed his warm hand on mine. "Before you leave, I need to explain one last thing about the *Gifts*. As *opikun*, you have three options…"

I looked at him. "Three options?"

"The *Gifts* belong to you." He cleared his throat. "Your first option is to keep them. And I prepare you to be the next Guardian."

I rubbed my forehead. "Lovely. My next option…?"

"Second, we find my grandson, Jason, birthright heir of the *Gifts*, and ask him to take your place."

I leaned my head back and closed my eyes. "Piece of cake. And third…"

Russell's voice took on a lower pitch. "While I don't recommend this last option, I must advise you all your choices…"

I sat up and stared at his frail hands.

"Return the *Gifts* to Ronald. Then, you will never have to deal with any of this ever again."

I rubbed the monogrammed handkerchief between my fingers and looked at him. "When do you need my decision?"

He blinked several times and shifted in his seat. "While I know this must not be easy for you. I must know your answer this morning. Before we leave."

20

RUSSELL

Alli's eyes widened as we sat outside Starbucks. "Mr. Garanski, I could never give the *Gifts* back to Ronald—especially after what you've told me about them." She turned and watched the cars waiting to turn left from Falcon Street onto Washington. "I love those trees in the middle of the boulevard, don't you? This area is just so quaint."

"Very quaint, indeed," I said, smiling.

She took a deep breath and turned back to me. "I'll keep the *Gifts* safe from Ronald. And help you get in touch with Jason. Where does he live?"

"I don't know," I said. "It's complicated. Do you remember the story of how his mother left Ronald?"

"Yes, but…"

"Jason was five. Almost twenty-five years have passed…"

"Okay, wait." Alli held up her hand. "You're saying I can give the *Gifts* to Jason? Who might be anywhere? And even *you*, of all people, have no idea where he is?"

I rubbed my forehead and tried not to clench my jaw. "There's probably another thing I need to mention…"

"There's more?" She raised her voice. "Please, don't spare any details."

"For Jason to become a Guardian through inheritance, he must receive the *Gifts* before his thirtieth birthday. Stipulated by the Guardian's Covenant centuries ago '…once an heir has passed the eve of the third decade after their birth, they forgo any birthright and the *Gifts* advance to the next of kin…' which means…"

"Finding him will be next to impossible. And, if we don't, I'll be stuck with those things. Right?"

I nodded.

"And let me guess, his birthday is at the end of October…" She paused and glared at me. "Which will give us about two weeks?"

"Actually, we have a bit more time." I cleared my throat. "Until the end of the year. About two and a half months…"

"Oh, well then. Let me just finish my coffee and muffin, and we'll get right on it." She closed her eyes. Tears ran down her cheeks. She wiped them with the back of her hand, opened her eyes, and looked at me. "I'm sorry. I'm not used to owning weird, ancient world-changing artifacts. Or having a large, irate man follow me around and threaten me. And, last I checked, I haven't been given a short deadline to find a missing person who will make it all better. I thought talking to you would clear everything up."

"I understand…"

"In reality, Mr. Garanski, I don't think you do. You see, I never take chances." She raised her hands above the table. "Look at me. I'm trembling and it's not because I'm cold. I've kept my hands in my lap to hide how terrified I am. I keep anxiety medication with me always, because… because I can't handle things. Not just weird stuff like this, but everyday life. Now, for some unknown reason, I'm pouring out my heart to you. I haven't even told Liz or Cheryl about any of this." Alli buried her head in her trembling hands and wept.

My heart ached for the *opikun*. I placed my hand on her head. "You might not think I understand, but I do. In more ways than you know."

She lifted her head and looked at me through red, swollen eyes. "What do you mean?"

"My son, Ronald, hates me. After an incident when Steven was about five, Ronald made it clear that I was to *never* cross him again. Knowing he would do everything in his power to obtain the *Gifts* for

Steven in the next few months, I was tasked with finding another *opikun*, at least until Jason was found. Ronald is a dangerous and shrewd man. I pushed through great fear and risked my life to keep the *Gifts* safe."

Alli pulled out the monogrammed handkerchief and held it.

"I'm sorry to put so much on you. But, I know in my heart you are the right person to be the protector of the *Gifts*." I glanced at my pocket watch. "Look at the time. You'll need to leave soon."

"Mr. Garanski, I'm not as courageous as you think I am." She wrapped her uneaten muffin in a napkin. "Until we find Jason, what should I do with the *Gifts*?"

"The *Gifts* are yours to use in whatever way you see fit. Just a word of caution, if you do use them, be careful."

Alli's eyes twinkled. "My roommate Cheryl hired a guy to help her find her missing dad. Maybe he can help us find Jason."

"I'll gather some information and be in touch."

Alli stood, offering her hand. "I look forward to your call."

Standing, I shook her hand, then tipped my hat. I took in a deep breath as I watched the *opikun* hurry down the wisteria-lined sidewalk. *I hope this ends well for all of us.*

21

ALLI

I was *so* ready for this day to be over. Not only did I drop, and shatter, a whole case of glass picture frames, I left my sweater in the shop. When I unlocked the front door again, I forgot to disarm the alarm. The shrill blasts about broke my eardrums. The owner received the alert on his phone about a possible break-in. After he arrived at the shop, he didn't waste any time telling me (multiple times) how I'd inconvenienced his evening. After apologizing and explaining to the police, I locked up, re-armed the alarm, and left. Thank goodness, it was Friday.

As I walked home, I passed rows of dogwood trees. Although the blooms had faded, the ruddy-colored branches were covered with leaves changing into multiple shades of pink. I plucked one off a low-hanging branch and crossed the street to my washed-out apartment complex. Trudging up the concrete stairs, my footsteps echoed against the narrow hall.

I arrived back at the apartment and took in the spicy aromas of hot dogs and jalapeño cheese. "Someone made dinner," I said, forcing a smile.

Nestled in a dark blue fleece blanket, Cheryl sat on the couch holding her favorite oversized mug. She licked the back of a large serving spoon while watching some old comedy show on TV and motioned toward the stove. “Saved a ton of zesty mac and cheese for ya. Made it with little cut-up wienies. You gotta try it.”

Liz sat at the kitchen table, spearing macaroni with a fork. She stopped in mid-stab and looked up. “How was your meeting with the old dude?”

“You mean Mr. Garanski?” I asked. “It was interesting, Liz. I learned a lot.” *Man, did I learn a lot.* I decided to risk Cheryl’s concoction and filled a bowl with gooey yellow pasta. Scraping the sides for hot dog bits hidden in the sauce, I grabbed a soda and pulled out a chair, joining Liz as Tippy Toes wound herself around my legs. “Russell explained a bit about the stuff I bought, and we talked about how I might get it back to his other grandson, Jason.” *Just enough information to satisfy her curiosity.*

Cheryl unwrapped herself from the blanket. “Sooo, tell us about the stuff and the Jason dude. Is he a douche like his father?” She slid her bowl onto the coffee table, then grabbed a handful of mini-candy bars from a bag tucked next to her on the sofa.

I snapped my fingers. “Hey, those are for the Halloween party.”

“Oh yeah? Do *you* really expect *me* to ignore these babies for the next ten days? Can’t be done. Not by you. Not by Liz. And, especially not by me. I’ll buy more before your party.” As she tore the wrapper, her piece of candy dropped on the floor. Bending over, she picked it up and pushed it in her mouth, smacking her lips loud enough for the neighbors to hear. “Mmmmmmmm.”

Liz rolled her eyes. “You are so gross. I’d never eat anything off this floor. Cat hair…”

“The wrapper was still on when it landed,” said Cheryl. “Lighten up.” She grinned at Liz, then dropped another piece on the floor for dramatic effect “So, did Garanski tell you why his freako son harassed us the other day?”

“Ronald wanted me to cave and return the antiques to him and his son, Steven,” I said. “Russell said he has anger issues.”

“Not surprised,” said Cheryl. She grabbed a handful of candy bars from the bag.

“The items I won in the auction belonged to Ronald’s other son,

Jason. We just need to find him first." I swirled my spoon around the bowl then glanced at Cheryl. "When you get a chance, I'd appreciate the name of your investigator person."

Cheryl jumped up. An assortment of candy wrappers fell from her lap. "Wow, a real-life mystery. A missing person and a bunch of family heirlooms… Maybe I can help, too."

I stared at the wrappers scattered on the floor, then at her. "Thanks. But, no. Giving me the name of your investigator will help more than you know." My chest tightened. I took a deep breath. "I know it's early, but it's been a long day. I'm going to turn in and start my new book. Come on, Tippy Toes. Time for bed."

My cat and I headed down the hall to solitude. I shut the door, then made a nest in my blanket for her. She settled in and closed her eyes. I opened my closet and removed a brown canvas storage box from the top shelf—my new hiding place for the *Gifts*.

Since I hadn't looked at them for a few weeks, it was almost like seeing them again for the first time. As I took out each item and placed them next to Tippy Toes, I wondered… What power did the quill hold? Running my finger along the broken nib, I felt the sharpened point and noticed ink stains along the edges. The quill appeared to be an ostrich feather—white, translucent, and spindly. Did Jane Austen really use this when she wrote *Pride and Prejudice*? It was difficult to imagine.

The top hat. I inspected the silky brim and held it up to my head. Would I be able to speak more eloquently if I wore it? *Not likely.* I placed it on my bed next to the feather.

Those glasses… Gandhi's? The perfect round glass lenses inside thin frames. Delicate and so beautiful. If I were to wear them would I see what someone was thinking? Or feeling?

No one was in the room but Tippy Toes. My anxiety surrendered to my curiosity. *Russell did say I could use them…if I was careful.* I slipped off my glasses and laid them next to my purring cat. Unfolding the fragile wire earpiece, I held them in front of my face, then slid the unbroken side over my ear. I squeezed my eyelids together and waited. I opened one eye, then the other. No lightning. Or thunder. I didn't feel different.

I jumped at a knock at my door. Liz popped in holding a piece of paper. "Hey, saw your light on. Cheryl wanted me to give you this before she forgot. Said something about the info you needed..."

Oh man, what just happened? As I stared at Liz, I read her thoughts... "It's a long shot. You're wasting your time..." *What?* I felt her nervousness. *She's been hiding the truth... Oh crap.*

Liz broke my concentration. "You okay? Your face is pale. Your forehead's all sweaty. Need some water or something?"

I gasped. "Yeah. I mean no. I mean... I'm okay. Don't need water." I tore off the round-rimmed glasses and flung them back in the bin. Everything was blurry. I couldn't shake the sensations of what I experienced. I felt strong and yet, weak at the same time. My heart raced. Everything moved in slow motion. I shuddered as Liz's thoughts mixed with mine.

"You sure you're okay? When I first came in you were fine... then you went all bizarro." She came over and stood next to me patting my shoulder. "I was only giving you Cheryl's message. It's not like I said the Ronald dude was at the front door."

I wiped my eyes and put on my own glasses. Everything appeared normal, or it resembled normal. My chest stopped pounding. My hands stopped trembling. "Sorry. That was kinda eerie. When you came in it was like I knew everything about you. Your feelings. Your thoughts... I knew... everything."

Liz scooted Tippy Toes out of the way and sat down. "What are you talking about? How would you know what I'm thinking? You can't read thoughts."

I stared at Liz and took a deep breath. "I'm not kidding. I felt fine, then when I saw you, I felt strange, and I... I knew..."

She peered in the bin. "Love your new glasses, very vintage-like."

The glasses? Thinking back to before Liz walked in. *I put on the glasses, and saw...* "Liz, something weird just happened. I need to ask you something."

Her eyes widened.

"We've been friends for a long time. I know you try to keep stuff to yourself. But..." *She's gonna hate me for this.* "Are you... pregnant?"

22

LIZ

I jumped up from Alli's bed. "What the heck did you just say?"

"Are you pregnant?"

I shoved my hands into my pockets and looked at the laundry-strewn floor. "How did you find out?" I glared at Alli. "No one was supposed to know."

"Liz, it doesn't matter how I found out. Can we please talk about it?"

I looked away again. For the first time since my father's murder, my throat tightened. *Don't cry.* I dug my fingernails into the palms of my hands. *Damn.* Ugly crying. No matter how hard I tried to think about something else, I couldn't stop. *Double damn. And now she's hugging me.*

"Oh, no," I said between sniffles. "I got snot on your shoulder."

Alli pressed a handful of tissues in my hand.

I stepped back and blew my nose, making an impressive foghorn sound. I laughed despite my bawling.

Alli wiped my cheek with a tissue. "You want to talk about it?"

"You mean my *it*?" I said, pointing to my belly.

Alli nodded. "What did Zack say?"

"He doesn't know." I sighed. "It might not be his. We broke up over a month ago. I was with… someone else since then."

"What do you mean?" Alli pulled a pillow off her bed and sat cross-legged on the floor.

"Remember that night I came home messed up?" I kicked clothes out of the way and sat next to her. "I was pissed at Zack and went to a bar. I picked up a guy. Or, rather he picked me up. His name was… Rex or was it Max? We were so drunk. He was a great kisser. And we hooked up in his car."

"Seriously?" she said. "That doesn't sound like you."

"Tell me about it. The next morning, I woke up in a strange bed with no memory of what had happened."

Alli's eyes widened.

I blew my nose again. "How could I be so stupid?"

"You weren't stupid. You were upset." She placed her hand on my leg. "When did you figure out you were, you know…?"

"Pregnant?" I grabbed another pillow and held it against my chest. "Remember that night you came into the kitchen after your bad dream and saw me drinking a soda?"

Alli nodded.

"I'd been feeling queasy for a while. The next day I bought a pregnancy test. I took it before everyone got home. It was positive. I thought I buried the tester thingie, along with my secret, in the trash."

Alli picked at a hangnail then looked at me. "When was the last time you were with Zack? It could be his, right?"

"About six weeks ago. That party was a month ago. It could be Zack's. Or Max's. It doesn't make a difference; I'm getting rid of *it* anyway." I clenched my jaw. "I have no business having a kid, especially when I slept with a bunch of guys. And, the only one I knew was a lying, cheating sonofagun."

"You know I'll support whatever decision you make." She let out a long sigh. "You going to tell Cheryl?"

I unclenched my jaw and took a deep breath. "I suppose. Maybe. I know she'll be okay with my decision. I just don't want to keep telling everyone about my get-back-at-Zack night." I tried to get up but had no feeling in my foot or ankle. I pointed to my foot. "Don't you just hate the pins and needles feeling when it wakes back up?" I winced as moved my toes.

Alli stood and nodded while scratching Tippy Toes behind her ear. "You going to be okay? About the baby-thing?"

While gripping the bed, I tapped my foot on the floor and attempted to stand again. "I'll sleep better tonight knowing I'm not dealing with this all by myself. Thanks for listening… and everything."

"That's what friends are for." Alli reached for my hand to help steady me.

As much as I wanted another hug, I avoided making eye contact. I scooted around her and headed to my room. *Stupid hormones*.

23

ALLI

Russell called me back first thing Saturday morning with what little information he knew about Jason. It wasn't much to go on since Jason's mom disappeared with him almost twenty-five years ago. All Russell knew was Jason's birthday and mother's name—Jennifer Garanski. I hoped the last name was unique enough to speed things up. I called Geoff and explained the dwindling time frame. While he encouraged me to stay positive, he had no idea how hard it was for someone like me.

In spite of all I'd been dealing with the last few days, I woke up in a good mood on Sunday. I jumped out of bed, dressed, then bounded into the kitchen to make myself a bowl of granola. I was determined to enjoy this day no matter what came my way. I glanced down at the cat asleep in my lap. "Such a good kitty. Yes, you are."

"Talking to the cat again?" Liz walked into the kitchen, poured herself a cup of coffee, then joined me at the table.

"You supposed to be drinking that? I mean, because… you know…"

She raised an eyebrow. "Thanks, Mom, for caring. I'm fine."

Cheryl's voice echoed down the hallway. "Hey everyone, guess what?"

"Here we go again." Liz rolled her eyes. "Be still my heart."

Cheryl rushed into the front room waving her phone at us. "I just got a call from Geoff. He found him."

My chest tightened. "Him?" *My him?* "He found Jason, already?"

"Just a second," said Cheryl. "Waiting for Darius to get his pants on." She turned and shouted, "Hurry up dude, you're gonna miss the big news."

Liz rubbed her forehead. "Now the whole neighborhood knows you have news." She stared at Darius as he wandered into the kitchen. "Thanks for sparing us any unsightly hair."

"No problem, Lizzy." Darius opened the pantry, took out a box of cinnamon toaster pastries, then tore open a pouch.

"Okay," said Cheryl. "We're all here. Geoff called…"

Liz rolled her eyes. "We got that part already."

"He found Jason?" I said.

"No." Cheryl sprinting over to Darius. "Geoff contacted my dad." She jumped up and down, then squeezed Darius until he grunted. "I finally get to see him."

"Awesome. Going back to bed." Liz motioned a high five on her way down the hall.

I ignored Liz then turned to Cheryl and clapped. "Wow, Cheryl. That's great. I'm so happy for you." I jumped up and joined them in a group hug. "When are you going to see him?"

Cheryl grabbed my arm. "We're leaving Wednesday and meeting Dad in Sacramento. He lives in Reno but figured it would be easier to meet in Sacto since they're expecting snow over Donner Pass. We were going to wait until after the Halloween party, but… I hope you don't mind. I'm too excited."

"Don't worry about it. Liz and I will still go. Sounds like he's also looking forward to seeing you."

Cheryl grinned. "He is. I found out he'd been searching for me. Kinda an ESP thing I guess. Isn't that cool?"

I hugged Cheryl again. "I'm really happy for you. Hopefully, Geoff will call me any day with news."

"He said he'd call as soon as—" A loud crash interrupted Cheryl. "What the?"

I ducked behind the kitchen wall.

Darius rushed into the next room. “Oh, crap,” he said.

I peeked around the corner and gasped. Light from our lamp reflected off countless shards of clear glass covering the rug. My eyes scanned the floor, pausing on a grimy, red brick laying in the middle of the living room.

24

CHERYL

I rushed out of my bedroom and down the hall waving my phone. "I just got a call from Geoff. He found him." Alli thought Geoff located Jason while Liz complained. I didn't care. Geoff found my dad and I was going to see him—this week. I was so excited I could barely stand it.

"What the?" A brick just crashed through our front window. "Darius…" My voice cracked. He bolted into the front room, then out the front door. Several sets of footsteps echoed off the walls.

Alli peeked around the kitchen wall.

"Are you okay?" I said.

"I think so." Her eyes widened. I noticed she pulled her medicine case from her pocket.

Liz ran back into the front room. She pointed to the brick and shards of glass spread across the rug. "What just happened?"

"Have no idea…" I leaned against the couch. My heart pounded. I needed to pee.

Darius charged back inside and slammed the front door. He leaned over with his hands on his knees and gasped. "Didn't see anyone. Lots of barking dogs. Somebody ran down the street. Need to sit."

Alli tip-toed over to the glass on the rug and poked at the brick.

"Look, there's something attached." She picked up the brick, loosened a rubber band, and pulled out a piece of paper. Narrowing her eyes, she held the paper close to the light. "If you know what's best. Give me my stuff."

Liz slammed her fist on the table. "That Ronald guy is really screwed up."

Darius grabbed my hand. "I'm sorry Cheryl, I really didn't see anyone."

"Hon, it's okay," I patted him on the arm, then turned back to the girls. "What are we going to do? This is worse than the battery thing."

Alli grabbed her phone. "Should I call the police and tell them about the brick?"

Liz glared at her. "Sure, Alli. Wonderful plan. By the time they come out to investigate, we'll all be dead." She grabbed her phone and punched at the number pad. "I'll deal with this."

I looked up at Darius. "Hon, maybe we shouldn't go. I don't feel comfortable leaving Liz and Alli alone. Maybe we should wait 'til things calm down."

"A brick," Liz shouted into her phone. "Yes. In my front room. Lots of glass… Fine, I'll hold." She looked over at us, "If we'd been shot someone would be here right away. But noooo, all we just have is a stupid brick."

Alli walked around the glass and stood next to me and Darius. "Don't you dare postpone your trip. Go and meet up with your dad. Have fun. Liz and I, we'll… be just fine. Besides you aren't leaving for a few days, things will calm down by then." She went into the kitchen and came back with a dustpan and broom.

Liz shouted into her phone. "No, we didn't see anyone…"

I looked at Darius. "What do you think?"

He shrugged. "Up to you, Hon. It's your dad."

"Damn that guy." I sighed. *I don't have a good feeling about any of this.*

25

ALLI

Even though there was a threatening note, the police concluded our "vandalism" wasn't directed at anyone specific, nor could they link it to Ronald. According to their report, he wasn't anywhere near our apartment. Ronald's statement said he and Steven were bowling. He even gave them a copy of his shoe rental receipt. The police believed him. I didn't.

Mr. Bainter, the landlord, fixed our window Monday morning. As he scraped the old caulk off the frame, he shared his views on today's youth and the "olden days." As he applied an even white line to the inside of the window frame, he shook his head, "Too many juvenile delinquents roaming the neighborhood..." As he inspected his own work, he added, "Life was much safer when I was growing up. We had chores to keep us out of trouble."

With the window fixed, Cheryl and Darius left for Sacramento on Wednesday. She was so excited she had to pee twice. I hope everything turns out okay and they have a great visit.

THE REST of the week flew by. Finally it was Saturday, the night of the big Halloween party. Liz was in her room getting ready. I was in mine, fussing with my costume. We agreed to keep our outfits secret until we headed out. I chose Snow White with a blue velvet bodice and cream-colored skirt just touching the tops of my black flats.

Liz walked past my door. "Hey, you ready yet? We need to leave soon."

I spritzed my hair once more, pushed it into place, and grabbed my tiny black purse. Enough room for my anxiety pills, tissues, and keys.

As I walked into the front room, I caught sight of Liz. "Oh, my goodness. You look terrible. I mean terrific." She wore a racy zombie outfit, complete with tattered black leggings, ragged dress, and high heels. "I love your face and hair. How did you do that?"

Liz's eyes widened. "Baby powder to make my face look pale. Then lots of dark makeup around my eyes for the sunken in look. I used to do make-up at the Diversionary Theatre. Remember?"

"Yeah, the one in University Heights. They have great productions," I said. "You're going to have quite a challenge combing out your hair."

"Tell me about it," she said. "It's a real rat's nest up there."

Laughing, I poked at the top of her hair. "Well, it's really a great costume. The real you."

"And you make a perfect Snow White." She dashed into the kitchen and grabbed a red apple. "Don't forget your poisoned prop."

"Thanks," I said shining it on my bodice. I bent down and stroked my cat's head. "See you later, Tippy Toes. We'll be back soon." I locked the door and we headed down the stairs to Liz's car.

HOURS LATER, as it began to drizzle, we arrived home from the party. I hadn't seen Liz laugh so much since before she and Zack broke up. We needed this night to relax and hang out with friends.

Liz closed her car door. "You see Beth? She looked great in that lady pirate outfit—grabbing all the guys with her hook."

I laughed as we walked up the stairs. "Thought I was going to split my bodice when she grabbed Brad's crotch. The look on his face—"

Liz started to say something but stopped as we reached the landing. She kicked off her shoes and bolted down the walkway.

I followed behind, trying to keep up. "What's going on?"

She paused outside our wide-open front door and looked at me. "Don't go in, Alli. Someone might be in there." She peeked inside. "Look at this place."

The ceramic lamp lay broken on the rug. Shards of broken dishes covered the kitchen floor. Twisted wooden picture frames rested against the fireplace. Torn pictures lay crumpled on the rug. Though most of the room was trashed, my eyes caught sight of six half-empty beer bottles neatly arranged on the counter. My chest tightened. I reached for my anxiety medicine and took a deep breath. "Oh, my gosh. Who did this? You don't think Ronald…" My head became fuzzy.

Liz reached for her phone. "I'm calling the police," she said. "I don't think Ronald would have gone to this extent."

"Oh no. Tippy Toes. Where's my baby?" I used my phone's flashlight app, shining it in all her favorite hiding places. "You can come out now. I'm here." I followed Liz as she ventured down our hallway.

She cradled her phone between her shoulder and ear as she looked around. "I'm tired of being on hold. Someone broke into our apartment. And you know what, they might still be in here." She covered the mouthpiece and winked at me. "That should get their backsides out here."

She stopped in front of my bedroom door and pointed. "Look. Another note."

I ran down the hall, pushed past her, and tore the paper off my door. "Oh my gosh. No. No. No." My heart raced. Running back outside to get fresh air, I collapsed on the cement walkway near our door. I couldn't breathe. Or think. Or talk. My eyes were blurry from sobbing.

Liz took the paper from my trembling hand. She read it out loud. "I have your cat. You have my stuff. Let's trade. You have until Monday night. You know how to reach me."

Though I didn't open my eyes, I sensed Liz sitting next to me. She took a deep breath and grabbed my shoulder. "Oh man. That sick idiot took your cat."

26

LIZ

Putting the final touches on my zombie costume for the Halloween party, I looked in the mirror, puckered my lips, and applied black-tinted lipstick. I stepped back to view the finished product. *Just like I feel. Crappy.* I thought morning sickness was before breakfast. But, no, I was living on crackers and flat soda all damn day.

Tonight, I was doing something to get my mind off my mess. Should it bother me that Zack doesn't know? Probably not. Why bring him into it when I don't even want to keep it. *But what if it is his… Stop.* I didn't want to cry again and ruin my make-up.

I passed by Alli's room. "Hey, you ready yet? We need to leave soon." I didn't know what she was wearing, but I was sure it was probably a nun or nurse or some Mother Teresa-type outfit. Geeze, I wished she'd step out on a limb and take a risk. I turned back as she came out of her room. Snow White. How appropriate.

As we drove home from the party, a light drizzle sprinkled the windshield with tiny glistening dots. "Alli, didn't you leave a light on when we left?" I asked while parking the car.

"I thought so. Why?" She dabbed her red lips with a tissue.

We got out of the car and went up the stairs. "What the—?" I kicked off my shoes and ran to the wide-open front door. The place was a disaster. Even though I tried to hold her back, Alli pushed past me looking for her precious cat. *This is crap.* I dialed 911.

"No, you can't put me on hold. Someone…" Damned if they didn't do it. Finally, the dispatcher came back on. "And you better send someone out. They're still here."

Alli grabbed a piece of paper off her door and ran. I found her collapsed on the rain-splattered walkway outside the door. Her cat was missing. Water from the roofline dripped in front of us. "Damn cops… they'd better be here soon." A neighbor peeked out her door. I sat next to Alli and waited.

A siren in the distance intensified. Soon a patrol car pulled into the parking lot. Flashing red and blue lights reflected off the wet streets. Two uniformed police officers, a man and a woman, bounded up the stairs with guns drawn.

A tall, slim policewoman with short hair stopped in front of us. "I'm Officer Jarmon. Are you okay?" A squat, mustached policeman waited just outside the door.

"I think so," I said. "But our apartment is totally screwed." Alli kept her head in her hands and rocked.

"You two need to stay here until we secure the area," said Jarmon. "I realize this is a bad time, but I'll need to ask some questions." After motioning for the male officer to go inside she holstered her revolver. She took out a notebook and pen as another car pulled into the parking area. I heard a car door slam followed by heavy footsteps coming up the stairs.

"Detective Hastings," said Jarmon.

"I was in the area and heard the call." Hastings looked at us, then back at the apartment. "Kidnapping? Burglary? Have you secured the area?"

I managed to stand and stared eye-to-eye at the dark-haired detective. "Yes, a kidnapping." I waved my hands and pointed inside. "And who knows if the idiot is still in there. This is the second time this week we called for help. Last time nobody paid attention."

"I'm sorry. And your name…" said Hastings.

"Liz, I mean Elizabeth Green. And that's my friend, Alli. That idiot took her cat."

Alli looked up. She stood, brushed rain off her not so snow-white skirt and leaned against the stucco wall.

The uniformed policeman came outside and spoke to Hastings. "The apartment is secure. Do you have an ETA on the Field Services Unit?"

Hastings and the policeman went back into the apartment and talked. I moved closer to the door when Jarmon stopped me. "Please be patient. Our forensic tech specialist will be here soon. We want to make sure we collect as much evidence as possible before you go back in."

The drizzle continued. I watched as drops from the roof made a puddle in a low spot in the walkway. Soon the policeman and Hastings emerged. Hastings took out his notebook. "I'd like to ask these women some questions." He glanced at the uniformed officers and pointed to the walkway. "You two canvass the apartment residents and neighbors across the street. See if anyone has security footage." They nodded. The policewoman knocked on doors on our floor as the policeman turned and went down the stairs.

"I'm Detective Jack Hastings. I'm with the burglary division of the San Diego Police Department. Let's go inside to get out of this weather; but, until evidence is gathered, please don't touch or move anything. Do you understand?"

We nodded.

Hastings led us back into our damaged apartment and closed the door. As we sat on the edge of the couch, he pulled up a chair and unbuttoned his jacket. After verifying the spelling of our names, he asked us a crapload of questions. About the apartment. Alli's cat. If we had any ideas of who might have broken in. Alli seemed okay, though she twisted a tissue and cleared her throat a lot while answering.

"Is it possible to get some water?" I asked. "Or use the bathroom?"

Detective Hastings nodded. "But, don't move anything."

"Don't worry. Just gotta pee and grab a bottle of water. Promise not to mess up your CSI stuff." I'd always thought those shows were stupid. Now, I wish I'd watched a few to have more of a clue about what was going on.

I walked back into the front room and heard Alli talking about her cat. She wiped her eyes with a bundled-up tissue. I couldn't imagine how she must be feeling. That cat meant everything to her. As I sat on the couch a loud knock came from the front door. *Holy crap, who can that be?*

27

ALLI

When I heard the loud knock on the door, my heart raced, and I struggled to breathe.

Hastings stood. "Would you like me to see who's there?"

I nodded, trying to hide my trembling.

The detective walked over and opened the door. "Hi, Bob." Then he turned back to us. "The forensic specialist."

Liz leaned closer to me and grabbed a tissue from the box on the coffee table.

"He said not to move or touch anything."

She glared at me.

Hastings walked over to us with a tall, middle-aged, African American man with salt and pepper hair. "This is Bob Llewellyn. He's here to take pictures and collect evidence. Bob will need elimination prints of anyone who had legitimate access to this apartment. Everyone's prints will be submitted to the system for identification which will help us identify any latent prints we find." Hastings waited until Llewellyn went down the hall then he sat in the chair.

I looked over at Liz, then back to the detective. "Cheryl and Darius won't be back for a few days. I don't think anyone else has been here lately."

"Except for our landlord. Remember, the broken window?" Liz shuddered. "How far back should we go?"

Hastings scribbled something in his notebook, then looked up. "The past few months. Can you think of anyone else who might have been here?"

Liz glared at me, then the detective. "Yeah… Zack. He was here until a month or so ago."

"That was Liz's boyfriend," I said. "But they broke up."

"Please try and contact him. It's important," said Hastings.

I watched him as he questioned us. He wrote left-handed and curled his writing hand over the notebook in a distinctive way. He also looked familiar. Did I pass by him in the grocery store? Was he a customer at *Framed*? It was driving me crazy. Dark hair, trimmed mustache, twinkling green eyes.

"Have we met?" I felt a blush rise in my cheeks. "I really feel like I've seen you before."

He tapped his pen on his notebook. "You know, I was thinking the same thing. But, I talk to so many people I figured it was a coincidence." He paused, then smiled. "Although, I would have remembered the Snow White outfit."

I stuttered. "Um, yeah. We were at a party…" *Yeah, I'm an anxious person who wears weird clothes. Geeze. I know I've seen that smile. Okay. Focus. He's trying to help me find my cat…*

"You mentioned something about a note?" Hastings said.

"It's in my pocket." I took it out and handed it to him.

"The message says to give this person their stuff to get the cat back. What stuff are they referring to?" Hastings added something to his notebook then looked at me.

Twisting my tissue, I blurted everything out. "The auction. An old man. I bid and got a box. He was really upset. But I paid for it. He threatened me. Cheryl's battery was dead. A brick. He took my cat…"

"Okay," said Hastings. "Slow down just a bit. First, who is "he"?"

"Ronald, um, Gara… Garanski. Ron Garanski. He runs a storage place across town. He started following me and doing weird stuff. I think he threw a brick through our window last week… it also had a note…"

Hastings crossed out something, then continued to write. "Another note? Did you notify the police?"

"Yes," I said. "We called—"

Liz pounded her fist on the coffee table. "I told them it was serious. But they didn't think so. They only took a report over the phone… So, Detective Hastings, is this serious enough for you?"

Hastings flinched, then nodded.

My chest tightened. "But we couldn't prove who threw it and… I still have that note too, if you want to see it," I said. "Oh… but it's in my room."

"That's fine. We can get it when Llewellyn is finished. I'll want both notes." He tapped his thumb on his notebook and sighed. "I'm sorry no one took you seriously. We might be dealing with a stalker. Please give me as much information as you can about Mr. Garanski. I want to question him…" He paused and looked up as Llewellyn walked into the front room. "Excuse me for a moment."

"I've completed my primary survey and walkthrough of the hallway and bedrooms." The forensic specialist's deep baritone voice resonated against our bare walls. "Most of the damage is confined to the middle bedroom and these rooms. I've created an evidence-free pathway leading to those areas. It will be a few more hours, at least." Llewellyn turned toward Liz and me. "I'm ready to take elimination prints when you're finished."

Hastings motioned to Liz. "Ms. Green, I should have everything I need from you. If not, I have your contact information. Don't forget to let…" He flipped back through his notebook. "Zack know we need his prints."

"I'll do my best to find him." Liz looked over at me, then up at Llewellyn. "I guess we can do mine now if you want." They headed to the kitchen table as I sat knee-to-knee with Detective Hastings.

"Now, where were we?" He reviewed his last entry. "Oh yes, I want to know more about the auction box. Do you have any idea why Mr. Garanski would go to all this trouble for it?"

I must keep the Guardian's secret safe. "All I know is that they are part of an inheritance. The guy freaked out over them." *I hate lying. He's so calm and patient. And kind.* "I'm sorry. I wish I knew more."

Hastings' eyes met mine. "It's too bad you came home to this mess. It's good no one was home. It could have been a lot worse than dirtying up your dress."

I look down at my costume, pulled the apple from my purse, and smiled. "At least I kept the poisoned apple. I'm starving."

"You should be able to get something else to eat after Llewellyn takes your prints. We'll get someone over to Garanski's place and question him. If need be, I'll get a search warrant. And about your cat…"

"According to that note, I only have until Monday night." I clenched my jaw to avoid crying.

"Do you have any recent pictures of her? It would help."

"Yes. I have lots of…" I grabbed my phone and swiped at the screen. "Oops, I think the battery died. Okay if I send them to you by email?"

"That would be great." He smiled. "I'll do my best to wrap this up as soon as possible. I know that probably doesn't help right now, but I'm bound by rules, regulations, and red tape. The three 'R's that make my job miserable—that and the never-ending paperwork."

He placed the notebook and pen in his jacket pocket, then took a business card from his front pocket. "My email is on here. Send me a few images as soon as possible." He fingered his mustache and smiled. "If you think of something else. Or something just doesn't seem right. Don't hesitate to contact me." He stood and helped me up. "I'll do my best to find your cat and whoever left the notes."

Llewellyn and Liz came back into the front room. Llewellyn motioned for me to join him at the table. "I can take your prints now if you're ready."

As Hastings walked out the door, he looked back at me and waved.

I'll figure out where I saw him. Even if it keeps me awake all night.

28

ALLI

Every time I drifted off; my racing heart woke me. I gave up on sleep when the dawn's light peeked through my curtain. "Come on Tippy Toes…" *Oh man. Don't cry. Don't cry.* I grabbed for a tissue. I sobbed again, intensifying my headache. *Poor baby, he better not hurt you or…*

I crawled out of bed, dressed, and headed down the hall. Liz was in her room shouting at someone. I didn't stop or listen. I couldn't deal with anything else.

I still hadn't figured out where I'd seen Jack Hastings, although it was recently. Things like that drove me crazy. Right now I welcomed any distraction. I pictured Hastings showing up at Ronald's place, busting down the door, and rescuing my precious cat. Then, he'd show up at the apartment, hand her to me, and I'd give him a big hug. He'd smile and… *What am I thinking?* I'm not interested in that Hastings guy. I want my cat back. And I want Ronald to rot in jail and leave me alone.

As I was making coffee, Liz trudged down the hall and into the kitchen.

"You sleep at all?"

"Not really." I sighed. "Coffee?"

She rubbed her eyes. “I guess. I didn’t sleep very well either. Maybe the coffee will help my stomach settle down. I, um… talked to Zack this morning.”

“How did that go?” Judging by what I’d heard through her wall, I didn’t really need to ask.

“Oh, you know. I told him what happened. He freaked out. He wanted to come by to make sure I was okay. I said no. We argued. I said things I regret.”

I stirred my coffee. “So, nothing’s changed since you broke up?”

“Nope,” said Liz. “He tried to tell me he didn’t cheat. I didn’t want to hear it. I told him I only called about the fingerprints. It was so hard talking to him.”

“So, you didn’t tell him about…?” I pointed to her stomach.

“Heck no.” She slapped her hand on the table. “Besides, I still don’t know if it’s his.” She shook her head. “That’s the last thing he needs to know about.”

I glanced at the wall clock. “It’s only nine? This day’s going to drag on forever.” I sipped my coffee. “I hope Detective Hastings calls soon with good news.”

“I noticed you watching at him last night,” said Liz.

“He was asking me questions. I was being polite.”

Liz smiled. “Doesn’t he have the most amazing green eyes?”

“Fine, I’ll admit he has cute eyes, but....” I stirred my coffee, then looked at Liz. “I can’t deal with anything except Tippy Toes. Maybe after he finds her, I can think about his eyes. But for right now—”

My cell rang, interrupting our conversation. I glanced at the caller ID. *Oh my gosh. Detective Hastings.*

29

JACK

I'd had one of the longest, most exasperating days of my career. It was late. It was raining. All I wanted to do was go home and veg in front of the TV. While picking up my favorite vanilla bean drink from a nearby Starbucks, a call came through about a burglary-kidnapping. I was a few blocks away. I rushed right over and found two gals sitting outside their torn-up apartment. The "zombie," Elizabeth, was rightly agitated, protecting her friend, "Snow White," Allison, who was completely freaked out. Allison's cat had been kidnapped. *Or, would that be catnapped?* Such a bizarre story.

I'd seen Allison recently. Though I could have passed her in a thousand different places, I never forgot a face. I was up half the night thinking about her, I mean, the case. *Focus, Jack.* What would have possessed someone to break in, take a family pet, and leave a note?

I called in a favor and got a search warrant for the Store-More building, arriving just as the office opened. An older couple in their late 60s stood behind the counter. I introduced myself to a woman wearing a grey cable-knit sweater over black slacks accentuating her bluish-grey hair.

She adjusted her glasses and looked me up and down. "I'm Betty Shears. This is my husband, Ed. The regular manager, Ron, asked us to fill in for him for a few days. Something about a family emergency in Ventura.

Ed cleared his throat. "We normally don't come in 'cept Wednesday and Thursday." He licked the palm of his hand, patted down a few stray white hairs, then put on a Padres cap. "Ron said he and the boy needed to leave right away. Called late last night, after me and the missus had gone to bed." I noticed a dark hollowness under his blue eyes. Looked like he hadn't slept in a while.

Betty picked up a chocolate donut and waved it as she spoke. "Never knew he had family in Ventura, much less any family, 'cept that old guy who comes around occasionally." She took a small bite, then wiped her hands on a paper towel. "Ron's not the friendliest if you know what I mean."

I took out my notebook and pen and jotted down a few quick details. "You didn't happen to see a cat hanging around his apartment?" I glanced behind them but couldn't see past the wall beyond the counter.

"A cat you say?" said Ed. "No cats that I know of. My wife swells up like a melon if she's indoors with one. Although, I have seen quite a few feral cats chasing mice and rats out back by the storage lockers." He pointed to a small RV parked inside the security gate. "We stay in the motorhome. The smoke in here is bad, so we live in our home-away-from-home when we're on duty."

I doubted they had any idea what was going on. And since Betty didn't look "swollen up like a melon," I figured they weren't harboring a kidnapped cat.

"Ron said to expect him back Tuesday," said Ed. "Should I have him call you?"

"Thanks. But no," I said. "I'll contact Mr. Garanski." They seemed like a nice couple. I thanked them for their time, left them my card, and asked them to call if they noticed a yellow and white tabby cat roaming around.

I got back in my car and drummed my fingers on the steering wheel. If the Garanski fellow took the cat, would he hightail it up the freeway and stash her somewhere? He gave Allison until Monday. He told the Shears he'd be back on Tuesday. Coincidence? I checked my

GPS. San Diego to Ventura was just under 200 miles, about four hours away. *Should I rush up there and investigate?*

On second thought, I'd wait until Tuesday, then come back to interrogate him. *Although, the idea of finding the cat, taking her back to Snow White... I would be her hero. Her knight in shining armor.* So I was a hopeless romantic. There was just something about Allison. I couldn't get her out of my mind. I should probably go back to her apartment and question her again…

"Hello, Miss Harper?" I cleared my throat. "Detective Jack Hastings, from last night? Oh good, you remember me. Sure, I'll call you Alli." *Oh my. I'm sweating bullets here.* "Um, if you don't mind, I need to come by and ask you a few more questions. Yes, this morning, if possible." *Mental note: change shirt, put on extra deodorant.* "Thanks. See you soon. Goodbye."

I decided to stop and pick up muffins and coffee. Just because this was an investigation, didn't mean we couldn't eat while we talked, right? *Now, where's my cologne?*

30

ALLI

I closed my phone. “That was Detective Hastings. He’ll be here in about an hour to ask more questions.”

Liz gave me the look. “Your cheeks are flushed.”

“Stop it. I’m flushed because… I’m upset about Tippy Toes. And… A detective’s coming over asking questions I don’t know how to answer.” I wiped my eye, catching a tear. “Liz, I need to talk to you. Before he gets here.”

“What are you talking about?”

“I need advice.”

“Advice?” she said, offering me a handful of tissues. “About what?”

“I need to tell you about stuff from the box. I can’t tell Hastings, not yet anyway. But I have to tell someone… You’re the only person I trust.” I motioned for her to follow me into my room. I closed the door, pulling out a long, narrow plastic storage bin out from under my bed. Opening it, I took out an old wool sweater and a rag doll my grandma knitted me, along with an embroidered satin pillow.

“What’s all this?” said Liz.

“It’s the stuff from the auction. I hid it so no one would find it. In case—”

"In case Douchebag did something stupid. Like break in and try to steal it?" said Liz.

"That's why I needed to talk to you before the detective arrives." I unwrapped the sweater revealing the broken quill pen and paintbrush. "I hid the glasses in my rag doll. And the leather journal is tucked inside the satin pillow."

"Clever," said Liz. "Wasn't there a hat too?"

"I hid that on the bottom shelf in the bathroom." I laughed. "I didn't think Ronald would look behind toilet paper and sanitary pads." I walked across the hall and brought back the hat, patting it back into shape.

"Okay… so the stuff is special." Liz rubbed the side of the broken paintbrush. "Are these things worth millions? Did they belong to some famous person? Do they have secret powers…?"

I took a deep breath. "Actually, Liz, they do have special powers."

"You're just yanking my chain."

I shook my head.

"You're kidding, right?"

"I'm in no mood to kid. I'm telling you the stuff from that auction is special. I'm still confused, but Russell said each item has a special power that is endowed to the user." I paused to collect my thoughts. "I know it sounds crazy, but I swear, I'm telling the truth."

Liz looked at the items, then at me. "Have you tried anything out? I mean, how do you know?"

I picked up the glasses. "Remember the other night when you came into my room? I was wearing these. I knew you were pregnant, right? How do you think I figured it out? I'm no psychic."

"Lucky guess?" Liz jumped up and grabbed the hat from the end of the bed. "This hat? Secret powers? Yeah right." She tossed the top hat on the bed and pointed at the glasses in my hand. "If I put those on, I'll know all the secrets of the world…"

Before I could respond, Liz grabbed the glasses.

"Careful… one side's missing…"

She put them on and closed her eyes. "If you are correct Allison Harper, soon I will know everything about you…" She opened her eyes and scanned me, starting at the top of my head. Before she reached my feet, she screamed. Yanking off the glasses, she tossed them on the bed and backed away.

"What's wrong Liz? What happened?"

She wiped perspiration off her upper lip. "I… I saw your thoughts… It was like I was in your head, feeling what you're going through. Alli, what just happened?"

Knowing I didn't have much time before Detective Hastings showed up, I gave Liz the shortened version of the story of the Guardians and the *Gifts*. I told her about Russell, and Jason, and why Ronald was bent on getting the *Gifts* back for Steven.

"Like heck, he wants them for Steven," said Liz.

"I agree. Now you know. And you must promise not to tell anyone —especially Cheryl. I probably put you in danger for just knowing. I don't want to involve anyone else." I rubbed my forehead. "My tension headache is coming back."

"As much as I'm thrilled you shared all this with me, you really need to call Russell and let him know what happened. I'm sure he'll have much better advice." Liz's eyes darted from the glasses to the top hat, and back to the quill pen and paintbrush.

"I did call him," I said. "Twice. Last night before I went to bed and this morning when I woke up. He didn't answer. And his voice mail was full, which was weird."

"How so?"

"It means he hasn't picked up any of his messages for a while. I'm concerned something might have happened to him too. What if he's in trouble like Tippy Toes?" I looked around the room. "I need to put this stuff away before Hastings gets here. I'm sure he'll ask about it. After all, this is what Ronald wanted in exchange for my cat."

"You don't have to tell him the whole truth, do you?" She pointed to the top hat. "Just say they're vintage antiques or something like that."

I put my arm around Liz. Instead of flinching, she put her arm around me. "Thanks, friend," I smiled. "I feel much better telling you the truth." I grabbed everything but the hat and shoved them back under my bed.

As I turned to take the hat to the bathroom, Liz caught my arm. "If those glasses really tell what someone is thinking, then you better face the truth." She looked me straight in the eye. "You've got a thing for the green-eyed detective."

I placed my hands on my hips. "What are you talking about?"

She winked at me. "When I put on the glasses I read *your* thoughts."

Though the room was cold, I wiped perspiration from my forehead. "I must have been distracted or—"

A knock at the front door interrupted me.

I glared at her. "Don't. Tell. Anyone." Then I turned and walked out of my room.

31

JACK

I walked up the apartment's flight of stairs carrying a variety of drinks. Caffeinated and decaffeinated coffee, hot apple cider, and, of course, Vanilla Bean, plus a bag of assorted muffins. *Like a Dunkin' Donuts delivery guy. Do they deliver? I don't think so. Why am I talking to myself?* Hopefully, the snacks will help her feel more comfortable talking… about last night, of course.

I held the bag under my arm and breathed into my hand. Damn, shoulda popped a breath mint. I knocked on the door and heard two muffled voices. The door opened. Allison stood there staring at me with her big green eyes. She wore jeans, a mint-colored blouse and a sweater with little roses on the collar. A bit different than the Snow White costume from last night.

"Hi, I'm Detective Hastings." *Great, Captain Obvious.* "I brought something to snack on." Alli stared at me, then cocked her head to the side. *Was it me? Or the food? Either way, it was kind of cute.*

"Please come in, Detective. How very thoughtful of you—" She stopped and snapped her fingers. "I just remembered where I saw you. At the Starbucks on Washington Street a few weeks ago.

"I do stop there quite frequently." I stammered. "Most mornings in fact."

"I knew I'd seen you somewhere before last night." She motioned for me to sit at the kitchen table, grabbed two plates, and placed one in front of each of us. "Napkin?"

"Yes, thank you." I took the hot drinks out of the carrier, lined them up in the middle of the table, and described them. "I didn't know what you wanted, so I got a variety…"

"Vanilla bean? My favorite." She reached for the tall cup but drew her hand back. "Unless it's yours."

"No, please take it." *Be still my heart. A vanilla bean lover like me. I wished I'd gotten two.*

She caught my eyes. "Did you find out anything? I mean, do you know about Tippy Toes?"

"Ms. Harper…" I began, taking out my notebook and pen.

"Please, call me Alli."

"Alli… I went by the storage facility this morning, but Mr. Garanski wasn't there. He'd called an older couple to take his place for a few days." I took a sip of my hot apple cider. "Did he ever say anything about any family in Ventura?"

She peeled the paper off a blueberry muffin and picked a piece off the corner. "No, we never spoke about family. Though Ronald's fath—"

"What was that? His what?" I said.

Alli shifted in her chair. "Ronald's father. His name is Russell Garanski. I don't know of any other family, other than Russell mentioning Ronald had two sons."

"Would you happen to have any contact information for Russell?"

She looked at me and sighed. "Just a phone number. I've been trying to call him since last night. His voice mail is full." Her eyes flashed fear.

"And that bothers you, doesn't it?"

"How did you…? I mean, yes, I've always been able to leave a message. But, this time, it's different."

"How so?" I leaned back and sipped my cider.

Her eyes widened. Her breathing increased.

"He's been different the last few times we've talked. Like he's not feeling well. I mean, he's old. But now, with his voice mail full, it…

well, I don't think he's picked up his messages for days…" She took a sip of her coffee, then wiped her mouth with a napkin. "He's my friend. I'm concerned."

The other roommate tiptoed into the kitchen. "I'm so sorry to interrupt you, but I need to eat. I'll just grab something and leave."

"No hurry, Ms. Green. I brought extra muffins and coffee… please help yourself."

"That's very kind of you… And call me Liz." As she picked out a muffin, I noticed her turn and wink at Alli.

Wonder what that was about? Scribbling in my notebook, I pinched off a piece of my cinnamon muffin. I popped it into my mouth while observing Alli.

She let out a long sigh, then rubbed the back of her neck.

"I'm sorry this is so stressful, Alli. I'm really trying to do everything in my power to find your cat." I wiped my hands on my pants. "Last night, you mentioned the person who left the note wanted certain items back in exchange for your cat. Would you tell me more about them?"

Liz coughed on her water. "Excuse me. Went down the wrong way."

Alli sat up straight. "Um, yes. What would you like to know?"

I seem to have hit on something. What are they not saying? I looked at Liz, then Alli. "I need the timeframe of when you acquired the items, to Mr. Garanski's threats, to the break-in. And, if it's not too much trouble, I'd like to see the items in question."

Alli stood and motioned toward the hall. I followed her back to her bedroom.

I made notes as she answered my questions and talked about each antique piece. She kept clearing her throat and wouldn't make eye contact. While I didn't think she wasn't lying, my gut told me she was holding something back. Her reluctance would only hinder my investigation. *How could I be her hero if she didn't trust me?*

32

ALLI

I was excited and relieved when I figured out where I'd first noticed Detective Hastings. Who could forget those emerald-green eyes? Or curly, raven-black hair? The thin mustache? And charming smile? It was when he picked up his order the day Russell and I had met at Starbucks.

After Jack left, I called Russell again… *Yes. I still call him Detective Hastings to his face. I can think about him as Jack, can't I?* Regarding Russell… I still couldn't leave a message because his mailbox was full. I ended up showing Jack the *Gifts* but didn't tell him the whole truth. Nothing about Jason being the rightful heir or how I'd hired an investigator.

I was in the kitchen fixing myself a sandwich when my phone buzzed. *A voice message from Russell. Thank goodness.* I called back without listening to his message. *Please pick up. Please… Oh no, it went to voicemail. Which was full…*

I dialed my voice mail to retrieve his message when my phone rang.

"Hello, Mr. Garanski? I can barely hear you. Are you okay?" His voice sounded like gravel. After a long pause, he spoke. He'd been ill. Stomachache… weakness. The flu, he reckoned.

"I'm so sorry I bothered you with so many messages… I had to talk to you." I told him about the break-in and the note. I tried to stay calm but ended up sobbing. "No, I promise I won't give the *Gifts* back to Ronald… Yes, I want my Tippy Toes back more than anything… Mr. Garanski, what should I do?" He took his time, then whispered three words. "Thank you for your advice. Please, get better… Yes, I'll let you know what I decide." The call ended.

"You okay, Alli?"

I twisted around. "You startled me, Liz."

"I'm sorry. I happened to overhear," she said. "Everything okay with the old dude?"

I placed my phone on the table. "Russell didn't sound good."

"That sucks," she said. "Was he able to give you any advice?"

"Yeah. He said to follow my heart."

"Sounds like the same words that started this whole mess." She grabbed a paper towel and filled it with cereal. "No clean bowls, didn't feel like washing one."

"He also said if I decided to give back the *Gifts*, he'd understand."

Liz glared at me. Cereal pieces bounced off the paper towel. "You can't do that, Alli. That Ron guy is a dangerous person. After you explained the *Gifts'* powers, I can't imagine what he'd try with his anger and stupidity. There must be another answer."

I rubbed my eyes. "I'm so tired of thinking. I can't come up with anything right now. Maybe Detective Hastings will find Ronald and Tippy Toes, and then everything will be better."

Liz sat up straight and snapped her fingers. "Does the idiot know what the *Gifts* look like?"

"I think so… Actually, I don't know. He never referred to them by name," I said. "Why do you ask?"

Liz stood and began pacing. "If he doesn't know what they look like, what would stop us from getting similar items, putting them in the box, and giving those to him?"

I gasped. "Are you saying we should deceive Ronald? What about when he—"

"Once he sees the stuff, he'll give you your cat. Let the police deal with the scumbag." Liz smiled. "It's a win-win for everyone, well except for him."

I thought for a while. "Do you think it could work?"

"It should. He won't know the difference between a thrift store top hat and the real thing until he inspects it. By then you'll have your furry four-legged friend." Liz winked at me. "And, your detective friend will catch our burglar."

"He's not my 'friend.' He's a professional detective." *But, then again, if the case was solved...*

"Whatever." Liz rolled her eyes. "Come on, we don't have much time. If we're going to get fake *Gifts*, we'd better get going. The note said you have until midnight tomorrow night."

"Let me get my shoes and jacket."

AFTER SCOURING SEVERAL THRIFT STORES, Liz and I came back to the apartment with bags of items that we felt would pass for the fake *Gifts*. Heading to my room to put them on the bed, loud pounding rattled the front door. I turned. *Jack?*

"I'll get it," said Liz.

I dropped the bags on my bedroom floor and rushed back into the front room, hoping to see Detective Hastings. Instead, the front door stood open. Liz gripped the doorframe, staring at something on the ground. I inched my way closer to her.

"What the..." She pointed to a white cardboard box laying in front of our doorway. There was an image of a cowboy boot with "Old West Boot Co." on the flap. The edges were sealed with packing tape.

My hands trembled. My heart pounded. Without thinking, I picked it up. The box wasn't heavy, but something inside rattled and slid around as I carried it to the couch. "Did you happen to see who left it?"

Liz shook her head. "I don't have a good feeling about this." She stood next to me and grabbed my hand. "Don't open it. We need to call your detective friend."

I backed away from the couch. Tears ran down my cheeks. "It can't be," I said. "He said we had until Monday night..."

33

JACK

Another unproductive day. It began at the Store-More tracking down Mr. Garanski, the prime suspect in the burglary/kidnapping at the Harper residence. Calls to his cell went to voice mail. *Indisposed? Hiding?* Either way, I'd talk to him when he showed up Tuesday. *If he showed up.* My cell rang. The caller ID indicated it was Alli. Maybe she received new information.

"Hello. Yes… Wait, would you repeat that?" She sounded hysterical. "You think it's… No, don't open it. It sounds like evidence. I'll be there in less than fifteen minutes. Promise me you'll wait…"

Dammit. Not how I pictured going back to visit. I was supposed to catch the bastard, rescue her cat, and save the day. Fine, I'm a hopeless romantic. In my line of work, hope is all I've got.

I glanced around the squad room and noticed Officer Jarmon making copies. She was on the scene last night and understood the situation. Plus, it would be judicious of me to bring a woman along in the event of a worst-case-scenario. I motioned to Jarmon. We left at once.

When we arrived, the door to their apartment was ajar. As I knocked, it creaked open.

Alli rushed up to me. "Detective Hastings, I'm so glad you're here."

"This is so screwed up." Liz pointed to the box. "Someone left this at our door…" She placed her hands on her hips and exhaled. "This better be a box of boots, or I'm—"

"Until we know for sure," I said. "Let's try to keep our thoughts positive." Even though I said it, I had a hard time convincing myself, much less the distraught cat owner and her over-protective friend. Noticing a few neighbors milling around outside, I signaled for Jarmon to close the door. I'm sure they were wondering why the police had shown up twice in twenty-four hours.

Alli's eyes were red and swollen. She held a wad of tissues in her hand. My heart broke for her. "You and Liz should wait in the other room. We need to take photos for the chain of evidence—before and after I open the box. Since I have no idea what I might find, it might be easier—"

"But…" Alli stammered.

"Alli, please go with Liz while Jarmon and I deal with this." I looked directly into her eyes. "I need you to do this for me." She nodded, then turned and followed Liz down the hall.

Jarmon took photos while I inspected the box. Once I heard their door close, I took out my pocketknife. "I hate this."

Jarmon nodded and wrote something in her notebook.

I examined the sides and corners of the box. "Whoever sealed it, didn't want it easily opened." I cut through the thick, sticky tape, one side at a time until the lid was movable. "You ready?" I said.

Jarmon winced.

I lifted the lid, peered inside, and gasped when I saw tuffs of matted cat fur and a collar.

Jarmon snapped several pictures. "Don't even want to know what happened to the body."

I replaced the lid and looked up at Jarmon. "I don't look forward to this next part."

Getting up, I walked to the end of the hall. "Alli, you can come back now."

Alli opened her door, and rushed up to me, searching my eyes for answers.

I shook my head.

Alli collapsed in the hallway, sobbing.

Liz sat next to her, wrapping her arms around her friend. After a few moments, Liz looked up at me. "I remember when Alli's mom gave her that cat. It was right before Mrs. Harper passed away. Tippy Toes made us feel a part of her mom was still with us… Now, it's like she died all over again." Liz turned, wiping her cheek with the back of her hand.

I stooped down next to Alli and placed my hand on her trembling shoulder.

She looked up at me with tear-streaked cheeks. "Can I see her…?" Her voice broke. She wiped back tears with her sweater sleeve.

I offered her my hand. "I'm sorry. The box only contained a collar and… Would you like me to bring it to you?"

She sniffed and wiped her eyes. "No."

We walked back into the front room as Liz followed. Jarmon stood in the kitchen. The box rested on the coffee table. One by one, the three of us sat on the couch.

I glanced over to Alli. "Would you like me to open it?"

She nodded.

Liz rocked and reached for Alli's hand.

I pulled back the lid and swallowed the lump in my throat.

Alli took a deep breath, then leaned forward. "This is all that's left?" She picked up the collar as tears streamed down her cheeks leaving small, wet spots in the matted fur. She looked at me, then Liz. "Remember when I got her?" Holding her hands a few inches apart. "She was only this big."

Liz nodded and looked away. She yanked a tissue from her pocket and wiped her eyes.

I closed my eyes and took a deep breath. "Alli, I need to take the evidence with me…"

Her big green eyes met mine. "If it will help catch whoever did this…" She stroked the pieces of fur with her finger. "What good will this do?"

I shifted on the couch. “While we don’t have much to go on, our vet who will run tests on the fur and collar. Hopefully, he’ll find trace evidence… We should have a gross report of the results in a few days.”

Alli continued to touch the matted fur.

Not wanting to rush her, I waited. When she sat back and turned away, I placed the lid back on the box, then stood and handed the box to Jarmon.

I turned my focus back to Alli. “I’m sorry. I know this doesn’t help but I promise to call as soon as I know anything.”

Alli nodded and was silent as Liz followed us to the front door.

Jarmon and I walked downstairs to the parking lot. I opened the trunk as Jarmon placed the box in the back of the car.

“What’s that?” asked Jarmon. She pointed to a piece of paper wedged in the bottom of the box.

Picking it up, I read it, then rushed back up the stairs. Out of breath, I pounded on their door.

Liz opened it. “What the…?”

“I’m sorry to bother you again. Where’s Alli?”

A few moments later Alli rushed into the front room, her eyes wild. “What’s wrong? Did you hear something?”

“No, but I found another note.” I held out the piece of paper. “This was stuck to the underside of the boot box.”

Alli gasped. “What does it say?”

Clearing my throat, I read it. “Got tired of waiting. Tough luck for kitty. I want my stuff or someone else’s luck will run out.”

I stepped back and stared at Alli. “Whoever took your cat won’t stop until they are in possession of those items you showed me. You and your roommates are in danger.”

Alli folded her arms across her chest. “I can’t believe he’d—”

Liz stomped her foot. “We all know who did this. Why can’t you go arrest the idiot?”

“I’m afraid it’s not that easy,” I said. “Right now, we don’t have any solid evidence against the person you believe is responsible. I put out an APB on his vehicle, but it’s been less than twenty-four hours. We’re not even sure of his location. We also must consider an accomplice. Someone we haven’t suspected yet. What about the older

Garanski? I still need to question him. Maybe he could shed some light on our investigation, including the brick incident."

Alli tucked her hair behind her ear. "Russell would never hurt me. Besides, he's sick. There's no way he could have thrown that brick or torn up our apartment."

Liz snapped her fingers. "But, he did follow you here—several times. How do we know he isn't part of this whole thing? Maybe he's faking being sick. Maybe he and Ronald are both—"

Alli held up her hand. "Stop. There is no way Russell would do that. He's the one who told me…" She stopped talking and appeared to be in deep thought.

"Okay, maybe I am jumping to conclusions," I said, my voice rising. "But, I don't want to take chances. As soon as I leave, I'm calling in extra patrol cars for this neighborhood. And for a while, I'll work close to this area so I can check in on—"

Alli balled up her fists. "Is that part of your job description… to keep an eye on me too? Like I'm the criminal?"

My voice softened. "No. I mean. I… I wanted to make sure you're okay. Because, I… care about what happens…" I stuttered, then regained my professional composure. "Alli, I want you and your roommates to be safe. I also want to catch the person, or persons, who threatened you. If they show up again, we'll have someone close by. Creeps like this don't make inadvertent threats. He, or she, killed once. As a detective that concerns me." I smiled, hoping she understood. "Please promise to call me if anything out of the ordinary happens. Or you think of something else." I cleared my throat. "And if it's okay with you, I'd like to stop and make sure you're both okay…"

Alli unclenched her fists and shoved them in her front pockets. "I'm sorry. This has been a terrible day. And now it's gotten worse."

"If it would help…" I said, "I'll bring coffee."

Alli caught my gaze for a just a moment, then closed the door.

Was it my imagination? Or did she just smile at me?

34

ALLI

I laid awake staring at the dark ceiling. Tippy Toes was gone. My sweet baby. I'd give anything to feel her wet nose snuggling my neck. I buried my head in my pillow and sobbed.

I didn't go to work on Monday, though I forced myself out of bed to eat a bowl of chicken soup and crackers. Only because Liz told me I had to have something. I managed half the soup, then wandered back to my room and shut the door.

THE FLUSH of the hall toilet woke me. I hoped Liz wasn't dealing with morning sickness again. Poor girl. Every night and first thing in the morning. She said she wasn't going to keep it. *Was she having second thoughts?*

I felt my phone buzz and glanced at the screen. "Good morning, Detective Hastings… Yes, I have some time this morning before work. Forty-five minutes, around nine? Okay… see you then." *Probably need a shower.* I sniffed my armpits. *Definitely a shower.*

I buttoned my sweater and walked into the front room. A few moments later, I heard the familiar pattern of knocks on the front door.

Two sharp raps, then two light ones. Jack and I set up a signal so I'd know it was him, especially if he stopped by after dark. *Yes, he has come by to check on me. Twice. We chatted too.*

"Good morning." Jack smiled and handed me a Vanilla Bean Frappuccino while keeping a tall coffee for himself. He wore a dark blue suit, grey shirt, and a multicolored tie decorated with autographed baseballs.

"Interesting tie."

Unbuttoning his jacket, he revealed the entire ensemble. "Birthday gift from my dad…" He took a sip of his coffee. "Sorry to call so early. I finally spoke with Ronald and wanted to fill you in."

My heart thumped even though I'd taken my anti-anxiety medicine an hour earlier. "You spoke to him?" Holding my drink with both hands, I nodded toward the kitchen table. "Maybe we should sit."

"Good idea," he said. He pulled out my chair, then his own. He sat after I was settled.

I studied his face waiting for him to talk. Even though my mind was racing, I noticed a small, deep scar right below his right cheekbone. I felt a blush rise in my cheeks and took a sip of my drink.

Jack cleared his throat. "Apparently, Ronald was in Ventura the last few days. Or went to a lot of trouble to make sure we knew he was there."

"I don't understand."

Jack stirred his coffee, then reached into his shirt pocket. He removed several folded receipts and laid them on the table. "I was waiting in the parking lot at the storage facility this morning when he arrived with his son. Ronald was remarkably calm as I asked questions. He even offered to have us talk in his apartment. I'd planned to serve the search warrant but decided to hold onto it since it didn't expire for a few days. I'd rather go back when he's not expecting me." Jack pointed to the pieces of paper and continued. "When he exited his truck, he shoved these in my hand, like he expected me to ask about his whereabouts."

I unfolded the receipts—Vagabond Inn, USA Gas, Del Taco, Wendy's. All from locations in Ventura dated between Saturday and Monday night. "Does this really prove he was out of town?" I held one up. "Golf N' Stuff for three people on Saturday night? That's the same night of the burglary. Now, I'm really confused."

Jack shrugged his shoulders. "I have one more thing to show you… A family photo." He handed me a grainy picture of Ronald, a tall, lanky young man, and some red-haired woman, holding golf clubs, taken in front of a castle.

As I held the picture, my hand trembled. "Maybe it's just me, but it seems like he went to a lot of trouble to prove he wasn't in San Diego. Who carries around a real picture nowadays? Most people keep photos on their phone. And those receipts…"

"I agree, Alli. It doesn't add up. Like I said, he literally handed these to me as he shook my hand. He was sure eager to prove he his whereabouts." He folded the receipts and placed them back in his pocket.

I studied the picture again. "You're sure this is the same golf course as the receipt?" I positioned the picture on the table in front of us.

Jack picked it up and studied it. "I double-checked the internet for pictures of the golf course. It's the same place, alright. But several things bother me."

I stared into his emerald-green eyes. "Such as?"

"First, this picture. Like you said. Most people use digital cameras. Why didn't he show me his phone? Was there something he didn't want me to see? And why print this one picture?"

I nodded. "And…?"

Jack drummed his fingers on the kitchen table. "It was the way he was so eager to give me everything. And how he shoved his son out the truck and made him help a storage customer. I requested to talk to the boy, but Ronald said he was slow in the head, and wouldn't be of much help."

I traced the rim of my cup with my finger. "Anything else…?"

"Yes. Ed and Betty, who took over for Ronald, said he left for a family emergency. When I questioned him about the emergency, he hesitated, then laughed it off. Told me he needed to visit an old girlfriend who happened to be in Ventura for the weekend. The emergency was, how to put this delicately, he wanted… Um, you get the drift."

I almost choked on my drink. "Sex?"

Jack blushed. He handed me a napkin. "I'm sorry, that was unprofessional to tell you so much information."

I wiped my chin. "I'm not upset at what you said. I'm just shocked anyone would want to… you know. With him?"

"I guess there's someone for everyone, eh?" Jack finished his coffee and blotted his mustache. "Probably should get back to work. I wanted to tell you about all of this, in case it would help you remember something about Ronald. I hope I didn't upset you."

"You didn't. I appreciate the visit…" I smiled and pointed to my cup. "And the coffee." As we chatted, I realized when Jack was around my heart didn't hurt as much. His soothing voice and inner strength brought me comfort. And the fact he offered to protect me… Well, who could say no to that? I walked him to the door. "Take care. Be careful." Feeling much better, I left for work with a more positive outlook.

AFTER A LONG DAY, I dragged myself up the stairs. Dropping my apartment keys and jacket on the kitchen table, I sat gathering my thoughts when I heard rattling at the front lock. I jumped up and reached in my pocket for my phone.

The front door swung open. Cheryl marched in. "We're back. Anything exciting happen while we were gone?"

My breath caught. *Yes. Too much…*

Darius traipsed in next navigating through the front room, banging suitcases against the couch as he headed for the hall.

Cheryl grinned at me and tossed her purse on the table. "Where's Liz? I can't wait to tell you both about my dad and show you pics of our trip."

I smiled but didn't say anything.

Cheryl came closer and gave me a hug. Pulling back, she held my shoulders. "You okay?"

I nodded. "You're home early. Thought you were staying until Wednesday."

"Dad needed to return to Reno—something about his job, and he didn't want to get snowed out over the pass. So, we came back. I missed you." She winked. "Did you miss me?"

"A lot has happened since you left. I'm sure you're excited about your dad, but we need to talk."

Cheryl pulled up a chair and sat. "Is it Liz? Or did jerk-face do something stupid again."

Darius walked into the kitchen eating a candy bar. He stopped, turned, and pointed toward the front room. "Didn't we have a lamp in there?"

"What's going on Alli?" Cheryl's voice rose. "Is everything okay?"

Darius stopped eating in mid-bite as the front door opened.

Liz walked in, closed the door, and came into the kitchen. "Hey, you're home." She looked at me. "Did you tell them…?"

Cheryl grabbed my hand. "What happened?"

I took a deep breath. "Weird stuff went down when you were gone." I shared the details of the burglary, ransom note, and losing Tippy Toes.

Darius touched Cheryl's shoulder. Cheryl wiped her eyes and blew her nose. "That jerk. I can't believe it. Now we have to worry about that weirdo coming back to get us?"

"I talked to Jack, I mean Detective Hastings, earlier today. He's working on the case and making sure we're okay."

Liz's eyes danced. "Oh, and did Alli tell you about her cop friend who vowed to protect her?"

Cheryl ran her fingers through her curly hair. "We're gone less than a week and look what happened. I'm so sorry about your cat, Alli. I can't believe it. It's just so horrendous."

I rubbed my temples. "My head hurts thinking about it."

Cheryl reached out and grabbed my hand. "Wait, what cop friend?"

I glared at Liz. "It's no big deal. Really. Detective Hastings was concerned. He came by to check on us." I looked at Cheryl and Darius. "Just be aware of your surroundings when you go out at night. Until things calm down—"

Liz interrupted. "Fingerprints."

I stood up. "Yes, I almost forgot. You and Darius need to get fingerprinted. They need to match our prints to figure out which ones belong to the person who broke in."

Darius finished his candy bar in one bite, then examined the tips of his fingers. "Cool. Like on TV."

"You better not give anything back to that jerk," said Liz. "He really screwed himself after what he did to Tippy Toes. He can rot for all I care."

Cheryl nodded. "I agree with Liz. You can't give in now…" She stopped talking to check her phone.

Darius turned and rummaged through the cabinets. "Wow, that's some heavy stuff. Maybe I should stay and protect you girls." He pulled an opaque plastic bag from the top shelf. "Look. Cheryl's secret stash."

Liz rolled her eyes. "Sasquatch—our hero. As long as we provide snacks, he'll be our protector."

Cheryl tapped my arm. "Did you see your email from Geoff? He cc'd me. It's about your Jason guy."

I picked up my phone and opened my email app. "Please read it. I'm too nervous."

We gathered around Cheryl as she cleared her throat. "Alli. Located Jason. Your info matched a man living in Bloomington, Minnesota. Call me ASAP for details."

I clapped my hands. "Finally, some good news. I'll call Geoff. Then Russell. Maybe I can finally get rid of those stupid things."

35

RONALD

"How many times I gotta tell you? Get your lazy butt out of bed." I grabbed Steven's pillow and tossed it against the wall. His head hit the mattress with a thud.

"Aw, Pops. It's barely eight. I thought Wednesday was our day off?" Steven rubbed his eyes, raised his head, and yawned. "Why you making me get up so early?"

"Listen, bonehead, not only is it Halloween, it's the end of the month. Time to dumpster dive while Ed and Betty are at the front desk." When I jerked a dirty, grey blanket off his body, Steven rolled off the bowed mattress and lay dazed on the carpet. "Ha. Such a nitwit. That's what you get for wrapping yourself up in your blankie." I kicked at a pile of dirty clothes with my snip-toe brown Stenson. "Get up. We head out in thirty minutes."

STEVEN CAME out of the bathroom buttoning his shirt. "Hey, Pops. Whatever happened to that cat you brought home the other night?"

"I told you, you was dreamin.' Was never no cat. I *hate* cats.

Besides Betty Shears is allergic to them. Remember?" I leaned my head sideways, cracking my neck.

Steven ran his fingers through his unruly hair. "Yeah. I guess. Didn't that guy ask about a cat when we drove up yesterday morning?" He opened the cabinet and grabbed a box of cereal. Reaching in, he pulled out a handful of multicolored bits.

I took a plastic bowl from the other cabinet and slid it across the table. "Where're your manners?"

Steven dropped his head. "Sorry, Pops… By the way, thanks for letting me show those new customers around while you and that guy talked. You tell him how proud you was of me?"

"Yeah. Told him you was my right-hand man." I slapped the kid on the back in a playful way. *Dumb as a rock and easy to distract.*

I finished off my first beer of the morning and tossed the can at the trash. As it rolled under the table and across the linoleum floor, I looked at Steven. "Finish up. We're wasting time gabbin'." I patted my shirt pocket, confirming I'd remembered my pen and small notebook, then I flipped the switch on the flashlight to check the batteries. "Don't forget them grabbers and trash bags."

"I never forget stuff, Pops." Steven tossed his bowl in the sink, then buttoned his coat as we headed out the door.

You best forget some stuff. If you know what's good for you. We walked back through the parking lot to the far end of the storage units. "Well, what do we have here?" I checked my notebook. "Unit 1454. Abandoned instead of paying." I pulled on the metal storage door. As it scraped across the pavement, I flinched and gritted my teeth. Damn noise. Gave me the willies.

I pointed to a spot on the asphalt. "Stay out here, Boy. I'll be a few minutes." Squeezing past the door, I entered the unit. I pulled out my flashlight and directed the beam inside the dusty ten by twenty-foot space. *I've eyed this one for a while.*

Inside, I noted an army-green, four-drawer filing cabinet, an oak chest of drawers with matching mirror, two awful orange and pineapple-shaped lamps, and a dozen or so file boxes. With a garbage bag and flashlight tucked under my arm, I yanked the lid off the first file box. *Bowie knives, take. Pictures of Granny, leave.* After I stashed the knives in the pocket of my brown corduroy jacket, I moved on to the next box. I tossed the lid aside, scanned the contents, and grumbled. "How many pictures do they have of that old broad?"

As the metal door creaked, I noticed light coming in. "Pops, you say something? Since I'm your right-hand man, maybe I can help." The sun backlit Steven's body in the doorway.

"Stay outside," I said. "I'm baitin' rat traps with poison." After Steven closed the door, I turned and sorted through the other boxes. I filled my bag, leaving unwanted or unsellable junk scattered on the concrete floor.

Next, I focused on the filing cabinet. The top drawer was locked, but I didn't let that stop me. Not as a self-trained locksmith. A trade that had come in very handy, especially lately. I removed a scuffed leather pouch from my jacket and worked my tools in the rusted lock. *Click.*

"Okay, let's see what was so important they locked it up," I muttered to myself. *Coin collection, take. Antique pin and gold pocket watch, take.* Looks like I'd be making a trip to the pawn shop. The dust stirred. I coughed and hurled a glob of spit into the corner.

As I opened the bottom drawer of the cabinet, my pulse quickened. I used my locksmith tools again picking the round silver lock with ease. *Hot damn.* Flipping open latches, I lifted the lid and gasped. *A .22 caliber Smith and Wesson, with a five and one-half inch barrel, wood target grip, and ambidextrous magazine release.* I turned it over in my hand. *And would you look at that? No serial number. I'm one lucky son of a gun.* I stroked the barrel and thrust it into my right back pocket, then pulled my jacket down and walked out into the sunlight.

Steven sat on the ground poking at an ant hole with a stick. "Geeze, Pop. That many rats?"

I chuckled. "More than you'd ever believe. Come on, we got other stuff to check." Glancing at my watch, it was only ten-thirty. More than enough time to continue.

Holding my nose as Steven dug through overflowing dumpsters, I pointed to pawn-worthy items. He didn't mind bending over the edge to snag our finds with the long-handle grabbers. Then, while he was busy separating everything, I inspected more neglected storage units under the guise of "preventing the ever-increasing rat population."

By noon my belly was grumbling and our garbage bags were full. We headed back to the apartment. While Steven fixed lunch, I inspected our loot for my pawn shop trip. I patted my right back pocket and smiled. *Although, some things were too valuable to pawn.*

36

ALLI

Work sucked. My life was at a standstill. Days had passed since I'd heard from Russell. And nothing from Ronald. The Garanski men were too quiet. The big phone call—from Geoff about Jason—turned out to be a bust. Same name. Wrong guy. The only thing I looked forward to was seeing Jack. He'd been over every night since he took what was left of Tippy Toes. With each visit, I became more attached, and more attracted, to him.

Lost in my thoughts, I stared at a shelf of stained pecan frames. Not a single customer in three hours. The first of the month was usually busy, but today was ridiculous. I closed up thirty minutes early and headed home.

After I walked in the door, I dropped my keys on the table. *What should I make for dinner?* In the mood for warm, gooey comfort, I set the oven at 350°, then scoured the cabinets. Flour, sugar, vanilla, salt, chocolate chips, brown sugar, baking powder and baking soda. I found three eggs in the fridge and put them on the counter. Wait… No butter? *Seriously? Could just one thing go right today?*

I cringed when my phone rang but smiled when I glanced at the caller ID. I swiped the icon and answered. "Hello, Jack." *Yes, I'm now calling him Jack.* "Tonight? Sure. That would be great. I was about to make cookies, but… The results. Oh… okay. I'll see you soon. Goodbye." My heart raced. I wanted to know, and yet, I didn't want to know. Either way, I knew I wanted to see Jack.

"Hey, girl." Cheryl walked into the kitchen playing with a black scrunchy. She twisted up her thick, curly hair and gathered it into a ponytail. "So sorry about the bad lead on that Jason in Minnesota. Geoff knows his stuff, but sometimes it takes a while."

I put the eggs back in the refrigerator and turned. "Yeah, I was really hoping for some good news. We have only two months to find him."

Cheryl frowned. "Most people make the cookies before they put everything away."

"Out of butter," I said. "Plus, Jack's on his way over."

Darius walked into the kitchen holding a TV remote. "Dead batteries. Got any more?"

I pointed to the cabinet. "Top drawer, left side by the sink." Filling the dishwasher with plates from the sink, I added detergent and closed the lid then glanced at Darius. "Find 'em?"

"There are C and D. Oh wait, here they are… nope, those are the little ones with three As." He continued to rummage through the junk drawer. "You ever notice that batteries are like boobs? The bigger the letter, the bigger the battery. Double Ds are bigger than double As. Not that I'm an expert… but just saying." He grabbed a handful of batteries and left the kitchen as Liz walked in.

"That dude is seriously strange. I only heard half of that conversation, but it was enough." She grabbed a soda from the refrigerator and sat down at the table.

As I made my way into the front room, I heard the familiar pattern of knocks and rushed to open the door. "Jack, it's good to see you… You're not dressed." I felt a blush rise in my cheeks. "I mean, you're not dressed up, like for work." *I'm such an idiot.*

He smiled. "I'm off duty." His green eyes brightened.

"Please come in." I turned toward the kitchen, "Jack, this is my roommate, Cheryl." While I made introductions, Darius strolled into the front room. "And her boyfriend, Darius."

Darius and Jack bumped fists. "Dude, they said you were a cop. That's so cool. I work at Hemp Friends Dispensary. Wanna beer?"

"Thanks for the offer. Maybe later." Jack glanced at Darius' hat. "Padres fan?"

"Is there any other team?" said Darius.

Jack chuckled. "I prefer the Diamondbacks."

Darius opened his mouth, but Cheryl snapped her fingers, then glared at him. Darius smiled at Jack and wandered into the kitchen.

Jack walked over to the couch and stood, waiting for me. I chose the middle cushion. Jack sat next to me and sighed as he removed a plain white envelope from his jacket. "I promised I'd let you know as soon as I received the lab results. Tonight I'm here unofficially. I didn't want to make you wait until my next shift."

Liz came in and sat on the other side of me. She reached for my hand as Cheryl and Darius settled on the floor.

Jack used his car key to open the top edge of the envelope. "This is known as the Gross Report. It includes a tentative findings, pending the lab procedures, plus comments from the veterinary pathologist."

I looked at Jack. "They didn't have much to go on…"

Jack cleared his throat, then read from the report "…hair follicles showed high levels of warfarin, brodifacoum, and bromadiolone…"

Tears welled in my eyes. "I don't know what any of that means."

He looked up from the paperwork. "Those are common forms of anticoagulants used in rodenticide… in other words, rat poison… very toxic…" Jack folded the letter and shoved it back in the envelope.

I grabbed my knees to keep them from trembling. "Do you think she was in pain?"

Jack placed his warm hands over mine and took a deep breath. "I'm sure she passed quickly. But, with so little evidence to go on…"

Liz pounded her fist on the floor. "He never intended to give her back alive, did he?"

Jack regarded Liz, then looked back to me. "She's probably right. I'm very sorry."

I slumped against Jack's shoulder and sobbed. My heart was so empty my chest ached. I tried to compose myself and took in a deep breath. As I glanced around the room, I spotted a framed picture of me and Tippy Toes on a shelf over the TV.

Liz followed my glance. She got up and walked over to the shelf. When she came back, she handed me the picture, then turned and wiped her eyes with the back of her hand.

Jack caressed my back. Out of the corner of my eye, I noticed a tear rolling down his cheek.

"Forget it," said Liz. "I need a drink. Anyone else want to join me?"

Darius and Cheryl went into the kitchen. They came back with a bottle of vanilla vodka and five shot glasses. With a trembling hand, Cheryl placed the glasses on the coffee table. Darius filled them.

Liz handed one to each of us as Cheryl raised hers. "To Tippy Toes."

"To Tippy Toes." We slammed back our shots and sat in silence.

Liz reached for the vodka and poured another round. She held her glass high. "To Detective Jack and his team. Here's to them catching the disgusting person who did this." Glasses clinked again.

I put my empty shot glass on the coffee table and pressed the picture close to my chest. Tears streamed down my cheeks. I looked up at Jack and whispered. "Please catch him. For me… and for Tippy Toes."

37

CHERYL

When I walked into the front room the next morning around eight, I found Alli half-asleep on the couch. "How long did Jack stay last night?"

She sat up and blushed. "Actually, he just left a few hours ago." She ran her fingers through her mussed-up hair.

"He spent the night?" I raced over and gave her a high-five. "Way to go, girlfriend."

"It's not what you think." She stared out the front window. "We just talked. He's a nice guy. He kept me company."

I pushed her feet off the cushion and plopped down on the couch. "He's also a heck-of-a-cute guy. And yes, very nice. Did I mention cute?"

Alli laughed and pulled her knees up to her chest.

"Those dark green eyes and curly black hair," I said. "And that bod. Bet he'd look great in a speedo. Don't ya think?"

She laughed again. "You better not let Darius hear you talking like that."

I enjoyed hearing her laugh after all she'd been through.

Alli let out a dreamy sigh. "He's not too bad to look at. And that little mustache… Like one of those old-timey movie stars." She rested her head on her knees. "I wish we'd met under better circumstances though."

"Yeah, that part sucks." I cocked my head to the side. "I noticed he put his arm around you." I leaned in closer. "Did he kiss you goodnight? Or rather, good morning, before he left?"

Alli lowered her knees and sat up straight. "A proper girl doesn't kiss and tell."

I snorted. "And I weigh ninety pounds naked. Come on. Tell me all the juicy details. You know I live for this kind of stuff."

Alli relaxed and pulled a faux fur pillow to her chest. "Well… After you all went to bed, we talked."

"And… I know there's more…" I made kissy lips at her.

"And then… It got late and I was cold. He pulled a fleece blanket up over me and asked if I wanted to snuggle."

"Such a gentleman."

"I must have fallen asleep. Next thing I remembered was him saying he needed to leave and go to work."

I tossed my head back. "You're making me crazy."

"And then…" She gave me a toothy grin. "He kissed me."

I bumped my shoulder against hers. "I want details."

Liz ambled into the front room and stood in front of us with her hands on her hips. "What's going on? I was trying to sleep in since I didn't have to be into work early today—"

"—Jack kissed Alli. Shhhh. She's giving details," I said.

Alli rolled her eyes. "There's nothing to tell. He kissed me and left for work. That's all."

Liz sat on the coffee table staring at Alli. "Bullcrap. There's always more when it comes to a first kiss. How long did it last?"

I also prodded. "Did he slip you the tongue?"

Liz teased. "Eyes open or closed?"

I leaned against Alli. "Come on, when was the last time a guy kissed you?"

"Fine," she said. "Just don't make a big deal about this. Okay?"

"Deal," Liz and I said together.

"Like I said, we sat on the couch. We chatted. About his family. And, my family. How he became a cop. When he made detective.

Originally from Stockton. Moved to San Diego. Brother lives in Carlsbad…"

Liz grabbed a blue, corduroy pillow from the couch. "Get to the good stuff or I swear I'll throw this at you."

Alli sighed. "He sat closer. And closer… Then, we snuggled." She paused, picking at her fingernail. "Then he kissed my earlobe. He smelled like musk. I felt all wobbly inside. Then, he kissed my neck. And my cheek, then…he brushed the hair from my eyes and leaned in. And… you know the rest."

"How romantic," I said.

Alli blushed.

I bumped her with my shoulder. "And you said nothing happened."

Alli dipped her head, then looked up. "Okay, I fibbed. I wanted to savor my secret before sharing the juicy details with you two."

I grinned. "Well, it's about time. Anything else you wanna reveal before I go wake up Darius? Best sex ever is after hearing about someone else's sex life."

Liz rolled her eyes. "Gross. I could have gone all day without hearing that."

Alli looked at both of us. "We didn't do anything except kiss. I mean, I wanted more and I'm sure he did too." She giggled and twisted a piece of hair behind her ear.

I squealed. "You are such a bad girl."

Liz slapped my arm and laughed. "Looks like we might be hearing Alli's headboard hitting the bedroom wall soon."

I looked at Liz. "Bout time, yes?"

Alli got up and headed into the kitchen. "You guys are disgusting. I'm sure nothing's going to happen for quite a while. If ever."

I followed her. "You might want to pick up some condoms—it's better to be prepared. In the meantime, I've got a bunch in the bathroom."

Alli grabbed two pieces of bread and popped them in the toaster. "I'll be fine."

Liz joined us. "Any of my cereal left or did the hairy beast eat it?"

I pointed to a box on the counter. "Still there. Darius wanted to raid the kitchen last night, but I kept him too busy to think about food."

Liz grabbed her cereal and a bowl. She turned to me and glared. "TMI."

Alli buttered her toast and added sugar to her coffee. "You two can plan my future love life. I'm going to finish breakfast then take a shower. I need to be at work by ten."

I patted her arm. "You want Darius to stop by today?"

Alli dunked the last corner of toast in her coffee and shook her head. "Jack promised to come by later, plus he assured me a police presence nearby. He hoped a black and white would deter Ronald from doing anything stupid." She picked up her coffee cup and headed down the hall.

Liz finished her cereal. She placed her bowl in the dishwasher then turned to me. "You find it weird that butt-wipe hasn't contacted her? I wonder what he's up to."

I glanced at Liz. "Every time I leave, I wonder if he's waiting for one of us. After this past weekend, who knows what he'll do next."

38

ALLI

The first week of a new month always means additional duties at work. Inventory, reconciliations, and ordering new stock. Usually, I didn't look forward to any of it. This time, however, it kept my mind off Tippy Toes. Only a few people came in and browsed, giving me time to work on my other tasks before lunch.

I glanced up at the antique wall clock. It was almost noon. I stood and stretched just as the shop door opened.

"Hiya, Princess."

"Jack, you're funny." My cheeks warmed as he approached. "It's not Halloween anymore."

"I couldn't resist. Even though you're in commoner's clothes, you're still the beautiful Snow White princess." He bowed and reached for my hand. "Since I'm on duty, I won't give you a kiss out here. But if we both happen to meet in the back…"

I felt the heat spread from my face to my neck. "I won't tell if you won't." I breathed in the musky scent of his cologne. "Do you have time to join me for lunch?"

His green eyes sparkled as his warm hand touched mine. "Sorry, can't stay long. I was in the area and wanted to see how you were doing." He released my hand as a customer walked in. "Any signs of trouble?"

"No," I said. "In fact, ever since I met you, things have calmed down. Maybe you are my knight in shining armor." I looked him up and down. "Well, at least my knight in a fine-looking, three-piece black suit."

"I don't know about that." Jack cleared his throat. "More likely the uniforms and cruisers around your neighborhood and workplace have been the deterrent."

"Whatever it is, I like having them, um, and you… around." I passed my hand over his and we locked pinky fingers for a brief moment. Walking over to a shelf I repositioned an out-of-place frame, then turned back and faced him. "I'm glad you're here. It means more than you know."

He smiled and his eyes crinkled. "I like being around you too, Alli. I feel like we've known each other forever, even though it's only been a week. You're so easy to talk to and—" His phone signaled an incoming call. "Crap. I've got to go. Promise to call you later." He brushed his fingers along my cheek, then left.

After eating a peanut butter and apricot jam sandwich, I went back to my tasks. During customer lulls, I kept myself busy in the back room doing inventory. I thought I was calm until I heard a loud thud from the front of the store. My heart raced. I vaulted into the frame area.

The copper-plated storefront door had blown open from a gust of wind. *Guess I'm still a bit jumpy.* After I checked the aisles, I walked over and pushed the door closed. I took in a deep breath, let it out, and settled myself behind the counter. The clock chimed five times, reminding me one more hour until closing time.

About thirty minutes later Cheryl poked her head inside the door. "Need help closing?"

When I spotted her red hair and orange sweater I grinned. "That'd be great. The wind's been blowing the door open, and it's freaking me out."

"Maybe we can figure a way to secure it." She looked around the floor, then turned back to me. "I thought you might want a ride home." She pointed toward the sky. "Looks like rain."

I glanced out the window and shuddered. "I've been in the back and never noticed. Thanks." I said, giving her a hug.

She patted my back. "Didn't think you'd want to wait at the bus stop if those clouds opened up—" A crack of thunder crashed overhead.

"Nice timing. I'm almost ready to go. Just need to put the ledger book in the back office." I rushed to the backroom and stacked papers and manila folders atop a burgundy, leather-bound book. On the way back to the front, my phone buzzed. I stopped and checked it. "Hold on a sec. Jack called. And Liz… I don't recognize this number. They left several messages." I pressed the voice mail icon and listened. "Oh no."

"What? What?"

I held up my hand and replayed the last message. "It's about Russell… He's in the hospital…" I made notes on a nearby scrap of paper, hung up, then looked at her. "Russell's at U.C. San Diego Medical Center in Hillcrest. They admitted him last night, but just found my number." I stuffed my phone in my back pocket, then took an anxiety pill from my pill box. I popped it in my mouth, swallowing it without water. "We need to get to the hospital."

39

ALLI

The hospital doors automatically opened and closed with a whoosh. Artificial wind propelled by exhaust fans blurred our conversation as Cheryl and I entered the U.C. San Diego Medical Center. Women wearing baggy green scrubs and men with clipboards and little plastic bags scurried past, distracted in their own thoughts. The pungent scent of rubbing alcohol assaulted my nostrils. An empty gurney waited in the hallway. *Reminds me of when Mom was in the hospital.*

I ran up to the first desk I saw. "Excuse me. I got a message…" I struggled to breathe. "Garanski? Which room…?"

A slender, blond-haired woman checked her computer screen then peered over her glasses. "Are you family?"

I gripped the counter. "Someone from your hospital called and left a message. Will you please help me?"

"Your name, Miss?" Her faded gold name tag read Olivia Barnes.

"Alli—Allison Harper."

Ms. Barnes scanned her screen and flicked the mouse with the tip of a bony finger. "Patient's name?"

"Garanski… Russell Garanski." I drummed my fingers on the counter and looked down the hall.

"Garanski," she said, her voice lowering. "He's in Cardiac ICU. Room 413—that's on the fourth floor." She pointed left, "You'll need to go that way, take the elevator and check in with the ICU charge nurse..."

We rounded the corner before Ms. Barnes finished her spiel. I scanned the hall for the elevator sign. A loud ding signaled we were close. We slipped inside the crowded cab as the doors closed. I pressed my back against the cold, silver wall and looked around. A woman in a wrinkled jogging suit held a shiny, blue ribbon attached to a *Get Well Soon* balloon that appeared to eavesdrop as it bobbed with the movement of the elevator. A well-dressed gentleman absorbed in his phone cursed under his breath. A young couple whispered to each other as he pushed the sixth-floor button multiple times. She held a pink floral arrangement and an overstuffed pink Teddy Bear. The sweet scent of baby's breath mixed with stale body odor hung in the air. Waiting for our floor, Cheryl leaned against me and grabbed my hand.

As the doors opened, we stepped out into the hall.

I took a deep breath. "Thank goodness that's over. I hate elevators about as much as I hate hospitals. And, I really hate hospitals."

Cheryl wiped her sweaty hands on her pant leg. "You aren't kidding. Let's find the nurses' station."

As we dashed down the hall, I gave Cheryl a sideways glance. "Did the lady downstairs say Cardiac ICU?"

She nodded, then stopped and pointed to a large desk located in the middle of the hall. Like the hub of a bicycle wheel, rooms at the end of each of the spoke-like aisles led to an open area. Several nurses busied themselves behind a desk, while others checked charts before setting off toward different rooms.

"Excuse me," I said to a pleasant, dark-haired woman behind the desk. "I'm trying to find room 413." I scrutinized her badge as I waited. It displayed a smiling face, credentials, and the name Maria Mercado.

Nurse Mercado checked her computer screen. "Your name?"

My heart pounded in my throat. "I'm Alli Harper. Someone called me a few hours ago. What happened to Russell? Is he going to be okay?"

The nurse stood. "I see you are listed as a contact for Mr. Garanski. He's in serious condition."

I gasped. "What happened? Why is he here?" I leaned on the corner of the desk to steady myself. Beeping came from a nearby room. A male nurse scurried down the hall.

Cheryl watched him disappear into a room. "That didn't sound good."

Nurse Mercado patted my hand, grabbed a clipboard, and motioned for us to follow her. "Let's go into the waiting area. It's more private."

We walked around a corner past the glass windows of the ICU patient rooms. Rhythmic beeping, irregular sirens, and coughing came from various areas. Visitors and nurses stood outside talking in muffled tones, some clutched each other's hands. Nurse Mercado pointed to a group of chairs in a brightly lit corner. On the opposite side of the room, a television played an old *Tom and Jerry* cartoon. An older Asian woman sat in a mauve, upholstered chair staring at the TV. Her head jerked as she fought sleep.

"Please have a seat," said Nurse Mercado.

"I want to know about my friend." I choked back tears and remained standing. "Why can't I see him?"

"I'll take you to him in just a moment. First, I wanted to advise you of his condition." She studied the chart in her hand. "Alli, it appears Mr. Garanski might have taken too much of his heart medicine…"

I grabbed Cheryl's sleeve and gasped. "Oh no, I can't believe it." My legs weak, I sunk into a chair.

"On October 31, a neighbor called an ambulance when he saw Mr. Garanski fall down his front steps. Apparently, he became dizzy and fainted while giving out candy to some children."

Cheryl put her arm around my shoulder as I leaned in closer to the nurse. "He's going to be okay… isn't he?"

Nurse Mercado lowered her voice, then spoke. "He's in serious condition. Upon evaluation, his doctor suspected he ingested an overdose of Coumadin."

"What?" I said.

"Coumadin," said the nurse. "It's an anticoagulant medication used by stroke and heart attack patients susceptible to blood clots." She cleared her throat and continued. "When he collapsed, he fell and cut his head. Because of the medication, he lost a lot of blood because it wouldn't clot properly."

"Oh my gosh," said Cheryl.

"It took a while to control the bleeding," said Nurse Mercado. "Mr. Garanski required quite a few stitches and several pints of blood."

Cheryl grabbed a handful of tissues from a nearby table and passed them to me.

I fought back tears. "He's got to get better… I want to see him." I jumped up and began pacing. "Please…"

Nurse Mercado stood. "I wanted you to be aware of his condition. He's still comatose and very weak. He's on oxygen and is hooked up to several IVs. It might seem grim, but please try to stay positive when you are in his room. Even though he appears to be asleep, I believe he can still hear—"

"This can't be happening. I turned to Cheryl. "First Tippy Toes, now…" I sobbed.

Cheryl wiped her eyes with a tissue, then pulled me close. "Alli, you need to pull yourself together. If he hears us bawling, he'll sense it." She stepped back and looked at me. "We need to be strong for him."

Nurse Mercado nodded. "Your friend is right. You must force yourself to be upbeat, no matter what you think or feel on the inside. That's why I wanted to prepare you, mentally and emotionally."

I nodded. First, I blew my nose and shoved the tissues into my pocket. Then, I squared my shoulders. "Okay. I'm ready."

Nurse Mercado led us back down the hall to room 413. I wiped my hands on my sweater and took a deep breath before I entered. Cheryl stood close, resting her hand on my shoulder.

As we walked in, Cheryl fanned herself. She unzipped her jacket, took it off, and tied it around her waist. Machines around the bed beeped and chirped. A screen above displayed heart rate and blood pressure readings. Four IV tubes snaked under the covers to Russell's pale body. A large sterile pad was taped over his left eye. His forehead and cheek were dark purple and swollen. I wiped beads of sweat from my upper lip and moved closer to his bed. His right eye was closed. An oxygen tube drooped under his nose.

I forced a smile. "He looks good. Don't you think, Cheryl?"

She nodded and stared.

"Hi, Mr. Garanski. It's Alli. Can you hear me?" He seemed to stir but didn't open his eye. I looked back at Nurse Mercado for guidance.

She gave me a thumbs-up. "You're doing great. Just keep talking. Remember, he can hear you." She started toward the door. "If you need anything, I'll be right outside."

I looked back at Russell. "Mr. Garanski. If you can hear me… This is Alli. I'm here. They called me and said you were in the hospital." I realized I was shouting at him and reminded myself to talk quieter.

Cheryl stood behind me. "Tell him I'm here, too. And that I'm sorry."

"I think he just heard you. Look…" I pointed to Russell's hand laying on the bed. His fingers twitched as we spoke. I reached down and took his hand in mine. I continued to talk, describing the weather. My week at work. Anything I could think of to keep speaking and stay positive. I even told him about Jack. "I met a cute guy…" I said.

I motioned to Cheryl to join in. She chatted about her trip to Sacramento and how she met up with her dad. She even shared a recipe for chicken tacos. She shrugged. "I didn't know what else to say."

Nurses entered and exited as we chatted. Even though we were only supposed to stay five minutes, Nurse Mercado told us not to worry. She said the company would do him good since no one else had visited. As Russell's vital signs improved, she gave us more time. One of the male nurses dubbed us "Russell's Good Luck Charms." I figured it was because Russell and I shared the unique bond through the *Gifts*.

When my stomach growled again, I realized we'd been at the hospital almost two hours. I looked at Cheryl and motioned toward the door. "Mr. Garanski, we have to go now. You need to get some sleep. I promise we'll come back again tomorrow." Holding his hand, I swore I'd felt his fingers twitch, although his eye remained closed.

As we rode the elevator down to the main floor, I breathed out a long, deep sigh. "I feel better now that we saw him. But I wonder…

Why did he take too much of that prescription? I didn't even know he had a heart condition."

Cheryl looked at me as we walked outside and stood under the overhang. The rain had stopped, although the parking lot was still wet. "I don't know. Maybe when he wakes up, you can ask him."

I checked my phone as we walked out to Cheryl's car. "Poor Jack, he sent three text messages. We left so fast I didn't get a chance to tell him about Russell. He's probably worried… Two voice messages from Liz. I wonder what's up?" I listened to the first one, then bristled. "Oh, crap."

Cheryl stopped walking. "Now what? Did Ronald…?"

I pushed the icon to call Liz. "Not Ronald. Zack showed up at the apartment. He demanded she open the door."

40

LIZ

I figured Cheryl forgot her key again when I heard a knock at the door. When I peered through the front window, I jumped back. My pulse quickened. I folded my arms across my chest and glared at him. "Zack? What are you doing out there?"

His muffled voice resonated through the wood. "Liz, please let me in. We need to talk."

I leaned in and yelled into the door jamb. "No way. You cheated on me. We're finished." I hated what he did to me. But because I was still attracted to him, I couldn't risk opening the door. I didn't trust my emotions or reactions especially if the baby was his.

"Liz, I didn't cheat." I heard a thud hitting the wall. "I'm not leaving until you open this door."

"Then you're going to be standing out there all night."

"It's cold out here. Please…"

I heard another voice. An exchange of muffled words. Though I pressed my ear to the door, I couldn't hear anything specific.

"I'll be back, and we will talk…" shouted Zack. His voice trailed off as I heard keys jingle in the lock. *Where's my phone? Damn. Left it on my nightstand.* I spotted one of Cheryl's jade Buddha statues on a shelf and rushed over. I held the statue ready to throw at whoever came through the door. *Instead of Karma biting you in the arse, it will knock you in the head.*

I took aim. "Who's there?"

The door opened and Darius walked in. He took a step back and waved his hands. "It's just me."

I relaxed my hand and returned the statue to the shelf. "Sorry, I thought Zack might have a key.

"He was here, but he left when I showed up. Everything okay?"

"I guess. Just glad you got here when you did."

Darius adjusted his Padres hat and stretched out on the couch. He grabbed the remote and flipped through the channels. "You seen Cheryl?"

The thought of making small talk with the hairy-thing didn't thrill me, but I forced a smile. "No, I have not seen Cheryl. She said something about picking up Alli because of the storm." Marching into my room, I grabbed my phone and punched in Alli's number. When she didn't answer, I left a voice mail.

I went back into the front room. Darius was knocking back a beer and was engrossed in a football game. *Thank goodness.* Didn't want to engage in any more pointless conversation. After making myself a ham sandwich, I headed back to my room. I put on long socks and wrapped up in my comforter. Once I ate, I must have dozed off.

I BOLTED UPRIGHT when my phone rang. "You're where? What happened?" Alli talked so fast, I couldn't catch everything. "Yes, Zack was here, but he left…" I yawned and rubbed my eyes. "Food? Sounds good. I'm sure Darius will want something also…" I held the phone away from my face. *Geeze, almost ten o'clock.* "And Jack. I'll let Darius know." *Great. More people to deal with tonight.* Looking down at my grumbling tummy, I hoped they'd hurry back with the food. *At least I don't feel like puking.*

I tossed my comforter on the bed and headed into the front room. Darius and Jack sat on the couch drinking beer and discussing football. "Nice to see you again, Jack."

He stood and smiled.

Such a gentleman. Alli found herself a good one. I just hope they aren't taking things too fast. *Who am I to talk?* Zack and I slept together after our first date. I let out a long sigh. *Seems like so long ago.*

I jumped when the door burst open. "Food is here," said Alli. She and Cheryl walked in and plopped their bags on the counter.

I walked over and inhaled the scents of cumin, garlic, and onions. I used to hate anything spicy—now I couldn't get enough of it. I searched through the bags and pulled out a few tacos, a burrito, and a handful of chips. I touched Alli on the shoulder. "Any news on Russell?"

Alli shook her head, then rushed over to the couch. Jack stood and embraced her.

Cheryl took several plates from the cabinet and turned to me. "He didn't look too good. He was still unconscious."

"What happened?" I set my overflowing plate on the table.

Cheryl shared the scant information the nurse disclosed. Piling an assortment of tacos and burritos on a plate, she took it to Darius, then came back and joined me.

"How did Alli take it?" I asked, biting into a juicy taco.

"She kept it together in his room but sobbed on the way home." Cheryl dipped a tortilla chip in her beans, pausing before she ate it. "I heard you had an exciting evening."

I nodded, then swallowed. "Yeah, it turned out okay. Thanks to your boyfriend." I wiped my mouth and picked up a burrito dripping with red sauce as Alli and Jack came in the kitchen.

Alli rested her hand on my arm. "You okay? I can't believe he showed up again."

I nodded and gave Jack a look. "After I called him about the fingerprints…" I cleared my throat, extra loud, for emphasis. "He's called me daily."

Darius walked into the kitchen and grabbed two beers. "You want another one, Detective Dude?"

Jack waved him off. "I'm good. Thanks."

"I was gonna kick his butt," said Darius. He puffed out his chest and gave us a toothy grin.

I rolled my eyes, though I was thankful Darius showed up. I wasn't ready to confront Zack. Not until I talked with Alli. I thought about asking her to wear the glasses again and tell me what I was really thinking. Now, since she was all freaked out about the older Garanski, my idea seemed stupid.

I looked around. Alli and Jack settled back on the couch watching TV. Cheryl and Darius headed down the hall arm in arm. I stifled a yawn. "Good night," I said to no one in particular. Without a response from anyone, I turned and walked down the hall, massaging my growing belly.

41

ALLI

Resting my back against Jack's warm chest, I scanned through the channels. "I'm glad you decided to stay."

"When you didn't return my messages, I was concerned." He kissed the back of my neck. "I'm sorry about your friend."

"I didn't get your texts until we were out in the parking lot. There was no Wi-Fi in the ICU. Everything happened so fast. I freaked out. Sorry I didn't call before we went to the hospital."

Jack wrapped his arms around my waist. "An overdose, you said?"

"As far as I knew, Russell didn't have heart problems." Taking in a deep breath, I savored the scent of Jack's musky cologne. I offered him the remote. "You choose something to watch."

"I'm good with quiet," he said.

I turned off the TV. The new lamp in the corner cast a warm glow over the room. Feeling drowsy, my senses heightened as Jack snuggled closer. I turned and faced him. He drew me in and rested his head next to mine. I closed my eyes as his curly hair tickled my nose and was thankful he was taking things slow, even though everything inside of me wanted to speed up. We'd only known each other little over a week and, under the circumstances, it didn't seem right.

"You're sure you won't catch heck at work for being here?"

Jack sighed. "Though I'm still investigating this case, they can't stop me from what I do on my own time." He stroked my arm with the tips of his fingers. "And I prefer spending my own time with you. That is if you don't mind."

"I don't." His fingertips reached my hand. We locked fingers and sat, holding each other. My stomach fluttered as I turned my head, exposing my neck. I trembled and hoped he didn't notice.

He kissed my neck, then my cheek. I let my hand drop to his leg. A wave of panic ran through me. What if he wants to spend the night? *Oh crap, I never bought condoms.* I caressed his leg. *I'm almost thirty and never done it. Should I tell him? He's probably got lots of practice. I've never even watched a porn movie. I need one of my anti-anxiety pills…*

Jack sat up and studied me. "You okay, Alli?"

"Um, sure." I patted his leg. "Why?"

He moved back and stood. "I should probably go."

"Did I do something to upset you?"

He smiled. "I was about to ask you the same thing."

"No, I… my brain gets weird sometimes." I gazed into his green eyes.

Jack took my face in his hands. "Alli, even though I've only known you a little while, you're very special to me. But, I don't want to mess anything up." He leaned down and kissed my forehead. "I thought I might have gone too far last night. I wanted to talk to you about it earlier but had to leave. Then I couldn't get a hold of you. I didn't know if you were mad or if something happened." He let out a long sigh. "I'd love to take this to the next level… But I don't want to rush you."

I let out a nervous laugh. "I was kinda worried you'd, you know… want to…" I felt a blush rise in my cheeks. "Never mind."

Jack locked eyes. "To be honest, I do. But, I want you to know I'm here for you emotionally, not physically. Does that make sense?"

I reached up and hugged him.

He held me against his warm body. We stood in the front room. Not speaking. Just hugging. For what seemed like forever. My body relaxed in his strong arms.

He pulled back a little bit. "I've never experienced this before. I mean, working on a case and feeling something. I don't want to screw this up…"

I looked up at him. "I was nervous about not being prepared." I used air quotes emphasizing the last word.

Jack laughed, using air quotes. "I wasn't prepared either." He kissed me on the lips. "Besides, if, and when, the time comes, I'd be too intimidated to… er, take this to the next level here with all your roommates in the next room." His breathing quickened as he kissed my neck and began nibbling on my ear.

I pulled back and fanned myself. "Jack, you're making me all crazy inside again." I pressed myself against him, slid my hands down his muscular back, and cupped his tight butt cheeks.

Jack whispered in my ear, letting the last word linger. "You're not helping my situation either, Princess."

Without warning, Darius stumbled into the front room and headed to the kitchen. He shielded his eyes. "Just getting a snack. Don't mind me."

We watched as he grabbed a box of cereal, released an enormous belch without apology, then stumbled back down the hall.

I shuddered. "Maybe we should head over to your place."

"Definitely…" Jack's eyes met mine. "You better leave a note. Don't want your friends to freak out if they can't find you."

I rushed into the kitchen, scribbled "Went to Jack's" on a napkin, and stuck it on the fridge with a flower magnet. Then I dashed to my room and grabbed my blue canvas bag stuffing it with my pillow, phone and charger, a change of underwear, and my best sleep-shirt. Then I hurried into the bathroom, snatched my toothbrush, make up-kit, deodorant, and one of Cheryl's condoms—okay, two, just in case—and shoved those in the bag. I stopped, looked in the mirror, and tucked a strand of hair behind my ear. *Stop fussing, you look great. There's nothing to worry about…* Just wish I'd never eaten that second bean burrito.

42

JACK

Alli and I left the apartment silhouetted by a full November moon. Wanting to attract as little attention as possible, things didn't go exactly as planned. First, Alli's footsteps reverberated on the concrete and metal stairs leading down from the apartment to the parking lot. Then I dropped my bundle of keys on the pavement. Not once, but twice, as I fumbled to unlock the doors of my grey Charger. As I retrieved the keys, our quickly-planned escape continued—until I set off the car alarm. An ear-splitting siren echoed up and down the street prompting a cacophony of barking from neighborhood dogs.

I let out a deep sigh. "Crap, now everyone knows we're out here. I just bought this car a month ago, and the alarm is so damned sensitive." Wincing, I chirped the key fob a few times to disarm the alarm. "So sorry."

I closed the passenger door and made my way to the driver's side. Stumbling on a soda can lying in the street, it shot across the pavement and crashed into the rim of a parked car. Another dog barked. A porch light came on. "Dang, can't a guy take a girl to his place without the whole world knowing about it?" I slid into my seat and looked at Alli.

She placed her bag on her lap then brushed her hand over mine.

"Someday, we'll laugh about this." She giggled. "It's actually kinda funny right now."

I was drawn in by her warm smile. Taking her hand in mine, I brought it to my lips and kissed it. "Glad you have a sense of humor, Princess. I hope things get better from here." I let go of her hand and started the engine.

"Oh no." Alli rubbed her hands together. "I forgot my jacket."

I turned the heater on high. "Would you like to go back and get it…?"

She laughed. "No way. I'm not going through all that again. Someone might call the cops. That's all we'd need." She warmed her hands by the vent and looked at me. "I just realized I don't know where you live."

"Mission Hills. From your place, it'll take less than fifteen minutes if I don't take the freeway." I shifted into drive and pulled away from the curb. Merging into light traffic, we headed west on Washington Street.

A few minutes later Alli turned toward me. "Everything okay? You're so quiet." As she removed her glasses, the light reflected in her eyes.

"Yeah, sorry." I turned and smiled. "I was thinking about something you mentioned earlier. Guess my detective-brain is always on duty, even when I'm off the clock."

"What are you talking about, Jack?" She put on her glasses. "Are you having second thoughts… about us?"

I smiled. "No. Not at all." I reached over and caressed her arm. "That part I'm sure of." I pulled up to a red light and looked at her. "It's what you said earlier about Russell. You mentioned he didn't have health issues." I accelerated as the light changed. "With the possibility of past alleged criminal activity, part of me wonders if there's a connection."

Alli sat forward in her seat. "I don't understand."

I pulled over to the side of the road and parked. "You mentioned something about an overdose of Coumadin and excessive bleeding. As I mulled over the information, something clicked just a few minutes ago."

Alli grabbed my arm. "What are you talking about?"

"After I received the necropsy report on your cat's fur samples, I did some research. Did you know Coumadin, an anticoagulant, is one of the main ingredients found in rat poison?"

Alli gasped and grabbed my hand. "Are you saying…?"

My heart raced. "If Russell was healthy, then a few days after your cat's death he developed symptoms consistent with the ingestion of rat poison, I can't help but think the two might be related."

"Do you think Ronald poisoned my cat… then his dad?" Her eyes widened.

"I don't want to jump to conclusions without evidence. The hospital will need to run specific toxicology tests on Russell. Plus, I'll need to get a search warrant for his home."

"Oh my gosh." Alli twisted her hair behind her ear. "You're freaking me out."

"I don't mean to scare you. I'm only trying to help." I patted her hand. "Alli, do you remember any other details? Try to think back and tell me everything."

"I don't know." Her voice became higher. "If Russell was poisoned, then he might… Oh, Jack, we have to go back and see him now."

As I shifted into drive, Alli began sobbing. I kept my foot on the brake, grabbed my phone, and called the hospital. Identifying myself, I requested to speak to the ICU charge nurse and explained my concerns.

"Alli, listen to me. They need your permission to run the tests." I held her close and whispered, "Hon, I need you to be strong right now. And, so does Russell."

She looked up and nodded as I released the brake. We headed back toward Hillcrest and the UCSD Medical Center. I gripped the steering wheel, working my way through traffic.

Alli touched my knee. "The nurse said he was bleeding. A lot. They had a hard time stopping it. She also mentioned something else…" She drummed her fingers on the seat. "He was unconscious. They figured it was from the head injury."

"You're doing great. Anything else?" I checked the GPS. *Only a few more miles.*

"Someone called 911 and said they'd found Russell collapsed on his front lawn. Supposedly he appeared dizzy and weak. Then fainted. That's all I remember."

The lights of the city blurred in the background. As I pulled into the hospital parking lot, Alli took off her glasses again and wiped her eyes. I jumped out of the car, took in a deep breath, and glanced up at the cloud-filled sky.

"Did I mention how much I hate hospitals?" she asked, reaching for my hand. We walked in silence through the emergency entrance.

I shuddered as we entered the elevator. "I'm not fond of them either." A male nurse leaned up against the chrome wall reading a dog-eared book. He looked up, nodded, and went back to his book.

Alli gripped my hand. "Fourth floor."

I pushed the button and sucked in my breath.

When we reached the fourth floor, Alli stepped outside and paused. "Last time we came in the other way. I'm not sure where the ICU is…"

I spotted a nurse and asked directions. An orderly led us around a corner and down a long hallway.

Alli tugged on my hand as we rushed to the nurses' station.

"Nurse Mercado…" Alli shouted to anyone nearby. "I have to see Nurse Mercado." A woman in scrubs turned and walked toward us. Alli stopped and pointed. "There's his room…"

Just as Alli got close to his doorway, an earsplitting alarm blared. A male voice announced over the loudspeaker, "Code Blue Room 413." Hospital staff rushed past us and closed the door. Someone pulled the curtains.

Alli screamed. "What's going on?"

No one paid attention to her. More people wearing scrubs rushed into the room, followed by a tall woman who appeared to be a doctor.

"Jack? What's happening?"

I held Alli close to keep her from the bustle of activity. Each time the door opened, she tried to pull away.

The alarms continued. The announcement repeated. "All nurses to Room 413. Code Blue Room 413."

Alli sobbed.

I trembled. We held on to each other waiting for someone to come out.

Soon, the activity died down and the alarms no longer shrieked. One by one nurses filed out of the room. Alli broke away from me. She squeezed past hospital personnel coming out the door. I caught up to her as she wailed and collapsed on the floor.

My eyes darted around the stuffy room. Machines no longer monitored vital signs. A male nurse filled out paperwork. I glanced at the older gentleman on the bed, his face already turning grey. A female nurse walked up to me. "I'm sorry. We did everything we could…"

Damn. Not the way I thought this evening would turn out.

43

ALLI

I saw Russell leaning against the stucco wall outside *Framed.* Walking through the front doors, I smiled. "I'm so happy to see you. Are you okay?"

He turned and gave me that wonderful, kind smile I'd missed seeing for the past month.

"How have you been?" I extended my hand to him.

"I can't stay long," he said. "I need to get back."

"But, you just got here. I have so many questions." As I pleaded with him, my eyes welled up. "Please, I have to talk to you." I moved closer, hoping to catch a whiff of his cologne. Something, anything to let me know it was really him.

Russell looked directly in my eyes. "Don't worry about me. I'm okay now." He reached out as if to touch my arm, then stopped. "I'm sorry," he said. "I need to go. Take care of yourself."

I leaned in for a hug.

He was gone.

I SAT UP IN BED, crying. *Was I dreaming?* It seemed so real…

After I wiped my eyes and blew my nose, I called Russell's phone. The same call I'd made each morning for the last three weeks. Though I knew he wouldn't answer, it helped to hear his voice on the greeting. I still couldn't wrap my head around it. First Tippy Toes. Then Russell.

I forced myself out of bed and dressed. Walking into the kitchen, I inhaled the aroma of fresh-brewed coffee. Darius stood near the refrigerator, drinking milk from the carton.

"Morning," he said offering me the carton. "Milk?"

"No. Thanks. It's yours now." Opening the upper cabinet door, I took out a coffee cup and a glass. "You always do that?"

"Most times." Darius wiped his mouth on his sleeve. "Is it a problem?"

"Yeah, kind of." I handed him the glass. "I prefer you use one of these." Filling my cup with coffee, I continued. "I don't like anyone drinking out of the carton. And Liz. With her hair and germ phobias… she'd freak out."

He dropped two pastries in the toaster, pushed down the button, and leaned against the counter. Smiling at me, he poured milk in the glass.

I nodded to him as I stirred sugar into my cup. I buttoned my sweater and settled outside on our shady patio with my coffee. San Diego was having one of the darkest, rainiest Novembers on record. Most of the time, I looked forward to grey clouds. Since Russell's death, the gloom only added to my misery. Over the past few weeks, my anxiety had gone through the roof. Panic attacks and nightmares woke me nightly. I couldn't concentrate. I couldn't do anything.

The patio door opened with a soft whoosh. Liz popped her head outside. "We're getting ready to head out. You riding with me or waiting for Jack?"

"Waiting. I'll see you over there."

Liz nodded and closed the door as I took a sip of coffee.

We were all meeting at Mount Hope Cemetery for a small memorial service for Russell. After the medical examiner released the body, everyone chipped in for a direct cremation. We wanted to give him a proper burial and paid for his inurnment alongside his wife who passed so many years ago.

Ronald has been scarce lately. He didn't even show up to claim the body. Makes sense since I was almost sure he poisoned Russell. The primary toxicology showed high levels of Coumadin. Due to the suspicious circumstances, Jack ordered a full autopsy which could take up to six weeks. I think he found something when they searched Russell's house after his death but didn't fill me in. Jack mentioned something about an "ongoing investigation," though that's never stopped him from sharing before.

Next Thursday is Thanksgiving. Except for Jack, I don't have anything to be thankful for. From taking me home the night Russell passed away, to coming by after work and on his days off, he'd been amazing.

I looked up as the door opened again.

"Heya, Princess." Jack leaned down and kissed me on the cheek.

I stood and hugged him. "I'm so happy you're coming with us."

He nodded and waited for me to lock up before we headed out.

JACK HELD my hand as we drove to Mount Hope Cemetery. I stared out the window and watched as the sun broke through the clouds over the Laguna Mountains and casted golden highlights on the sprawling city. I smiled, listening to him sing along with the radio. It was some oldies tune, and although he missed a few words, he didn't care.

As we entered the gates of the expansive grounds, we stopped to read an unobtrusive brown granite monument.

Mt. Hope Cemetery
A PUBLIC CEMETERY FOR ALL PEOPLE

I TURNED TO JACK. "Russell will be near a lot of famous people. City founders, mayors, a governor of California, a famous author. Even Civil War generals are buried here."

"Is that so?" He smiled. "Quite fitting for your friend."

I nodded. We drove past sprawling oak trees, elegant palm trees, and soldier-straight junipers on acres upon acres of monuments. The short, squat granite markers reminded me of faded, grey chocolate bars poking out of the ground. Tall, slender vertical monuments stretched toward the heavens. Russell's cremains were interred in his wife's grave which was located near a majestic oak tree.

We made our way up and down the cemetery streets, passing groups of bike riders headed the opposite direction. As we heard a loud ding, ding, ding, we stopped when red lights flashed and crossing gates lowered to block the road. I smiled as we watched the cherry-red San Diego Trolley glide over the tracks that crossed through the cemetery.

I pointed. "There's Cheryl and Darius. Oh, and Liz too."

Jack pulled his Charger near Cheryl's car. We got out and walked over to meet up with them. A gentle breeze pushed puffy white clouds across a cerulean sky. Curled oak leaves drifted down along the path. The scent of fresh cut grass tickled my nose.

Cheryl motioned for us to gather under the oak tree, just a few feet away from the Garanski plot. For the first time in weeks, my chest didn't tighten. This was one of the most peaceful places I'd been to in a long time.

"Thanks for coming. I really appreciate how you've all been there for me the last few weeks…" My voice cracked. I reached into my pocket and fingered the monogrammed handkerchief Russell gave me the morning we met for coffee. Closing my eyes, I took a deep breath. "…Russell was a special friend. Even though I'd only known him for a few months, he was like my grandpa… He…" My shoulders shook. I began sobbing. Turning, I buried my face in Jack's chest. His strong arms held me as I heard mourning doves calling to each other. Quite fitting, I thought.

When I composed myself, Liz and Jack stood on each side of me. Liz held the long stem of a dark red rose. Jack put his arm around my waist. The three of us watched as Cheryl and Darius took a few steps, then arranged a spray of cheerful orange and buttery-yellow chrysanthemums on a granite headstone bearing the name of Agatha Garanski.

"This is so screwed up," said Liz. "His idiot son should be in a grave somewhere…" She wiped her eyes with a crumpled tissue. The breeze kicked up a pile of leaves and sent them skittering across our feet.

Jack looked over at me. "Do you want to…?"

"I can't," I said. "Not yet. In my mind, he's still here. Just not answering his phone."

Liz cleared her throat, walked over, and laid her rose next to the mums.

As she walked back and stood next to me, I caught a familiar scent. My heart raced. *Old Spice?* The same cologne Russell always wore. *But how? Where?* I turned and followed the haunting aroma. My eyes widened. A Firebird sat parked a few sections away from us. A tall, lanky guy leaned against his car, light reflecting off his neon sunglasses. I elbowed Liz in the ribs and motioned for her to turn around.

She balled up her fists. "What is Zack doing here?"

44

ZACK

What a horrible month. After Liz called about their break-in and how the police needed my fingerprints, I wanted to come clean and share the details about my family search. But, she never returned my calls. Visits to her apartment became hostile shouting matches. Even Darius, who I thought was my friend, threatened to kick my butt.

Funny how you don't really know people until something happens. Liz and I had been doing great. I planned the proposal, even bought the ring and everything. But, once she thought I was cheating, everything changed. All I ever wanted was to find out who I really was.

After years of searching, we finally located the man I'd been looking for. As I watched him from a distance, I realized I really only knew two things about him—where he lived and that he wore Old Spice cologne. I even bought a bottle of the stuff, figuring we'd have something in common when I found the nerve to talk to him.

I finally gathered my courage and drove to his house on Halloween night. I pulled up to the curb and let the engine idle. *It's now or never, Zack.* I shut off the engine when I saw him sitting outside on the porch handing out candy to the kids. He looked up and noticed me. He stood, smiled, and started walking down the stairs. It was like he knew me—

maybe even expected me. About halfway down, he stumbled, then collapsed.

I shut off the engine, jumped out of my car, and ran to him. There was so much blood and he was unconscious. I called 911, said I was a neighbor and gave them his address. Once I heard sirens, I ducked out of sight. I didn't know if my dad might be nearby and I sure couldn't let me see me.

I tried to visit Gran-Dad in the hospital that night, but he was in Cardiac ICU. I overheard the nurses say he was in grave condition. When I asked to see him, they said family only. Even though I was family, I couldn't risk it if someone else in the family showed up. I returned the next night and paced around the E.R. entrance while trying to devise a way to see him. That's when Cheryl and Alli rushed in. I left before they spotted me.

The next time I went up to the hospital, they said he'd died. That really sucked. After all those years of searching… *Why didn't I have the balls to talk to him sooner?*

Online, I found a brief obituary. It mentioned something about Mount Hope being his final resting place. I'd been out every day since they buried him with my grandma. Sitting on the soft grass under his big tree, I'd talk to him. That's why I was out here today. Then Cheryl, Darius, and Liz drove up. And Alli and some guy. I figured they were visiting some relative or something. But then they gathered around his grave…

My heart raced. Confused, I leaned against my Firebird hoping they wouldn't see me. Then Alli turned. Our eyes met. She elbowed Liz. They glared at me. *What the... ?* How did they know my gran-dad, Russell?

45

ALLI

I wasn't looking forward to our memorial gathering for Russell. Then I noticed Zack and everything got weird. Liz bolted toward him, followed by Darius. Jack looked at me. I didn't know what to do. Before they reached Zack, he'd taken off in his Firebird, leaving a swirl of leaves and a cloud of exhaust behind him.

"I just can't believe…" Liz stomped back and brushed the dust off her jeans. "What a jerk."

"You know," said Jack. "I can help you file for a restraining order if he keeps bothering you."

"I've been thinking about it." She sighed. "I really figured he'd give up by now. But showing up here? Today of all days."

Darius came back breathing hard. "I would have kicked his butt."

Cheryl stroked his beard. "I know you would have, Sweetie."

Liz turned to Cheryl. "I'll wait in your car until you're ready." She looked at me. "Sorry…"

I glanced down at her stomach, then back up to her face. "No need to explain." Liz, Cheryl, and Darius trudged back to their car. Jack and I watched them drive away.

"I'm ready to go," I said to Jack. He slipped his arm around my waist and we walked back to his car.

He pulled out of the cemetery and drove down a tranquil street. I stared out the window listening to Jack's steady breathing. I figured he was deep in thought and didn't mind the silence. I thought about the last month. How wished I could wake up from this nightmare. Until we found Jason… I'd be the next Guardian.

After a quiet drive home, Jack and I arrived at the apartment. We walked in and found Liz, Cheryl, and Darius in the front room eating pizza. I peeked in each of the three large boxes on the counter, then turned to Jack. "Pepperoni? Vegetarian? Or, Meat Lovers?"

"I could go for a slice or two." His eyes crinkled and his little mustache lifted just a bit, exposing a subtle smile.

I handed Jack a plate, placed a few slices of pepperoni on mine, then sat at the table and picked at my food as he sat and joined me.

Cheryl jumped up from the couch and rushed over to us. "When's the last time you checked your messages, Girlfriend?"

"Before we left, I guess. My phone's been on silent. Why?"

"Well, check them now," said Cheryl. "I just got a text from Geoff. He's been trying to reach you all morning."

I turned my phone over and noticed the notification light blinking. Multiple text and voice mails. I dialed his number then stood up and paced as it rang. Once. Twice. *Please pick up. Arggggg. Voice mail.* I started to leave a message when my phone vibrated. "Oh, he's calling…" *Do I swipe? Hit End?* I answered it but hung up on him by mistake. I threw my head back and groaned. "I can't believe I just did that."

My phone vibrated again. "Hello, Geoff? Hold on a second…" I held my phone between my ear and shoulder as I motioned for something to write with. Jack pulled his pen and notebook out of his pocket, flipped to a clean page, and held it while I wrote.

"…Sorry. Didn't mean to hang up… What was that? You did?" I took a deep breath. "Are you sure?" I scribbled as Geoff talked. "Okay, that number again… 928… okay… 6653? In Arizona… Flagstaff? That's amazing. Not that far away." I pointed to the paper and gave a thumbs-up. "And this time you're positive? Wow, that's great." I ended the call and re-read my notes.

Cheryl squealed and grabbed my hand. "He found Jason, didn't he?"

I turned to Jack. "Actually, he found Jason's aunt… which is a start. And, she's less than eight hours away in Flagstaff."

Cheryl gave me a hug. "Oh Alli, I'm so happy for you."

I closed my eyes and sighed. *If Russell had only known we'd been so close to finding Jason.*

46

ALLI

I'd just found out Geoff located Jason's aunt in Arizona, about a day's drive from San Diego. It was nearly the end of November. Only five weeks to find Jason, explain the situation, and have him take over as the next Guardian. At least that was my fantasy ending. Reality—it would probably be much different.

Cheryl touched my shoulder. "Darius and I will postpone our trip if you need someone to take you to Flagstaff."

I turned and looked at her. "No. This will be your first Thanksgiving with your dad in a long time."

Liz pointed at me with a piece of pizza. "You can't go by yourself."

Jack set his slice on his plate. "I used to live near there, in Bellemont. I was on loan to the Flagstaff PD for two years through the DEA. Afterwards, I came back to the San Diego PD." He wiped pizza sauce from his mustache. "It's a beautiful area. Pine trees, mountains, snow. I wouldn't mind heading back for a few days."

As much as I wanted Jack to take me, I didn't know if I could trust him with the truth.

Liz gathered her trash. "I don't mind going. With the four-day holiday coming up, I might be able to swing it by asking for an extra day off."

Standing, Cheryl opened the refrigerator. "Do you think it would be a good idea to leave the place empty while we're all gone?" She passed a beer to Darius, offered one to Jack, then looked back at me. "Then again, if Jack goes with you, and Liz stays… No telling what you-know-who might do if he knew she was all alone."

I finished my soda. "Are you referring to Zack or Ronald?"

She tucked a curl behind her ear. "Liz shouldn't be alone if either shows up."

Darius looked up at me from his pile of pizza. "Alli, why don't you and Lizzy go? Maybe Jack would consider staying here while you're gone." He grabbed the top piece and ate half in one bite. "Then the place wouldn't be empty."

"Wow, Darius." I tossed my empty soda can in the recycling. "That's a great idea."

Cheryl bent over and hugged her boyfriend. "That's my sweetie. Food fuels his brain."

Liz snorted. "By the way he eats, he should be a friggin' genius by now."

Darius shrugged and kept eating.

"I need a nap." Liz headed down the hall giving a half-wave goodbye to whoever was watching.

Jack grabbed his beer as we went into the front room and settled on the couch. "I hope you didn't mind me mentioning Flagstaff," he said. "I wasn't trying to be pushy or anything…"

"No, that's fine." I patted his leg. "I'm worried about what will happen when I get there. I mean, what if Jason's aunt doesn't want to talk to me?"

"I don't understand why you can't contact her by phone. Find out where he lives. And mail the stuff." He slipped off his shoes and placed them under the coffee table. "Wouldn't it be easier than wasting a trip?"

I shook my head. "I can't. Plus, I'd rather tell her about Russell in person. It's bad enough I have to share the bad news, but the way it happened…"

"Alli, is there something else going here?" Jack avoided my glance, then cleared his throat. "I'll respect your privacy if you don't want to tell me, but I need to ask."

I looked at Jack. "Whenever I ask about Russell's death, you change the subject. Did you receive the toxicology report and not tell me?"

Jack let out a long sigh. "I didn't want to share until I had all the facts."

I stammered. "Jack, I've only known you for a little while, but part of me feels like I've known you forever." *That sounded so cliché.* "I'm not sure I should do this…"

Jack leaned in close. "If you're in danger, I'd rather know so I can protect you." He grasped my hand. "Will those items also put Jason at risk?"

"As long as Ronald is around…" *Yes, he'll be in terrible danger. But how can I tell him?*

Jack pushed up his sleeves. "Hon, I wish you'd trust me and tell me what's going on." He patted his shirt and pants. "Look no badge. Just me. Everything we talk about is off the record. Okay?"

I drew a small circle on his pant leg with the tip of my finger. "You're going to think I'm really crazy. And you might not even want to be friends anymore."

"Princess, don't worry about what I think. I'm concerned about you and what you've gotten yourself into." He caressed my cheek with the back of his fingers. "Please trust me."

I met his gaze and swallowed hard. "Follow me." I took Jack's hand, leading him down the hall to my bedroom. My heart thumped harder as I closed my bedroom door and walked over to my closet. As he sat on my bed, I opened the closet door and removed a green canvas bag, my newest hiding place for the *Gifts*.

Taking a deep breath, I told Jack about the auction. How I met Russell. When Steven opened the storage unit. Bidding on the *Gifts*. I recounted how Ronald harassed and threatened me. I took out the leather journal and shared the story of the Guardians. I explained why I had to find Jason.

Jack sat in silence, nodding as I shared each piece of the puzzle.

I placed the glasses on the bed and stopped talking. “Bet you think I’m a freakin’ mess, don’t you?”

Jack looked up at me. “If what you say is true, then prove it.” He picked up the glasses, studied them, and handed them to me. “Put these on. Then you’ll know if I’m really holding something back about the case.”

My hands trembled. I stared at Jack, then at the thin, round-rimmed glasses. I removed my own glasses and handed them to Jack. I took a deep breath and closed my eyes as I placed the Guardian’s glasses on my face.

I hesitated for a moment. As I opened my eyes, I looked at Jack. His outline started out fuzzy. Little-by-little his features came into focus.

He gazed at me, expressionless.

I studied his face and scanned his heart. Then, what felt like an electric bolt shot through my entire body. I jumped and gasped. “Oh no. I don’t believe you. That’s a lie.”

47

JACK

Alli finally confided in me. She explained how she had met Russell and about the Guardians. Sounded like some sci-fi story. An ancient group who passed on special powers? *Did I believe her? Not really.*

With an explanation of why Garanski might be after her, I'd keep an open mind. If she put on the glasses and told me something no one else knew, I'd reconsider.

She handed me her glasses. The "special" glasses looked like something from a thrift store. I watched as she closed her eyes, put on the round spectacles, and took a deep breath. As she stared at me, I felt like I'd been prodded with the end of an electrical wire. My fingers tingled. My head buzzed. My chest ached. I reached for the nightstand to steady myself.

Alli gasped. "Oh no. I don't believe you. That's a lie." She stood in front of me trembling.

I reached for her hand. "What's a lie?"

She took a step back.

I stuttered. "What are you talking about?"

"Russell didn't do it." She folded her arms across her chest. "He didn't kill Tippy Toes. How could you even think that?"

I shook my head in disbelief. *Did she read my mind? I'd never told anyone of my suppositions.* "I never said Russell…"

She glared at me. "You didn't have to. I felt your thoughts and what was in your heart."

I forced myself to take a deep breath. "Alli, what exactly did you see?"

"You think Russell killed Tippy Toes. You found the rat poison on the workbench in his garage… And you also found her I.D. tags, didn't you?"

Oh no. My mouth went dry. My mind raced. The wind picked up outside. Leafless branches scratched against the bedroom window.

"And, the brick… The one that broke our window… You found an empty space in one of the brick columns on Russell's front porch."

"Alli, I can explain." I ran my fingers through my hair. *She knew everything I'd been considering. And in perfect detail.*

She wiped her cheek with the back of her hand. "I can't believe you. Thinking Russell would do such a thing? From the beginning, it was Ronald. Ronald threatened me. Ronald threw the brick and took my cat. Ronald poisoned Russell…" She collapsed into my arms and sobbed.

I held her close. I wanted to say something. Anything. To let her know I believed her. If she figured all that out by putting on the antique glasses… *What else did she know?*

"Hon, listen to me." I pulled back, looking in her face. "What you felt or saw was true. I've been dealing with those facts since we searched Russell's house. I couldn't tell you because I wanted to invalidate them first."

Alli looked up at me. "So, you really don't think Russell did it?"

I sat on her bed, motioning for her to join me. "My job is to connect the dots. At first, the dots pointed to Russell, which in my professional opinion was too convenient. Yes, we found rat poison and your cat's tags on his workbench. Yes, we found a brick missing from one of the columns on his porch. And yes, his death might have been an accidental overdose of blood thinners, but I didn't believe any of it." I brushed tears off her cheek.

She glanced at shadows of the dancing branches on her wall. "Do you believe me about the *Gifts*?"

I smiled. "I believe you. It means my theory refuting Russell as a suspect is even more plausible. First, the guy was in his 80s. I don't think he hoisted a brick through your front window from downstairs, in the dark. I don't even think I could have done it. Second, if Russell had wanted the items, you would have given them back without hesitation. Correct?"

Alli nodded and smiled. "Of course."

I touched her hand. "And third, and this has bugged me most… In all my years of investigating, no one has ever been as eager as Ronald to hand over evidence of their whereabouts. Most hesitate or ask for a badge, then search through a wallet or glove box."

Alli relaxed her shoulders and let out a long sigh. "Thank you."

"For what?"

"For telling me everything. Even the stuff about Ronald. Thanks for being someone I can trust."

My arms relaxed around her waist as I leaned my head against hers. "I needed to come clean. You knew everything anyway." I smiled, then sighed. "Now to prove Russell innocent, while proving Ronald guilty. And, until I receive that toxicology report, I can't do a damned thing at all."

48

RONALD

Rain splattered against the windows of our apartment above the Store-More. Almost midnight. I'd just finished cleaning the small-caliber gun I'd found in one of the units a few weeks ago. Sitting on the edge of my unmade bed, I held the weapon under the dim light of my bedside lamp, inspected it, then laid it on the mattress.

Just the right size for "protecting" my assets. Smirking, I ground my half-smoked cigarette into the nearby ashtray. I stood up, shoved the gun into my back pocket, then grabbed my jacket off the worn carpet. As I walked toward the front door a flash of lightning lit up our small, dismal front room. Steven was asleep on the couch, twisted in a heap of blankets. A crack of thunder rattled the window. He startled and sat up.

"That you, Pops? What time is it?" He yawned and squinted at the cable box. "Where ya going so late tonight?"

I stopped. "Why you doing sleepin' on the couch? Wet the bed again?" I let out a horselaugh then went toward the door. Turning back, I asked, "And since when do I have to tell you my business? I can go anywhere I want, any damn time I want. That clear?"

"Yes, Pops. I was just wondering… since you been going out after dark a lot."

"You been spying on your old man?" I lurched over to the couch, raising my fist above his face.

"No. No, Pops. I haven't." Steven cowered and pushed himself up against the wall. "I swear. I didn't see nothing."

"Weren't nothing to see anyway." I lowered my hand. "And stop swearing. Jesus, haven't I told you to watch that mouth. I see why your momma left you. Dumb as a rock and ain't no use to nobody." I started toward the front door again. "Now you get back to your own bed. If I find you in here again, they'll be heck to pay."

As I left the apartment, I zipped up my jacket. A wind gust pushed across the parking lot. A tumbling tin can caught on a wet chunk of paper under my truck as I opened the door. "Damn this cold, wet weather. Least there's no moon. Easier to keep an eye on things, undetected."

I drove the streets, taking the backroads to their apartment. A familiar path, I'd repeated every night since my first "visit." My locksmith tools opened their door, just like I owned my own key. Since no one was there, I made myself at home. Drank a beer, watched some T.V., even played with the kitty cat.

After a few more beers, I smashed a few plates, broke a lamp, and rummaged through each room. Since I couldn't find what was mine, I decided to take something of hers. I never planned to give her the stupid cat back.

As for the old man—he deserved it. Took Steven when his crazy mom left with Jason. Never did forgive the bastard. He always kept his distance from me. But, when I spotted him watching the girls' apartment that night the brick landed in their front room, I couldn't let him point the finger at me. It was his fault for getting involved.

Figured the rat poison would be perfect. Probably never knew why he was getting sicker. Every time he left his house, I'd help myself into his place. Half-filled a crapload of his pills with the poisoned powder, then put 'em back in his prescription bottles. And just for the heck of it, I left the box of poison on his workbench. Like I always said, "No one messes with Ron Garanski and gets away with it." *Damn fools.*

Oh, and taking that brick from his front porch. *Brilliant.* And everyone thought I'd amount to nothing. *Fooled them idiots.* With the old man gone, the girl gots no one to help her when I come calling with the shiny friend in my back pocket.

I'd been watching her apartment, hanging around the dumpster waiting for the dumb boyfriend to take out the trash. He talked up a storm once I introduced myself as the new downstair's neighbor. Almost expected him to invite me up for beer and weed. That woulda been a hoot. According to the boyfriend, he and the fat broad are headed out of town. Spending Thanksgiving with family. *Whoopie.*

He also told me the two gals would be by themselves for a few days. Even suggested I look in on them to make sure they were safe. Something about some dude who might be hanging around… and maybe I could watch out for him. *Idiot.*

I'll make time to visit the helpless women when they're all alone. I can wait a few more days to get what's mine. And, it won't bother me none if no one's alive at the end of my visit. This Thanksgiving, I'll finally have something to be thankful for.

49

LIZ

Looks like I'll be headed to Flagstaff with Alli on Thursday. I requested the Monday after Thanksgiving off, giving us five full days. Assuming one-day travel time there and back, we'll have three days to locate Jason's aunt, explain everything, and find him. Then Alli can dump her box of problems on them and be done with it. At least that's the plan.

Speaking of planning, I need to deal with my "problem." The little one who's causing my belly to pooch out. I'm pretty sure it's Zack's. Even though I did that one-night fling, I'd already missed my period. Now, I was at least three months along.

At first, I wanted to get rid of it. Get rid of everything reminding me of the cheater. Now that I wasn't retching daily, I might want it. But then I'd have to deal with the daddy. *Why did I get myself into this mess?*

I looked up as I heard several knocks on my bedroom door. I kicked a week's worth of laundry out of the way and pulled it open. Alli stood in the hall.

"You busy?"

I shrugged. "Just contemplating life. What's up?"

"I wanted to go over our travel plans." She peered over her glasses at me. “Do you have chains? You know, in case it snows? I’d planned on bringing an ice chest with snacks and water, blankets, my pillows, jacket, gloves, phone charger…”

“Whoa. We’re only going to be gone a few days. Yes, I have chains. And no problem with snacks and water; but you do remember I have a small car. Right? And we can’t bring everything and still have room for us. How about a few changes of clothes, something in case it’s cold… and don’t forget the box—”

Alli pulled out a long piece of paper and pointed to an entry. “See, listed right there under pillows. “Sanitary supplies.” My code word for the *Gifts*.”

I looked over the list. “What about real sanitary supplies? I assume you’re bringing those because you’re always prepared for every situation.”

“Oh, yeah.” Alli smiled and held up the paper. “Right here, under ‘Necessaries’ which include tampons, pads—thin and regular, wet wipes, toilet paper, paper towels, tissues, baggies—large and small, plastic utensils, paper plates…”

“Oh, my freaking goodness. Are you serious?” I grabbed the list out of her hand and tossed it on the bed. “Glad I didn’t have to travel with you in a covered wagon. I’d have been walking alongside it to make room for all your crap.

“It’s important to be prepared.” She placed her hands on her hips. “And, to be honest, that’s only one list. I have two more in my room…”

I rolled my eyes and dropped on my bed. “I don’t even know how to respond right now.”

Cheryl walked by and popped her head inside my door. “Looks like we’ll be heading out tomorrow morning. With a seven-hour drive and half the population of California headed north, we figured best to leave Tuesday instead of Wednesday.”

I looked at Cheryl. “Just out of curiosity, what are you guys taking on your trip?”

She pulled out her phone and scrolled. “Deodorant, change of clothes, box of cereal, candy bars, and toothbrush…. Why do you ask?”

"Toothbrush? Oh crap," said Alli.

I rolled my eyes.

As Alli rushed down the hall Cheryl turned to me. "Where's she off to?"

"Adding more stuff to list number one or two. Or both." I sighed.

"This is an important trip," said Cheryl. "It might finally mean an end to all the terrible stuff she's been dealing with."

"I agree," I said. "But do we really need to bring every type of paper product known to mankind on an eight-hour trip?"

"Well, you never know what you might need." Cheryl laughed. "Remember that last trip Darius and I took to Sacto? The gas station restroom didn't have toilet paper. Boy, was I glad I kept tissues with me." She shoved her phone in her back pocket. "So, you two going to be okay? I mean, until you leave?"

"She said Jack would stop by after work tomorrow." I kicked some clothes against the wall. "We'll be fine. It's only one night."

Cheryl sat down next to me. "Ronald's been too quiet. I have this weird feeling that he's up to something. And I don't want you guys to be in the middle of it."

Sitting up straight, I rubbed my hand across my pelvic area. I'd been cramping most of the day but tried to ignore it. *Normal ligament stretching, right?* Man, that last pain almost took my breath away.

I stood, gripping the doorframe. "Cheryl, I need to use the bathroom. Let's talk later." Gritting my teeth, I limped across the hall.

Something was wrong.

50

ALLI

I'd been in my room packing when Liz stumbled in.

"I need you to take me to the emergency room." She pointed at her tummy. "I'm bleeding."

My heart raced. "But, I can't drive. I mean I can. But… can't Cheryl take you?"

She took her time lowering herself on my bed. "Cheryl doesn't know anything about it…" Her jaw tensed as she sat.

"Are you in pain?"

"Since this morning. Alli, please help me."

The thought of driving sent a bolt of adrenaline through my entire body. *I can't do this.* On the verge of a panic attack, I looked at Liz. "Give me a second." I scooted across the hall into the bathroom. Reaching into my pocket, I took out my pillbox. I opened it, counted out one and a half anti-anxiety pills, then took them with a big gulp of water. *I can't tell her about my panic attacks. Not now.*

Liz stood outside the bathroom waiting for me. She hesitated, then regained her composure and continued into the front room. Thank goodness Cheryl and Darius were in Cheryl's room. We didn't have to answer any questions about our late-night trip.

Once we left the apartment, I helped Liz down the stairs. After buckling in, I started the engine, took a deep breath, and put it in "drive." The car crept forward. I slammed on the brakes, causing us to lurch forward. Liz moaned. She didn't yell at me, thank goodness.

"Do you even know where we're going?"

She sucked in her breath and let it out. "Yes." She took in another deep breath through her nose. "Straight two blocks, then left on El Cajon about a half mile. It's on the right side. You can do this. I believe in you, Alli."

I focused on the street. The other cars. My own breathing. As I stopped at each corner, I glanced over at Liz. Her arms cradled her tummy. Her eyes appeared to be closed. I forced positive thoughts into my brain. She couldn't lose the baby. Not like this. Not now.

I stopped for a red light still gripping the steering wheel. "We're almost there. Just a few more blocks."

Turning toward the window, she groaned as I pulled into the parking lot.

Fortunately, the small hospital was close and it was nighttime—a quick drive with minimal traffic.

I pulled into a space near the entrance. Turning off the ignition with damp, trembling hands wasn't easy, but I managed. Jumping out of the car, I ran over to Liz' side and helped her out. As we walked through the sliding doors, I caught the scent of rubbing alcohol and latex.

I shuddered as I gazed around the half-full room. A man comforting a small, crying child leaned against one wall. A woman dozed in a wheelchair; one arm covered with a large, blue bath towel. Faint music played a soft, soothing melody. A long fish tank brimming with colorful, neon fish illuminated by muted lights stretched along a side wall. I helped Liz over to a row of empty seats and waited until she was settled.

I rushed up to the front desk and stammered. "My friend…" I turned and pointed. "I think she's losing her baby." My voice left me as I burst into tears.

51

LIZ

I saw blood. My knees went weak. My body wouldn't stop trembling.

My heart raced as Alli drove me to the hospital. The waiting room part wasn't too bad. But, when the ER doctor poked and prodded my abdomen, I moaned. When he gave me a pelvic, I gritted my teeth. When he did the ultrasound… *I was so embarrassed.* They made me drink all that water, then pushed on my bladder. I didn't mean to pee all over the exam table.

The good news: He found a strong heartbeat and said there was a fairly good chance I wouldn't lose the baby. The bad news: He put me on bedrest for two to three weeks, maybe even longer. He said my OB/GYN would know more after an appointment… and more poking, prodding, and ultrasounds.

I was discharged just after midnight. We left the hospital, greeted by a full November moon. I took in a deep breath. Charbroiled burgers from a nearby fast-food restaurant mixed with decomposed, wet leaves in the gutter. Anything was better than the sterile odors inside that hospital.

Alli smiled and patted my shoulder. "I'm glad your baby is okay."

She leaned in close to me. "You need your rest. Your health is much more important."

Her words were comforting, but I heard the catch in her voice. I'm sure she must be disappointed I couldn't take her to Flagstaff. But, under the circumstances, we both knew the trip could put me back in the hospital. Or worse, I could lose my baby.

Fine. I said it. My baby. I didn't want to lose my baby. Especially after I saw arms and legs and heard the heartbeat. The doctor estimated I was about fourteen to sixteen weeks along. Far enough along to know it was Zack's. Far enough along I was wearing loose blouses and stretch pants. Far enough along that I wasn't going to be able to keep this secret much longer. *Damn.*

"YOU OKAY?" Alli's voice interrupted my thoughts. "Need some help getting up the stairs?" She'd parked at our apartment, opened my door, and reached for my hand.

"I can walk, thanks." I stood and steadied myself. Once we got inside, I noticed Darius' snoring, or was it Cheryl's? Didn't matter. At least everyone was asleep. All I wanted to do was change into my pajamas, climb into my own bed, and sleep.

Alli bustled around the kitchen. "Can I make you something? Tea? Food?"

"Just something to drink. Then bed." Before I finished talking, she'd grabbed a glass, filled it with ice and water, and handed it to me.

I placed the glass on the counter. Stepping in close, I wrapped my arms around her. "Thanks." It was the only word I could manage. If I'd told her how much she meant to me, I'd have choked up. If I'd said I knew she had to fight through her anxiety to take me to the hospital, I'd have sobbed. And if I'd explained how sorry I was for letting her down about Flagstaff, we'd have both been bawling.

But right then, I wanted a hug. A warm, comforting "Alli hug." And at that moment, in the kitchen, after midnight, I was safe. My baby and I were protected. And that's all that mattered.

52

ALLI

After a fitful night's sleep, I tossed off the covers and checked my phone. Six o'clock. Cheryl and Darius would be gone in a few hours. Liz made me promise not to tell them about last night's ER visit. She knew Cheryl would postpone their trip and insist on taking me to Flagstaff.

Now what? With Cheryl and Darius gone and Liz on bedrest, time was running out. *Should I ask Jack?* He knows about the *Gifts* and his way around Flagstaff. But, then I'd worry about Liz.

What if Zack showed up? Or even worse, Ronald? Maybe I should ask Zack to go with me? Then he wouldn't bug Liz. And Jack could check in on her and… No, that's a stupid idea. What would Zack know about Flagstaff? What would we talk about? *Zack, I've got these special items. I'm trying to return them to the grandson of an old guy. They have special powers…* What was I thinking? We had nothing in common.

I needed to get up and start the day. Maybe the answer would magically appear during my shower. If Liz could give me a hug, then anything was possible.

I CAME into the kitchen and got caught up in the middle of a farewell group hug with Cheryl and Darius. "I'm so happy for you both. Have a wonderful trip," I said.

"I left some pumpkin cookies in the fridge," said Cheryl. "I'll miss you. But, I'm so excited you'll be headed to Flagstaff." She hugged me again. "Call me each night. And, text when you find Jason's aunt… and when you finally meet Jason."

I forced a smile. "Will do."

Cheryl grabbed her tote bag. "I know you'll find him, Alli." She walked over and stood by the front door. "I just feel it in my heart."

Darius finished his bowl of cereal. He wiped his mouth on the back of his sleeve, belched, farted, then shrugged. "Better now, than in the car. She'd punch me in the arm."

"I'd punch you just because." Liz walked into the kitchen not missing a beat.

Darius sauntered over and gave her a quick hug. "I love you too, Lizzie." He grinned, then picked up a small suitcase and walked out the door behind Cheryl. As they paused in front of the window Cheryl punched his arm. She turned and gave us a thumbs-up, laughed, and they walked out of sight.

I looked at Liz. "How are you this morning?"

"Okay. Still feeling crampy. But, better when I rest." She poured a cup of coffee and sat down at the table. "What are you going to do about Flagstaff?"

I sighed. "Well, I thought about asking Zack to go. At least he'd be out of your hair."

Liz gave me the look.

I held up my hand. "Just kidding. We have nothing in common… The other thought is to ask Jack. But I hate leaving without anyone to take care of you."

"You need to get to Flagstaff," she said, stirring her coffee. "Call Jack. See if he can get a few days off."

"But what about Zack?"

Liz let out a long breath. "I probably should tell him about the baby." She looked up at me. "It's his, you know."

"Are you sure?"

She nodded. "When the ER doctor told me how far along I was, there was no doubt in my mind. And, if I'm going to keep it, he might as well know."

"Change your mind about him?"

"More like a change of heart," said Liz. "Watching that ultrasound last night made me realize we're talking about a little life. One that's half his. As much as I hate him for cheating, he deserves to know." She stared at her coffee. "When I thought I might lose it, I realized…"

"You still love him, don't you?"

She looked up at me and nodded. "I don't know about the future of our relationship, but I do know I need to tell him. Holding onto this anger isn't good for me. Or the baby. Besides, if I tell him, maybe he'll be around. Then, you won't have to worry about that jerk doing something stupid."

"Well, that's a solution I hadn't considered." I glanced at the clock on the wall. "I need to be at work in an hour." I patted her on the arm, then left the kitchen and walked down the hall. When I got to my room, I plopped on the bed. Scrolling through recent calls, I found Jack's number. I hesitated for a moment, then swiped the call icon.

"Morning, Jack," I said. "Do you have plans for Thanksgiving?"

53

ALLI

Jack didn't have any challenges getting the time off to take me to Flagstaff, especially after he told his captain the trip might offer clues and help solve a case. One problem solved. I hoped finding Jason's aunt was as easy.

I arrived home from work and found Liz asleep on the couch bundled in her grandma's handmade quilt. The faint aroma of buttered popcorn hung in the air. Liz stirred as I closed the door. She sat up, rubbing the sleep from her eyes. "Hey, how was work?"

"Same old stuff. People want frames. People don't know what kind of frames they want. People then inspect, move, touch, replace, and smudge every frame on every shelf until they find the perfect one that calls to them. I think I'll rename the holiday from Thanksgiving to FramesGiving since everyone in San Diego County must have purchased frames today."

Removing my shoes and socks, I shoved them under the coffee table. Settling on the end of the couch, I propped up my bare feet and flexed my toes. "So glad to be off these footsies. Don't think I sat for more than five minutes all day, not even during my lunch hour."

"That sucks." Liz ran her fingers through her hair, patting down stray pillow-head hairs. "You get a hold of Jack?"

"Yes. They gave him the time off since he happened to mention it was part of one of his open cases."

Liz pushed the quilt to the side of the couch. "Awesome. Did you see Cheryl's text? They arrived in Reno just before it started to snow." She held her phone in front of me, displaying a picture of Cheryl and Darius building a scrawny snowman. She swiped the screen again. "Here's one of her and her dad."

"Look at her smile," I said. "Haven't seen her that happy in a long time."

"Yeah. I'm really happy for her and the furry beast." Liz sighed. "She deserves all the happiness the universe has for her."

I looked over at Liz. "You do, too."

She shrugged. "I've done some dumb stuff. Karma's got a right to bite me in the butt."

"I think we've all done stupid stuff." I wiggled my toes and stared at them. "Hey, you hungry? I think we have all the makings for chicken tacos."

Liz nodded and attempted to get up. "That sounds really delicious."

"Don't move. I'll fix dinner." I placed my phone on the coffee table, got up, and headed to the kitchen. "You just relax. Or sleep. Or something."

After we ate and I washed the dishes, Liz and I watched old Christmas movies on a cable channel. All romance. All with happy endings. All of them made me cry. Just once, I'd like to watch a movie without crying at the end. I think Liz might have teared up a bit too, but she'd never admit it. Plus, she was distracted with her phone.

"Can I get you anything before I go to bed?"

She rechecked her phone. "Naw, I guess I'm headed that way also. I don't mind my bedroom at night, but during the day it gets kinda lonely cooped up back there all by myself."

I stood and walked over to the window. As I began to draw the curtains my heart raced. I dropped back behind the curtain and peered out the side of the window.

"What the heck are you doing?" Liz asked.

"That truck. Over there. Across the street." I pointed my finger without moving my hand. "I'd swear it's Ronald's."

She stiffened. "You sure?"

"Not completely." I hung back and looked again. "Someone's sitting in it. Looks like cigarette smoke coming out of the cracked-open window." I dropped to the floor and shimmied over to the slider. Raising my head a few feet, I scrutinized the late model truck parked under a solitary crepe myrtle.

"What do you see?" said Liz.

"Shhhh," I whispered. "Turn off the light."

I heard Liz's footsteps on the rug.

Darkness enveloped us.

Something touched my leg. I stifled a yell.

"It's just me," said Liz.

"You about gave me a heart attack."

Liz pressed up against me as we sat on the rug and peered out the slider. The truck cab was backlit by a nearby streetlight. Everything inside was dark except for the end of a glowing cigarette.

Liz grabbed my leg again. "Maybe I'm just paranoid. But, this might be a good time to call Jack."

I patted my pockets. "I don't have my phone." I moved my hands back and forth along the floor around us. "Where's yours?"

"Over by the couch." I heard Liz crawling away from me then slapping the floor and the top of the coffee table. "Found yours." She crawled back and shoved it into my outstretched hand.

I took it from her and pushed a button. "What the…?" I shook my phone then hit it on the rug. Nothing.

She tugged on my leg and pointed. "Someone's getting out of the truck."

I stared across the street. A large man exited the truck. After closing the driver's side door, he put on a cowboy hat and buttoned up his jacket. The streetlight reflected off something in his hand.

I elbowed Liz. "He looks like Ronald." My heart pounded in my ears and my body stiffened. "Where's your phone? My battery's dead." We watched. He waited for a car, then strolled across the street.

I heard Liz crawl back toward the couch. "Here is it. Oh crap. I dropped it, and it slipped under the couch."

"Trade me places." As I crawled back over to the couch, she passed me. “You keep an eye on him while I get your phone.” I lay on my stomach and reached under the couch. I felt the end of it… at the tip of my fingers. But, the more I tried to grab hold of it, the more it escaped my reach. I patted the top of the coffee table for a book, the remote, anything to extend my reach.

“Alli.” Liz’s voice became higher in pitch. “He’s coming up the stairs.”

My fingers found a magazine. I rolled it up and swiped it under the couch. It contacted with the phone. Just. A. Little. Bit. Closer.

“Alli…” Liz went silent.

Keys jangled outside the front door. The doorknob rattled.

As I shoved my hand under the couch, I groaned. My sleeve had caught on a spring. I had the phone in my hand, but now I couldn’t move my arm.

The doorknob rattled again. Then something thudded against the wall outside.

A muffled yell came from behind the door. “Son of a…”

54

ZACK

Liz called and wanted me to stop by after work. I said I'd be there sometime after eight. Things were going good until Joe, one of the other restaurant servers was a no-show. Usually, I didn't mind the extra hours and a hundred bucks in tips. But getting to Liz's two hours late? *Damn. Talk about walking into a big mess.*

Between Liz's phone call and work, I was still trying to wrap my head around Gran-dad's passing. It was such a freaky coincidence how Liz and her friends were at the cemetery. Did they know the person buried next to my grandparents? Somehow, I felt it was more than a coincidence after seeing Cheryl and Alli at the hospital.

I'd never met my grandma. And I only remember little things about Gran-dad. Like how he used to tell me stories in Polish—one about Babcia, another about Babushka. While I didn't understand the words, I loved how he changed his voice for each character. Now he's gone, and I have nothing. Well, maybe the hope of something since Liz called.

I left the restaurant at about ten. The chilly November breeze felt good after running tables all night. No clouds, just a scattering of stars winking at me. Like they somehow understood I was going on a trip that would change my life forever. With a half-hour drive to Liz's apartment, I thought about calling, then I reconsidered. Didn't want to give her any chance to cancel.

I was making pretty good time until I came up the offramp. Traffic was backed up for over a mile. I drummed my fingers on the steering wheel and craned my neck to see if there was another exit. Nope. Had to wait like everyone else.

Being stuck in traffic gave me time to go over some questions in my head. How should I greet her? Was it okay to hug? Should I talk about Gran-dad? Better not. She might think I was going for sympathy. Finally. The exit was in sight. I headed straight a few blocks, then turned right.

I practiced out loud. "How are you doing? What's new in your life?" *Note to self, make this about her, not about me.* I took a deep breath and exhaled as I drove up to the apartment. Oh, man. Need more time. I circled around the block again.

On the second time around, I found a spot a block away and parked. I checked my teeth in the mirror and patted down a stray hair with spit. I armed the alarm and marched down the street rehearsing my apology in my head. *Liz, sorry I'm late. Traffic... Someone didn't show up at work...* I rolled my eyes. They all sounded lame, even to me.

As I climbed the stairs, I noticed someone in a bulky jacket fiddling with a doorknob. *Wait. That's Liz's door.* My heart raced. "Hey. What are you doing?"

A man turned. He looked at me.

I froze. My gut twisted.

Our eyes locked.

He dropped a small case on the landing. "Son of a... " he said, rushing away from me.

55

JACK

Work had been crazy, so I was thrilled when Alli asked me to take her to Flagstaff, especially if the trip would give me a break in the Garanski murder case. I was grateful to leave town for a few days. Plus, it gave me another chance to be Alli's Prince Charming. *Yep, still a hopeless romantic.*

After going over the details of Russell's toxicology report, I chatted briefly with Alli. The same rodenticide that was found in her cat's fur was also found in Russell's blood. Commonly used to kill rats and mice, it was highly toxic to humans and especially pets. *Damn.* I had to decipher who poisoned them, and how.

I called Alli again later that afternoon, but her phone went to voice mail. *Probably on silent during work.* Hours later when she still didn't answer, I became concerned. With Cheryl and Darius out of town and Liz not feeling well, I planned to drop by her apartment. Besides, we needed to firm up our Flagstaff plans.

I finished my paperwork around ten. Walking outside, I took in a deep breath of the invigorating, chilly November air. I looked up… no clouds in sight. Just a sky full of twinkling stars.

It would be much colder in Flagstaff. After checking the weather report, I didn't think we'd get snow, but one never knew. I still had chains, at least we'd be prepared.

The freeway traffic was light and I was making good time. Crap. Spoke too soon. The offramp was backed up for a mile or more. I used my Bluetooth to call Alli again. Still no answer. *Damn.* Wish I could flash my lights or something to part the traffic. Since I wasn't on an "official call," I waited out the mess like everyone else. *Why do I live in such a big city?*

Only 75,000 people in Flagstaff compared to the one million plus here. Different lifestyle. Fresh air. Mountains. Friendly people. I'd move back in a hot second, though I'd miss the ocean. The smell. The food. The mesmerizing surf pounding on the sand. Sadly, being so busy I visited the beach less than the tourists who came once a year. Come to think of it, I couldn't remember the last time I'd scrunched sand between my toes and watched the sandpipers chase each other away from the sand crabs.

The traffic moved forward. Still slow but making progress. I didn't miss the snow of Flagstaff, but I missed the slower lifestyle. When I was there, I took time to do things. Like, visit the Grand Canyon. *What a sight.* Got a lump in my throat. Tears flowed. I couldn't do a damn thing to stop them. Felt like a doofus, but what can I say. It was the hopeful romantic in me. Maybe Alli and I will have time to see it.

The offramp. *Finally.* I headed straight a few blocks, then right. Now to find a parking space. Not easy this late… A man just ran across the street and jumped in a truck. *Perfect timing.* I waited as an oncoming car passed, their lights blinding me for a second. I blinked, then pulled into the truck's spot and parked.

As I climbed the stairs, I spotted a suspicious male. *Is that Liz's ex-boyfriend?* I waited and observed. Standing outside their apartment, he crouched down, picking up an object from the walkway. He stood and knocked on their door.

As I walked toward him, adrenalin surged through my gut. "Hey. What are you doing?"

He looked at me.

Our eyes locked.

Son of a ...

56

LIZ

Alli's arm was still wedged under the couch.

I didn't have the strength to help.

A muffled voice resonated from the outside our front door. "Son of a…"

Scuffling. Then heavy footsteps echoed down the hall.

I jumped and turned on the light when someone pounded on the front door.

"Liz. Open up it's me, Zack."

Peeking through the front window, I observed my ex-boyfriend and Alli's boyfriend eyeing each other. Seeing only them, I realized it was okay and opened the door.

"Seriously dude…" Zack folded his arms across his chest. "… she invited me."

"It's okay, Jack." I took in a deep breath. "Guys, we need some help in here.

Jack pushed past Zack. "What happened? Where's Alli?" Both guys stopped inside the front door and stared at the couch.

Alli turned toward us, her face flushed. "I'm stuck."

Zack rushed over and grabbed the far end of the couch while Jack grabbed the end closest to the door. They nodded to each other, then lifted.

Alli twisted her arm free and sat up for a moment. After rubbing her arm, she grabbed my phone and handed it to me.

The guys nodded to each other again and lowered the couch, letting it hit the floor with a soft thud. Jack turned to Alli. "What happened? Are you okay?"

She rolled her eyes as she brushed off her pants. "Long story. But forget about that… Did you see him? He was trying to break in."

Jack stepped closer to Alli. "What are you talking about?"

Zack waved a leather case. "A guy dropped this when I came up the stairs."

Stepping closer, Jack looked up at Zack. "May I see that?"

Zack nodded and handed it to him.

Jack fingered the outside and turned it over. Opening it, he showed us the contents. "A lock-pick kit." He scrutinized Zack. "You see who dropped it?"

Zack ran his hand through his hair and hesitated. "A guy. In a jacket, I think. He was messing around with the door when I came up the stairs. I yelled, then he dropped that and ran. Probably went down the stairs at the far end of the landing."

Jack pulled out his pen and notebook. "Did you get a good look at him, enough to provide a description?"

Zack cleared his throat. "It was dark. Didn't see his face… just the shape of his body as he turned…."

"It was Ronald," Alli said. "Liz and I saw him parked across the street." She motioned at me. "We watched as he left his truck and came up the stairs, didn't we?"

I nodded to Alli then glanced at Zack. "Guess it's good you got here so late. No telling what that idiot would have done if he'd broken in." I turned toward Jack. "Glad you were here too. Didn't either of you see him outside?"

Jack dropped the leather case on the coffee table, then fingered his mustache. "I remember a guy running across the street as I looked for a parking space. I couldn't see his face, though, because an oncoming car's headlights blinded me for a few seconds." He turned to Alli. "Hon, are you positive it was Ronald?"

Alli's voice trembled. "I knew it was him. I tried to call you, but my phone was dead. Then I knocked Liz's under the couch. I was stuck and couldn't move. I didn't know what we were going to do. Liz was supposed to be in bed..." Her voice broke.

Jack went over and embraced Alli, caressing her hair.

I glanced at Zack. It was the first time we'd been together without yelling in months. With all the excitement, I realized I'd forgotten to introduce him to Jack or even offer a proper hello. What should I say? *Hi, Zack. Good to see you. You're going to be a daddy.* Probably should rethink that.

He caught my gaze, nodded, and winked.

Oh man. That wink. Those eyes. My heart raced. My tummy fluttered. Not a baby-flutter, but an excited-to-see-you flutter. I smiled back.

Zack took a step closer.

I nodded.

And another step.

I nodded again.

He stood in front of me and reached for my hand.

I accepted.

With one smooth movement, he pulled me into his warm embrace and held me.

Resting my head against his chin, I slid my arms around his shoulders. My hair caught in his bristly stubble.

His fingers stroked my neck as his warm breath tickled my cheek.

Alli's voice appeared somewhere beyond my sphere of caring. "Hey, we're gonna leave you guys alone. Jack and I need to talk..."

I zoned out on the rest of her words. Pulling back from Zack, I motioned toward the couch. "We should talk."

He nodded.

I took a deep breath. *I don't care about the past. I hope he forgives me and wants our baby as much as I do.*

57

ALLI

When I glanced up, Liz and Zack were hugging.

"Hey, we're gonna leave you guys alone. Jack and I need to talk about our trip…" I doubt they heard me. We headed down the hall to my room.

Jack stopped just inside my door. "Tell me about the person you saw tonight."

"I know it was Ronald." My hands trembled as I spoke. "He was at the door, fumbling with the lock. I tried to call, but…"

Jack pulled his phone from his back pocket. "This is Hastings. I need you to check on something for me. The Store-More off El Cajon Boulevard." He nodded at me. "Get inside the gate… Yes, where the manager parks… Tell them you're looking for a suspect. Do whatever it takes, get inside, then find a late model Chevy pickup. Check to see if the engine's still warm… Don't ask the resident any questions. Call me after you leave… Thanks, I owe you one."

Pushing my suitcase to the end of my bed, I sat. "Is that legal?"

"It's legal to search for a suspect on the run. Especially if the officers on pursuit "think" he's hiding inside a storage facility," he said, using air quotes. "I can't go because Ronald knows me. It's better to have them go in on official business. Hopefully, it won't raise suspicions."

"How can we leave for Flagstaff…?"

He fingered his mustache. "If we don't, you won't find your Jason person."

"I'm worried about Liz. She's not supposed to get stressed. She's…" *Crap.*

"She's what?" He sat next to me. "Something I need to know?"

I looked over at him. "I'm not supposed to say anything." *Oh, that was good. Admit I'm holding on to a secret, to a detective.* I ran my fingers through my hair. "It's nothing, really." *And that's sure to convince him not to press for more information.*

Jack flashed a smile at me. The one that melts away my secrets. He reached over and caressed my cheek.

Oh my gosh, really.

He leaned in close. Brushing his cheek against mine, he whispered in my ear. "You know you want to tell me."

Resist. It's not up to me to tell him about Liz.

He kissed my neck.

I can't handle this. My will slipped away as he kissed my shoulders. I let out a long sigh. Then a small moan. I pulled back. "Is this how you extract information from alleged criminals?"

He smiled.

I nodded. "Fine. I'll tell you if you promise not to breathe a word to anyone."

He held up his hand like a courtroom witness. "I promise."

"Fine."

Jack winked. "Fine."

I leaned in close. "Liz is…"

His phone buzzed. He held up a finger as he answered. "Hastings. Yes… You went by…. Entered the property… The truck… You don't say? No, don't do anything. Good work. I'll call you back if I need any more information. Thanks." He looked over at me and cocked his head. "The truck's engine was still warm. Apparently, Garanski had just arrived back home. And, he was in a foul mood."

58

LIZ

Zack and I stood in the front room facing each other. The kitchen clock ticked away the minutes. It seemed like forever since we'd been happy. Taking in the sweet scent of his cologne, I shifted my feet trying to conceal my wobbly knees. The lamp in the corner softened our faces and cast faint shadows on the rug.

"Liz, I want to explain…" he said.

I shook my head. "I don't care about the past." Walking over to the couch, I sat and patted the spot next to me. "I just want to move forward." The cushion sunk as he sat. Our legs made contact sending a tingle up my spine.

"There's something I need to tell you." His eyes widened. "About myself."

I touched his lips. "Shhhh. I don't want to know. It's not important."

"But…"

I took a deep breath, then continued. "I have something to tell you."

Zack recoiled. "It's another guy, isn't it? You found someone else." He looked away from me.

"No… Even though I was so damned pissed at you, I… I never stopped loving you."

He turned back, his lips quivering. Wiping his eyes with the edge of his sleeve, his face brightened. "Really?"

I nodded.

He leaned in, but I moved back and held up my hand. "Wait…"

He straightened as his eyes followed my movements.

I braced myself and continued. "When you stopped calling, I figured you'd found someone else."

"No…"

I placed my hand on his leg. "Please, let me finish."

He nodded.

"I never wanted to talk to you again," I said. "Then after the break-in, I called about the fingerprints. As soon as you answered the phone, I wanted to apologize, but I couldn't control my hateful words." I reached for my water bottle and took a drink. Focusing on the ticking of the clock, I took a moment. *For goodness sake, don't cry.*

"Then," I said, "You started following me. I saw you everywhere. Across the street. In the parking lot at work. Down the street from our apartment. Even the cemetery, which wasn't cool at all—"

"—I can explain," he said.

"It doesn't matter anymore. The thing is, something happened. A few days ago I realized I didn't want to lose you. I couldn't lose you." I moved my trembling hands over his. Closing my eyes, I took in a deep breath and let it out. I opened my eyes, smiled, and looked up at him. "I really don't know how to say this any other way. Zack, I'm pregnant."

59

ZACK

My stomach twisted as we sat down on the couch. I wanted to explain how I'd left my home in Flagstaff to find out who I really was. How I'd found, then lost my gran-dad before I talked to him. How I still loved her more than anything. How I never meant to hurt her. And how there'd never been any other woman.

Liz placed her soft, trembling hands over mine. She closed her eyes and took a deep breath. She opened them and smiled. "I really don't know how to say this any other way, but… Zack, I'm pregnant."

My eyes widened. My heart raced. "Say what?"

"I'm pregnant. A baby. Yours…"

Yesterday, I thought she hated me. Tonight, we're having a baby. I stood up and paced. "Are you sure?" I stopped and sat back down on the couch. "When… how did you find out?"

She grabbed a tissue and wiped her eyes. "I've known for a while. Right after we broke up. I… I didn't even know if I was going to keep it…"

I clenched my jaw. "And you never thought I'd want to know?"

"Hold on Zack. I need to tell you everything." She took a deep breath and continued. "I didn't know what to do. We weren't together.

What did I know about raising a baby? I can barely boil water. But, earlier this week, I started bleeding..."

I squared my shoulders. "Are you okay?"

"Yes."

"And the baby?"

She touched my hand. "The baby is fine too. I just have to take it easy for a while. What I was trying to say, was that in the ER, when they did the ultrasound, and I saw…"

Liz began crying. I felt hot tears running down my cheeks, too. I leaned in and held her against me until we both stopped trembling.

"Are you sure you're both okay?" I said.

"The doctor wants to keep an eye on me. More ultrasounds and more appointments until the bleeding completely stops. He put me on bedrest and said no stress."

I laughed. "That's not going to be easy."

She looked up at me with big, hopeful eyes. "You don't hate me, do you?"

"I've never stopped loving you."

Liz scooted up on my lap and wrapped her arms around my neck. "I love you, too," she said.

My whole body relaxed. For the first time in months, I could breathe without a lump in my throat. I thought I'd lost her. Then when I lost my gran-dad, my heart ripped in two. As much as I wanted to tell her everything, I decided to let it go. She didn't care about my past. She loved me, and that's all that mattered.

I pulled back a bit. "So… when are we due?"

She grinned and placed my hand across her tummy. "Next May, on the 23rd, my father's birthday."

My voice broke. I managed a smile. "I'm so happy." I motioned for Liz to sit back on the couch, then fumbled around in my pocket for a while. As I pushed the coffee table back and slid off the couch, I turned, then balanced my weight on one knee.

She covered her mouth with her hands.

I held the little white box in front of her. "I bought this a while back, hoping to give it to you on our anniversary. I brought it with me tonight, just in case…

"Liz, I've loved you since the first day we met. I fell in love with you as we ate sandwiches. I fell more in love with you when I realized how much we shared in common. I loved you then and I always will." Opening the box, I clutched the diamond ring in my right hand as my left hand held Liz's. Tears ran down my face but I didn't have a free hand to wipe my eyes. I didn't care. Nothing would stop me from asking the question.

"Elizabeth Green, will you marry me?"

60

ALLI

Early the next morning, as Zack snored on the couch, Jack and I tiptoed through the front room with my bags. With Zack still at the apartment I felt better about leaving. At least Liz wouldn't be alone. *Yes, Jack also spent the night. But he stayed in Cheryl's room so we could head out at the early hour of three am.*

Thankfully, traffic on the freeway was light but as much as I tried to nap it wasn't happening. To help pass the time, Jack played a variety of CDs, including The Beach Boys and Queen. Normally a baritone, he strained his voice hitting the high notes, making me giggle. I, in turn, lowered my voice to cover the bass line.

Our first stop was Phoenix, a sprawling city in the middle of the dry, monotonous highway. We made good time arriving at the Denny's at eight o'clock along with other wearied holiday travelers.

Greeted by a cheerful waitress and the mouthwatering aromas of strong coffee and smoked bacon, I scooted into a corner booth next to Jack and studied the menu. As I looked over the breakfast selection, I realized it would be the first year Liz, Cheryl, and I wouldn't be together for our holiday brunch tradition. Ever since Cheryl moved in, we always made a special meal—bacon, pancakes, eggs, and Cheryl's famous potatoes that included tiny, whole red potatoes, diced yellow onions, sliced green bell peppers, and some exotic spice from an envelope she kept hidden in her room.

Jack touched my arm. "Hon, you ready to order?"

I looked up and smiled at Stacey, our waitress. "So sorry, yes. Eggs, scrambled dry, hash browns, and whole wheat toast, extra butter, please. Oh, and coffee. Lots of coffee."

She nodded as she filled my cup. "You two headed somewhere special for the holiday?"

I took a sip of the warm, bitter liquid, and waited for my brain to wake up. "We're going to Flagstaff."

"Beautiful this time of year," she said before leaving with our orders.

Jack leaned against me. "You doing okay?"

I nodded. "Just tired." As I spoke my phone alarm buzzed. I pointed to the time. "See, now it's time to get up."

Jack kissed me, then emptied three sugars into his cup and stirred them into the dark liquid. "I'm used to getting up all kinds of weird hours. Not that I like it, it just comes with the job."

We finished breakfast and headed out again. The rest of Arizona was nothing like I'd pictured. Driving through pine-covered mountains, my ears popped several times trying to adjust to the new altitudes. Patches of dirty snow soon appeared on the side of the road. As we climbed higher, the temperature dropped and Jack turned up the heater.

"It's so pretty," I said.

"Nothing at all like San Diego. I loved it here. Even considered asking for a transfer, until I met you." Jack moved his jaw back and forth, then forced a yawn. "Right ear won't pop."

I opened a piece of gum and offered some to him as I twisted my jaw. "It's my left one. Drives me crazy when they're uneven." The gum helped until we went further up the road.

"Look, more snow." I pointed to the pine trees. "You know, I've always wanted to see it snow. Like when it actually comes down."

Jack slowed and focused on the road. "Loved the snow. Hated the black ice."

"Black ice?"

"Water that freezes in the shaded parts of the road. The frozen patches create serious driving hazards. If you happen to drive over one you can slide and lose control."

I sat up and checked my seat belt. "That doesn't sound like fun."

Jack gripped the steering wheel. "Once, I hit a patch going only twenty miles an hour. The car slowly turned sideways and slid down a hill. I couldn't steer…"

"Why didn't you hit the brakes?"

Jack glanced over at me. "Would have made things worse. I had to keep calm and wait. The car stopped when it slid off the road and bumped against the side of a mountain. If I'd been on the other side of the road, I'd have gone over a very steep embankment."

I gasped. "You made that up."

"True story."

My eyes focused on the side of the road. "Now, I'm not so sure I want it to snow."

Jack let out a nervous laugh. "According to the outside temperature indicator, it's over thirty-two degrees. Nothing to worry about it right now.

"Right now? So that means I need to worry about it later… Like in an hour, or tonight, or tomorrow?" My heart rate increased. I dug in my pocket for an anti-anxiety pill. "By the way you're gripping that steering wheel, I think I need to worry about it now."

As Jack slowed going around a curve, the back end of the car slipped.

"Oh my gosh, what was that?"

Jack took a deep breath, then glanced over at me. "Alli, we're going to be okay. Look at the highway. See the water running across the road? That means the ice is melting, which is a good thing."

I gripped the seat and practiced my breathing. *No, don't have a panic attack. Jack can't see me freak out.* I pulled on my collar. I struggled to breathe.

"If I avoid the shadowy areas, we'll be fine."

I squeezed my eyes shut. They popped open. I scrutinized the road. Each time I noticed a stretch ahead in shadows, my chest ached. *What was I thinking? We're wasting our time. I'm not cut out to be a*

Guardian. I'm a failure. My hands trembled. Adrenaline shot through my body. My forehead beaded up with perspiration.

I pointed at the dash. "Turn down the heater."

"Hon, we're almost there. It's okay."

I clutched Jack's leg. "Stop the car. I have to get out."

61

ALLI

Jack pulled off I-17 and stopped on the shoulder. The car shuddered as other vehicles sped past.

My hands trembled. I fumbled with the handle.

After turning off the ignition, Jack leaned across me and opened my door.

I jumped out and stomped around, crunching snow under my sandals.

Climbing across the front seat, Jack caught up to me. Waiting until I stopped, he held me.

"I'm sorry," I said, sobbing. "I was so scared. You must hate me."

"Hon, it's okay. You don't have to explain anything." Jack rubbed my back. "I understand. More than you know."

I sniffed, then rested my head against his shoulder. "What do you mean?" My breath hung in the air. My teeth were chattering though I wasn't sure if it was from my anxiety, the bitter cold, or both.

"Can we get back in the car and talk?" Jack brushed his warm fingers against my icy cheek. "Don't want you to get sick."

I nodded as he climbed back in on my side and maneuvered into the driver's seat. I settled into my seat and closed the door. "If you don't mind, I want to roll the window down a bit. I need some fresh air."

"Anything for you, Princess."

I giggled. "I can't believe you still call me that." Staring out the open window, I watched little clumps of snow fall from nearby pine trees and plop on the side of the road.

Jack placed his strong, warm hand over mine. "I'm sorry last month was so terrible. No one should ever have to go through what you did. But, you are strong. Much more than you think."

I looked at him blinking back tears. "I'm not strong at all…"

"Yes, Alli. You are. Don't let that little voice in your head tell you otherwise."

I rolled my eyes. "I can't help it. That voice is loud and strong. And it never lets me forget my failures."

"Hon, I know how hard it is to deal with anxiety."

I opened my mouth, but Jack continued.

"Yes, I do know. I work with people all day who suffer from panic attacks. Plus, I used to suffer from them also."

My voice trembled. "Why didn't you tell me before?"

"Probably the same reason you never told me. I didn't think you'd want to be with me anymore."

I shook my head. "But, I don't feel that way about you at all."

"I don't feel that way about you either. I love, um, love being with you." Jack held my hand, then cupped my chin as he kissed me. "You ready to go find Jason?"

I nodded. "Thanks. It will be better now that I can tell you how I'm feeling. It was so hard hiding it… Being afraid you might find out." As Jack started the engine, I rolled up the window and rubbed my hands in front of the heater vent. "Just a bit colder than San Diego."

Jack laughed. "A lot colder."

A SHORT TIME later we arrived in Flagstaff and settled in the motel I'd booked for the next four nights. To be considerate, I made sure it included two beds. We still hadn't slept together, and with everything else going on, I didn't want to walk in and discover only one bed and be stressed out about first-time sex. We only had Friday, Saturday, and Sunday to meet Jason's aunt, locate Jason's mom, find Jason, and convince him to be the next Guardian. *Piece of cake. Right?*

The IHOP was just across the parking lot from the motel. Even though the temperatures hovered in the mid-thirties, we walked. I was so glad to be out of the car. Jack and I enjoyed a traditional Thanksgiving dinner with all the fixings. There was enough left for a midnight snack, so we took a doggie bag back to the mini-fridge. In the room, Jack relaxed on his bed flipping through the TV channels. Though I wanted to watch something with him, I couldn't stop yawning. Heading into the bathroom, I took a hot shower and changed into my flannel pajamas.

Jack smiled as I emerged. "Happy Thanksgiving, Princess."

I held out the bottom corners of pajama top and twirled in a circle.

He jumped up from the bed, came over to me, and bowed. "May I have this dance?"

I felt a blush rise in my cheeks and nodded.

He took my hand and began humming, probably a song from an animated movie, but I couldn't remember which one. It didn't matter. Pressing his hand up against the small of my back, he swept me around our makeshift ballroom and even dipped me a few times.

I giggled and breathed in the scent of his musky cologne. Our hips swayed together. He kissed my neck and then my cheek.

"Too bad I don't have my Snow White costume," I said.

Jack leaned back and winked. "I was just thinking the same thing. Although, that would have been much harder to remove…"

I stopped dancing and looked at him, my eyes wide. "What was that?" *Yikes, I forgot to put condoms on the list.*

"I meant…" Jack stammered, his cheeks turning rosy-pink. "You know, to be more comfortable… for sleeping in…"

"Is that really what you meant?"

Jack cleared his throat. "Well, yes. I mean. Kinda. Although… We are here. Alone. No roommates…"

"I didn't bring protection."

He crinkled his nose and smiled. "I did."

62

ALLI

I stirred and sensed Jack's warm body behind me. We'd fallen asleep and awakened in the same position. *How romantic.* As I stretched, he slipped his arm around my waist and hugged me. Then he kissed my neck.

"Morning, Princess," he whispered. "Sleep well?"

I let out a deep sigh and giggled. "Best sleep in a very long time… Thanks to you."

He brushed his fingers down the side of my body. "I like waking up next to you, too." He kissed me again on the neck, then rolled over. Hopping out of bed, he headed into the bathroom.

I watched his bare, furry butt disappear behind the door, then got up and slipped on my pajamas. Even though we'd made love, I wasn't ready to be seen in all my unclothed glory. Especially in the daytime. At least, not yet. After Jack finished, I went into the bathroom and took a shower. Today was the big day. The chance to meet Jason's aunt and end my stress.

ALTHOUGH MY STOMACH GROWLED, I only managed a few bites of a dollar-sized pancake covered in warm butter and maple syrup. As I glanced around the busy restaurant, I nibbled on a piece of thick, smoky bacon, hoping the protein would help ease my pounding head. Waitresses carried plates of eggs, sausage, and fried potatoes to other hungry customers. Unfortunately, the only thing that tasted good was my coffee. I finally gave up and offered my breakfast to Jack.

After I finished the second cup of coffee and Jack devoured my pancakes, he paid the bill, and we set out for Jason's aunt's place. My notes showed we were looking for a Debora Freison. She supposedly lived in a double-wide mobile home north of town at the base of Mt. Eldon, about a half hour from where we were staying. As we turned off Highway 89 onto Snowflake Drive, my heart rate increased.

I brightened as we entered the residential area. "Look at all the cool street names. It's like we're at the North Pole." I pointed as Jack drove us through narrow streets lined with brown and beige mobile homes. "Look there's Hollygreen, Snowflake Way, Christmas Tree Lane, and St. Nicholas Circle." Surprised to see gravel instead of green lawns, I noticed tiny, pink rocks poking through melted snow patches, creating unusual patterns in front of each house. Portable basketball hoops surrounded by dirt-smattered snow mounds stood like sentries near driveways. Snow drifts concealed the bottoms of wooden mailbox poles and frosted the sides of each house. In most directions, the tall pines hid our view of the mountains. But, heading down Wintergreen, the snow-capped mountain stood tall in front of us.

"Wow, that's amazing," I said.

"That's why I loved living here," said Jack. "I never got tired of that view."

We pulled up in front of an avocado-green, double-wide mobile home and parked just beyond an overflowing trash bin sitting askew on the sidewalk. A curtained window with skinny brown shutters looked out at us like a closed eye waiting to wake up. A small red pickup sat parked under the carport—hopefully, a sign that someone would be home. As I got out of the car, I took in a deep breath. The scent of pine invigorated me.

Jack glanced up and down the street. "Are you sure this is the correct address?"

"It's the one Geoff gave me. Said it was where Debora lived for over twenty years." As we walked up the driveway, I pointed to a rectangular, silver mailbox on a post. The name "Freison" was painted in black ink.

He looked at me. "You ready?"

I smiled and steeled myself. "Not really, but we've come this far. Be kinda ridiculous to go home now." We walked up to the dull-green front door. I raised my hand and gave three loud knocks on the wood frame.

No answer.

Crap.

I knocked again, harder, making my knuckles sting.

Still no answer.

Just as I was about to knock a third time, the door opened. A woman in her late-forties stood in the doorway holding an overstuffed trash bag in each hand. The scent of cinnamon wafted from inside the house.

"Sorry I took so long," she said. "Needed to run back and grab the donations." After dropping two bulky, plastic bags on the porch, she brushed a wisp of dark blond hair out of her twinkling blue eyes, then pulled her burgundy cable-knit sweater tight around her thin waist. Noticing a delicate silver chain around her neck with a small locket attached, I wondered whose picture was inside.

"I'm sorry," I said. "Donations?"

She smiled. "Clothes for the local school. Someone called and said they'd pick them up this morning."

I wasn't sure what to say and began stuttering. "Oh… we're not here for the… clothes."

Jack stepped back from the bags. "Are you Debora Freison?"

Her eyes widened. Her smile faded. "Who are you?"

I offered her my hand. "My name is Alli. Allison Harper. This is my friend Jack Hastings. We're so sorry to bother you. I'm looking for a Debora Freison. It's about her nephew. Are you Debora?"

"My nephew?" Her voice turned frantic. "Who are you? Why are you here?"

I forced a smile. "I'm trying to find Jason Garanski. I was told you are his aunt. We've come all the way from San Diego. I have to find him." My hands trembled. I watched her eyes change from fear to anger.

She kicked at one of the trash bags. "Jason *was* my nephew."

Jack looked at me, then back to the woman. "I'm sorry, we didn't mean to upset you, Ms. Freison."

She glared at both of us and shook her fist. Spittle flew from her lips. "Jason and his mother are dead. You've wasted your time. Go back home and leave me alone." Then she turned and marched back inside.

63

JACK

As Debora shut the door, Alli shouted. "Wait. Please help." Her legs gave out. She sank down on the porch and sobbed.

I bent down and tried to help her up. "Hon, it's okay. We tried."

"No." Alli shook her head. "Jason? His mom? They can't be dead. I've already lost Tippy Toes and Russell…"

"Did I hear you mention Russell?" Debora opened the door a crack. Then she came back outside and stood next to us. She offered her hand to Alli.

With me on one side and Debora on the other, we helped Alli stand. I looked over at Debora. "Did you know Russell?"

"Yes. A long time ago. I'm sorry for my reaction. After Jason and his mother, Jennifer, were killed… I haven't trusted anyone. But when you mentioned Russell… It's cold out here. We should go inside and talk."

Debora led us into her warm, cinnamon-scented home reminiscent of my mother's hot apple pie. My mouth watered as I recalled the buttery crust and thick apple syrup oozing from the V-shaped slits. Now I craved a thick wedge. As my mouth watered, I shook off the tempting image and looked around. Hardbound books stacked in piles lay everywhere around the front room. A basket of half-folded laundry rested up against the couch. An old black and white movie was on television.

Debra grabbed the remote and muted the TV. “Please sit,” she said. “Take off your coats. Can I get you something warm to drink?”

“Water is fine unless you have coffee,” I said as I helped Alli take off her sweater. I removed mine and laid both across the end of the couch.

“I can make some in a jiffy.” Debora turned. “What about you, dear?”

“Coffee is fine. Thank you.” Alli looked over at me with questioning eyes.

I shrugged. I didn’t know what was going on either. First, the woman about kicks us out of town, then she invites us in.

Debora returned to the front room a few minutes later with a wooden tray. On it were three cups, a coffee carafe, and a plate of lemon wafers. “Please accept my apologies. I just… Well, it’s a long story and it still hurts.”

She filled a cup with steaming coffee and gave it to Alli. Then she filled and handed another cup to me.

I took a sip and swallowed. “Thank you.”

Alli placed her cup on the coffee table and looked up at Debora. “You mentioned you knew Russell?”

“Um, yes. The boys’ grandfather. Nice man. Tried to help out the family until the father pushed him away.”

Alli sat up straight. “You mean Ronald?”

Debora nodded and stared at a pile of books. “Such a cruel man. Jason and his mother came here to live with me… she needed to get away.” She paused and took a drink of her coffee. “He killed them—well, had them killed. That was over twenty-five years ago. Car accident… Buried over at Citizen’s Cemetery… So senseless.”

“I’m sorry for your loss,” I said. As I sipped my coffee, I wondered how Alli was dealing with this news.

Alli looked at Debora, then me. “Could we go out there? Pay our respects?” She cleared her throat. “We’ve come all this way. At least I could have some closure.”

Debora stared at the tray, then selected a lemon wafer. "How did you say you knew the Garanski family?"

"I didn't." Alli shifted and crossed her legs. "Let's just say I came upon Jason's inheritance and wanted to make sure he got it."

Debora gasped and dropped her wafer on the carpet. "So sorry, arthritis." She leaned over and picked it up, placing it on the tray away from the other cookies. She excused herself and walked into the kitchen.

I looked at Alli.

She shrugged.

I wasn't sure what happened either.

Debora hurried back, gathered up the cups and tray with trembling hands, and took them into the kitchen. When she returned, she sat on the edge of the wingback chair next to us. "Storm's coming in soon. If you want to visit their graves, we better make haste before it hits." She stood, grabbed her coat, and stood by the front door, gripping the knob.

Thinking back to the weather forecast I'd pulled up on my phone this morning, it had predicted cold, but clear, weather through the weekend. While freak storms were possible… *Why did Debora want us out of the house? And, why were her hands trembling?*

64

ALLI

I climbed into Jack's car and buckled my seat belt. "Did you notice how she wanted us to follow her out to the cemetery? Like right this second?" Checking my face in the mirror, I noticed a lemon crumb in the corner of my mouth and brushed it off.

"Why were her hands trembling?" Jack pulled away from the curb and fell in line behind the red truck driven by Debora Freison, Jason's aunt.

I stared up at the mountain. "All this way, just to go visit more graves." As much as I didn't want to go to this cemetery, I needed to see it in person and believe Debora. I didn't think she lied… Though at this point, I didn't know who or what to believe.

As Jack turned back onto the highway, he pushed the button on his Bluetooth. "This might be a long shot… But, I have an odd feeling…" Changing lanes, he stared forward while making his call. "Is this Stacey? Jack… Jack Hastings. Yes, it's been a while. Hey, I need you to look up something for me. No… in Flagstaff. On vacation. Okay, a working vacation." He laughed and looked over at me. "See if you can find info on a 963." He looked at me and whispered, "Fatal car accident." Raising his voice again, he continued, "Last name Garanski. George-Adam-Robert-Adam-Nora-Sam-King-Ida. Got that?

Good… Would have been about twenty-five years ago. Interred at Citizen's… What's that? Yeah, I need it like yesterday. There's a steak dinner in it for you… Great… Call me back on the number on your caller ID."

I looked over at Jack and raised my eyebrows. "What was that about?"

"Just called in a favor with my old boss. I want to know if they have anything about that accident. Something about how Debora's whole demeanor changed once you mentioned the inheritance." Although he kept his eyes on the road and the red truck, he reached over and patted my thigh. "Just my gut telling me she's hiding something."

"What if there's nothing about the accident? Would that prove she was lying?" I slipped my hand over Jack's, weaving my fingers through his.

"No. It doesn't. But, since it's an uncommon last name, I'm hoping something shows up. And soon. The cemetery is just ahead." He lifted his hand and pointed to a sign on the road.

Before I could reply, Jack's phone rang.

"Hastings… What do you have? That's interesting… Anything else? Yeah, in town through Sunday, leaving early Monday. Let me call you back… Thanks, Stacey."

My heart pounded in my chest. "What? Tell me what she said."

"Actually, she's a he. And he found a report about an accident on the I-17 matching my information. According to that report, a car registered to Jennifer Garanski was parked on the side of the road. A semi came along, lost control, plowed into the back of it rupturing the gas tank. The semi cab caught fire on impact. The male truck driver didn't survive. The Garanski car also erupted into flames. An adult female and male child died; their bodies burned beyond recognition."

"Oh my gosh, that's terrible." My thoughts swirled inside my brain. If Ronald did that… killing my cat and his own father would have been easy. *Would he really go through all that trouble?* I looked over at Jack as he slowed and pulled to the side of the narrow road inside the cemetery. "So now what?"

Jack turned off the ignition and set the parking brake. "We get out and follow her." He opened the door, then turned to me. "By the way, do you have those special glasses with you?"

"In the trunk, why?" What was Jack thinking? Did he want me to use them on Debora? Did he think she was lying? *How could a woman lie about something so terrible?* I didn't think it was appropriate, but when he popped the trunk I dug through my overnight bag, found them, and handed them to Jack. "No pockets in my sweater," I said, watching my breath drift away.

"Wait until I give the signal," said Jack. Then he walked toward Debora.

What signal? I looked around. Citizen's was much smaller than the cemetery in San Diego. Instead of palm trees, it was like a forest. Lots of tall pines everywhere. Not as many giant headstones, just grave markers and lots of marble benches under the swaying trees. I shuddered. I couldn't feel the tip of my nose. I hated being cold. And, I really hated cemeteries.

I tried to catch up to Jack as he was trying to keep up with Debora. She marched along at such a quick pace; it was hard to keep up with either one. Jack looked back at me, then sprinted to the middle of an open area covered in dead, yellowed grass that crunched under our feet. I soon realized sandals were not the best choice for walking in the cold, lifeless areas of a dilapidated cemetery.

Finally, Debora stopped. She looked around. First left. Then right. Then she took off again. Although, this time she walked. *Thank goodness*. She stood silent in front of a grave marker and pointed. "There." She turned away and focused on something in the distance.

Jack and I edged closer. It was a flat, grey headstone with "J. Garanski. Loving Mother and Son" engraved on it. No birth or death dates. No full names. Just one initial and last name. Of course, Jason and Jennifer do begin with "J."

"No names?" I blurted out, then cupped my hand over my mouth.

"Didn't have the money back then for a proper marker. Figured this would do if he tried to find them." Debora rubbed her hands together, then took a pair of mauve knitted gloves from her pocket and put them on.

Jack cleared his throat. "How did you say they passed?"

Debora looked up. "I didn't."

I stepped closer and then leaned down and brushed pine needles from the headstone. "Do you mind telling us about it? I'd like to know."

Debora hesitated, then swallowed. "Police said they must have stopped on the side of the road. Car trouble or something like that. A semi came by, lost control, and… Car and semi caught fire. Everything burned up before anyone could get there. She had told me her ex was after her and thought he might do something stupid to get back at her for taking the kid. She'd only been here a few months…" She sucked in a deep breath, then let it out, watching the wind carry her words away.

My heart ached for her. I reached up and placed my hand on her shoulder.

Debora flinched and moved from me, never turning around. "What's done is done. He can't hurt them anymore. You saw the grave. Now go home and let them rest in peace."

Jack nudged my arm. Handed me the glasses, he whispered, "It's time."

I removed my glasses and gave them to Jack. My throat tightened as I closed my eyes and put on the *Gifts* glasses. I opened my eyes, focusing on Debora. My feet burned as hot bolts of energy shot up from the ground—through my sandals, legs, body, and out through my hair.

My chest ached.

My head pounded.

I saw Debora's thoughts.

Or, should I say, Jennifer's?

65

ALLI

After using the glasses, I observed Debora. I knew from her thoughts she was Jennifer, Jason's mother. *What should I say? And how should I say it?* She had just shared how Jason and his mother were killed in a freak accident. Now, we were in front of their final resting place, with her standing next to us.

I pulled off the *Gifts* glasses and handed them back to Jack. With trembling hands, I tried to put on my glasses but dropped them on the pine needles. As I bent over to pick them up, I whispered, "It's her."

Debora rubbed her gloved hands together. "It was nice meeting you. Sorry I couldn't be of more help." She turned, then marched past us toward her truck.

Oh man, it's now or never. I steadied myself. "Wait… Jennifer."

She stopped and turned back; her eyes narrowed. "What did you call me?"

I walked toward her. "You are Jennifer. You didn't want us to know because you're afraid. You're still hiding from Ronald because if he knew you were alive, he'd come back."

"That's not true…" She looked at me, then to Jack. "How did you know…?" Her eyes widened. She balled up her fists. "*I'm* Debora. *I'm*

Jason's aunt. They're dead…" She paused, then collapsed on the cold, hard ground and sobbed.

I sat down next to her. "I didn't mean to frighten you. I'm sorry you've been holding onto this secret for so long. I know you're terrified of Ronald. He's horrible."

Debora curled into a ball. Her shoulders shook. She wailed, "No. You can't know. No one knows the truth. Not even Jason."

"Then you really are Jennifer?" I asked.

She raised herself to a sitting position and nodded.

I let out a long breath. "Please believe me. I'm not here to hurt you. I just need to find Jason. It's a long story… there's not much time."

Jennifer looked at me. "Only until January, correct?"

I gasped. "How did you know…?" I glanced over and noticed Jack standing next to me.

Jennifer pulled off one glove, pulled a tissue from her pocket, and wiped her eyes. "After Jason was born, Russell told me about the inheritance. How it belonged to Jason. How he needed to claim it before he turned 30.

"After years of abuse from Ron, I took Jason and left in the middle of the night. I figured we'd be safe with my twin sister, Debora and her son Zackary. Both boys were born in the same year and had similar features.

"At first, Jason and I never ventured outside. After a month went by with no contact from Ron, we began to settle in. I changed my license and registration to the Flagstaff address. Got new license plates, the whole bit.

One day, Deb's son was ill. She needed to take him to the doctor. When her car wouldn't start, I gave her the keys to my car… I never saw them again.

"When the state troopers came upon the accident, they ran the plates. The police showed up saying they'd found Jennifer's car on the side of the road. They must have assumed I was Debora when I answered the door. They said my sister Jennifer and her son died in a horrible accident. Both vehicles burned. The occupants unrecognizable.

"I contacted Russell and told him what happened. He suggested I stay in Flagstaff and assume my sister's identity; otherwise, Ron would continue to hunt us down." She wiped her eyes again and blew her nose in the tissue.

"Since no one in Flagstaff knew us, Jason and I became Zackary and Debora Freison. I used their birth certificates for identification. Except for Russell, no one knew. I thought we were safe. But when you asked about my nephew, I freaked out. I thought something happened to my son."

My heart pounded in my ears. "So, Jason is still alive?" *Please let Jason be alive.*

"Before I answer, tell me how *you* got *his* inheritance?"

I explained how I met Russell at the storage facility and then bid on the box. Then I shared how Ronald threatened me and broke in. How Tippy Toes was taken and how Russell was also killed. "And that's how I met Jack. He was the detective investigating the whole case." I sighed. While it was all true, it still sounded like some bizarre movie plot.

Jennifer looked at Jack, then back to me. "I'm sorry you got involved. Ron seemed okay when we dated. But as soon as we were married, his abuse began. By the time Jason and Steven came along, he was out of control. I couldn't take it anymore. I came to Arizona where I thought we'd be safe. But the accident… I've never forgiven myself for my sister and nephew's deaths. If they hadn't been in my car…"

Jack cleared his throat. "Ronald must have known you were here."

Jennifer picked up a pine needle and broke it into small pieces. "Yes he did. He intimidated or used someone else to carry out his threats. Whoever he hired to do his dirty work must have thought Jason and I were in the car that day. It was too much of a coincidence." She shuddered. "All because he wanted that damned inheritance. Bastard."

"I'm sorry," I whispered.

She looked up at me. "I'm sorry for you. I remember Russell telling me something about "the things," or whatever he called them. I don't remember much, just that I needed to protect Jason until he was old enough. Then he could receive what was supposed to be his." Jennifer picked up a handful of pine needles and sorted them by size.

Adrenaline shot through my body. I blurted, "Where is Jason?"

She looked at me. Her eyes welled up. “I don’t know.”

“But, he’s alive, right?”

“Four years ago, he said he was leaving for college, but deep down inside I knew he went looking for Russell. After he left, I realized he’d found some papers… I thought I’d hidden them better…” She stood up and brushed dirt and dry grass off her jeans. “A few weeks ago I talked to Zackary, I mean Jason. He sounded upset but wouldn’t say why. He’s never told me where he was, for our safety.”

I tossed my head back and groaned. “So, he is alive. But no one knows where he is. I’ve got one month. We’re no closer to finding him than we were months ago.”

Jack stood and reached for my hand.

I got up and leaned against him. “I’m sorry,” I said. “It’s just so frustrating. If I can’t find him, then I’m stuck with the…”

“Is that how you knew who I was?” Jennifer folded her arms across her chest. “You have his inheritance thingies. You knew all along.”

“Actually, I just found out a few minutes ago when I used one of the, um, thingies. I really believed you were Debora, that was until you freaked out when I mentioned the inheritance. I’m sorry. I needed to know before we left.”

“It’s okay.” Jennifer looked down at my feet. “If I were in your, um, sandals, I’d have done the same thing.” She smiled.

Jack squared his shoulders. “I don’t suppose you have a recent picture of Jason?”

Jennifer shook her head. “Only the one when he was about five. Otherwise, I’ve never kept any, just in case. It’s been terrible. Always looking over my shoulder. Always afraid.”

I pulled my sweater tighter as the wind picked up. “So, if I’m to understand you, now I need to search for a Zackary Freison—the real Jason Garanski?”

Jennifer brushed her hair out of her eyes and nodded. “Part of me hopes you don’t find him. But, the other part of me does. If Ron really did murder Russell, then Zackary, I mean Jason, deserves what’s rightfully his. But if Ron were to know….”

I looked over at Jack, then back to Jennifer and smiled. “Must have been a popular name thirty years ago. My friend's boyfriend is a Zack."

Jennifer put on her glove pushing it tight around her fingers. "When Deb was pregnant, she wanted to come up with a regal name for her son. She settled on Zackary, with a "k" instead of an "h" after Zackary Taylor, the twelfth president. She thought it was so unique but was surprised when three other boys with the same name showed up in her son's kindergarten class. I guess it was very popular."

Observing the sadness in her eyes as she talked about her sister and nephew, I walked over to Jennifer. "Mind if I give you a hug?"

She reached out and embraced me, patted my back three times, then stepped back. Her gesture gave me goosebumps. My mother always hugged me and added three small pats to my back before she let go. Being so close I noticed her bright blue eyes and freckled nose. *Did Jason have his mother's features? Would I know him if I met him in person?* Who was I kidding? Even if he came into my frame shop, I'd never recognize him.

66

CHERYL

"Out of my way." I rushed up the concrete stairs ahead of Darius. After nine-plus hours in the car, my bladder ached. Though the drive wasn't too bad, it was *too* long. Flying would have taken less than two hours, but Darius preferred traveling by car.

Opening the front door, I tossed my bag on the couch and continued down the hall. *Wait. Was that Zack in the kitchen?* On the way back, I walked past Darius carrying suitcases to my room.

"Hey," he said. "You see who's back?"

It was Zack. Liz stood and hugged me. *Did I just come home to an alternate universe where Zack and Liz were back together? And Liz was nice again?*

My mouth gaped open. "How's it going?"

Zack reached over and fist-bumped Darius. "Doobie Dude."

Darius responded, "Z-Man." He offered Zack a beer, then they headed into the front room. A few minutes later, they were watching some sporting event, yelling at the TV like old times.

I looked at Liz, pointing toward Zack. "You guys back together?"

Liz hugged me again. "Yes. And I've got more news to share when Alli comes home."

"Not fair making me wait." I laughed and took a soda out of the refrigerator. "When do you expect them?"

Liz sat down and finished eating. "Alli called this morning when they left Flagstaff." She glanced at the wall clock. "Should be any time now."

I leaned in to Liz. "Did she say if they found Jason?"

"She didn't. Just she'd tell us everything when they got here."

"You have any problems with you-know-who?" I asked.

"Not that I noticed. Of course, Zack and I stayed in the other room a lot." She giggled, then added, "I'm supposed to be on bedrest. Doctor's orders."

"Are you okay? I didn't know you were sick…" I turned as the front door opened. Jack and Alli walked in carrying their overnight bags.

"Glad to see you guys made it home safely," I said.

He nodded, then turned his head as the guys yelled at the TV. "Zack's still here? That's a good sign."

"You've met?" I scratched my head. *When did that happen?* I opened the fridge and offered Jack a beer.

He accepted, then headed into the front room.

Alli caught Jack's eye and smiled, then turned back to us and pulled out a chair. "Time to catch up with my besties."

Before she sat, I gave her a hug. "Missed you, Girlfriend."

"Missed you, too. How was Reno?"

I clapped my hands. "Awesome. I have a whole family living there, brothers and sisters, and nieces I never knew about. It was so cool."

Alli smiled. "So, your dad remarried?"

Sitting down at the table next to Liz, I tucked a curl behind my ear. "Years after he left my mom and me." I took a sip of soda. "Forget about my trip, what about Jason? Did you find him?"

Liz put down her soda. "I've been waiting all weekend for this…"

"No, we didn't." Alli stood and opened the cabinet, grabbing a box of cereal. She poured some into a bowl and sat. Picking through the cereal, she looked up. "But we did meet his mother."

I slapped the table. "Oh, my. Are you serious? What did she say? Did she tell you about Jason?"

Alli paused. "It's really complicated. Apparently, Jason left. She doesn't know where he is. Geoff couldn't find them because they have different names… to protect themselves from Ronald."

Liz looked at Alli. "Makes sense. Did she tell you his new name? Or give you his phone number?"

Alli sighed. "She said his name was Zackary …"

Zack yelled from the front room. "Someone talking to me?"

I yelled back. "No, just watch your game." I shrugged my shoulders. "That thing is up so loud…how did he even hear us?"

Liz shrugged, got up, and put her plate in the sink. "So, you have his name, that's something. What about a contact number or email?"

Alli pushed the cereal around in her bowl with her finger. "She wouldn't give me any of his personal info. She did say she'd contact him and give him my number." She wiped her eyes. "I'm so frustrated."

I leaned over and put my arm around her shoulder. "You have no idea where he is?"

Alli shook her head.

Liz looked at Alli, then at me. "Damn. But, at least you know how to get a message to him. Did you tell her about the, um, inheritance?"

Alli nodded. "She seemed to know about it. But, she also knew Ronald would do anything to keep it from Jason. She was still terrified of him, even after all these years."

I looked at her. "Do you blame her."

"I haven't even told you about the accident…" Alli looked up as Darius came into the kitchen and grabbed a handful of beers. "…or how she faked their deaths yet."

Darius stood behind me. "Who was in an accident and pretended to be dead?"

Liz looked up at him. "No one. We're talking about… a movie."

He sighed and left the kitchen.

I grabbed Alli's hand. "This is crazy."

"More than you even know. Jennifer… his mom's real name. Not Deb…" She paused as Zack and Darius strolled into the kitchen.

"Halftime," said Darius. Zack's getting pizza. You gals want in?"

Zack strolled into the kitchen and stopped behind Liz, massaging her neck. “You tell them your news yet?”

She blushed. “Alli was sharing about her trip. My news can wait.”

Darius eyed Zack. He came up behind me and began rubbing my neck. “You tell them your news yet?”

“Not yet.” I blushed. “Shhhhhush.”

Alli looked at me, then Liz. “Wait,” she said. “You both have news? What’s going on?”

Zack held up his finger while he placed the pizza order. He turned his mouth from the phone, “Wait before you say anything… I’ll be done in a sec.”

Darius called out to Jack. “Hey, Jack Dude, come join us for the news.”

Jack walked in and placed his hands on Alli’s shoulders. “What news? Is this about our trip?”

Alli patted his hands. “So, who’s going first? Liz or you, Cheryl?”

At the same time, we pointed to each other and said, “You.”

Liz rolled her eyes. “Seriously?”

Darius rubbed the stubble on his cheeks, then looked at Liz and me. “Why not say it at the same time?”

Alli stood. “Great idea. I’ll count down. When I reach one, you both share your news. Agreed?”

Liz sighed. “Fine. Just hurry up.”

Alli looked at us. She raised her hand. “Three. Two. One…”

Liz smiled. “I’m pregnant, and Zack and I are engaged.”

I grinned. “Darius and I are moving to Reno.”

67

JACK

Alli and I didn't talk much on the way back to San Diego. Going through the Arizona mountains, she stared out the window, focused on the road. Once we hit the long, flat expanses of highway, she slept. I understood her quiet, somber mood. Even though Jennifer, Jason's mom, promised she'd contact her son, who knew if she'd follow through, or if Jason would even call. Jennifer's fear of Ronald was justified. If it were me, I wouldn't want to put my kid in danger.

As we headed into the apartment with our bags, Alli dashed off down the hall. Cheryl greeted me, and after offering a beer, took me into the front room where Zack and Darius were arguing over a play in the game. The Dolphins and Panthers were tied with less than three minutes left in the half. The ref threw a flag on the line of scrimmage.

"Offside," said Darius.

Zack pointed to the TV. "False start."

Cheryl stood in front of the TV, drawing protests. "Zack, this is Jack. Jack, Zack. Now go back to your game."

I sat on the edge of the couch. "Gutsy move."

Darius held up his fist. "Jack-Man."

I gave the obligatory first bump, then nodded at Zack. Last week, I almost arrested him as he stood outside the front door. Hope he didn't hold a grudge.

Darius snorted. "Ha, it was offside."

I chuckled. That guy's such a goofball, but he's got a big heart.

Darius elbowed me during a commercial. "How was the trip?"

"Good." I settled back in my cushion and drank my beer. "Glad to be home. Just missed a big storm coming in."

"Where'd you go?" asked Zack.

"Flagstaff."

He sat forward and peered around Darius. "Oh yeah. Got family there?"

"Went to locate a friend of Alli's."

"I grew up there," said Zack.

The commentators came on and began discussing the ref's call. As Zack sat back in his seat, I leaned forward to get a better look at him. "I lived there for a few years also when I was with the DEA," I said. "Where'd you go to school?"

Zack finished his beer. "Homeschooled. Mom didn't care much for the school system."

Darius perked up. "Dude. You went to school at home? Who was your teacher?"

Zack smiled at Darius. "My mom." Zack turned to me. "Pizza sounds good. What about you?"

During a quiet moment on the TV, I heard Alli mention the word "Zackary."

Zack must have also heard it because he turned toward the kitchen. "Someone talking to me?"

Cheryl yelled back, "Just watch your game."

"Time for another cold one. Anyone else?" Darius stood and walked into the kitchen.

I couldn't help but wonder if… No, that would be too much of a coincidence. I pulled out my phone and did a quick search. According to one site, over 162,593 men had Zackary as a first name—the 397th most popular. *Why was I a statistics freak?* I didn't know much about Zack, other than he lived in Flagstaff. And was homeschooled. That would fit if Jennifer didn't want him in the school system. *Though, the odds of him being Alli's Zack were practically nil.*

My curiosity got the best of me. "Hey Zack, didn't catch your last name."

He looked over at me. "Thomas. Why?"

"Just wondering if I'd met you when I lived in Flagstaff."

"Worked at Brix as a server. Maybe you ate there while I was at work?"

"Possible." *Let's see if I can tip the odds in our favor.* "And your mom's…?" The ref's shrill whistle interrupted me.

"Halftime." Zack jumped up and headed into the kitchen.

Darius followed, then shouted to me. "Hey, Jack Dude, come join us for the news.

Damn. My question would have to wait.

68

ALLI

Although it was good to be back home, I couldn't shake my despair. Meeting Jennifer gave me a shred of hope. I'd given her my number. I hoped she'd follow through. *Who was I kidding?* Ronald assumed they were dead. She wanted to keep it that way. With everything I knew about Ronald, I wouldn't blame her.

Seeing everyone helped. Zack and Darius watched football like old times. Hopefully, Jack and Zack would be okay after all of Liz's trash talking about him. *Do guys even remember that stuff?* Give 'em beer and football. They bond instantly.

Cheryl and Liz wanted all the trip details, and although I shared some, I couldn't go into the particulars. Cheryl didn't know much about the *Gifts*. Just telling them we were close, but not successful would help satisfy their curiosity until Liz and I could chat.

My mind drifted as they talked about their Thanksgiving weekends. My thoughts went back to Jennifer. The accident. The faked IDs. How Jason thought he was Zackary Freison. If Jennifer contacted her son, she'd have to come clean on the lie she had created over twenty-five years ago. And that's before she mentioned the inheritance. With only a month left, why would she put him in danger just to help me? Someone she never knew existed until a few days ago.

As I shared bits of my story, Liz and Cheryl asked questions.

Liz seemed most curious. "So, did she tell you his name? Or give you his phone number?"

I sighed. "She said his name was Zackary…"

Zack yelled from the front room. "Someone talking to me?"

Cheryl yelled back. "No, just watch your game."

How did he hear that over the racket of the game? For the last three years he only referred to himself as Zack. Although… my name is Alli, but my legal name is Allison. Maybe Zackary was his "kid" name… the one only grandmas and aunties used.

The guys came in. Zack said something about ordering pizza. As he ordered, Liz and Cheryl announced they had news to share. Since no one could figure out who should say theirs first, Darius suggested I count down for a double-reveal.

With Zack off the phone, I raised my hand. "Three. Two. One…"

As Liz said, "I'm pregnant, and Zack and I are engaged," Cheryl said, "Darius and I are moving to Reno."

I stared at Cheryl, then at Liz. "Wait. What did you both say?" I was thrilled and shocked. *Should I congratulate Liz or question Cheryl's decision?*

Liz waved her hand in front of us, showing off her sparkly ring. "We're getting married."

Cheryl spit soda on the table. "You're pregnant? When did that happen? I mean… I'm really happy, but what the… ? We were gone less than a week."

The guys patted Zack on the back and offered congrats. They opened more beers and toasted the happy couple.

Darius fist-bumped Zack. "Guess I should call you Z-Dad now. Congrats, Dude."

Cheryl stood and hugged Liz and Zack. "I'm so happy for you," she said, pulling back. She stared at Liz's tummy, then bent over placing her face next to Liz's baby bump. "Happy for you too little baby whoever-you-are."

Liz and Cheryl joined me at the table. I placed my hand over Cheryl's. "You're really moving? I don't know what to say… I mean I'm happy about your new family… But…" Fighting tears while relaying our Flagstaff trip story, I couldn't hold back any longer. I let go as they streamed down my cheeks.

Cheryl squeezed my hand while grasping Liz's. "You two are still family. You were my only family all these years… I don't want to leave. But I need to… I want to know my dad's family."

I blew my nose. "It's what you've always wanted."

Liz wiped her eyes. "Promise to stay in touch? Especially now that we're expecting…"

Cheryl nodded.

"How soon are you leaving?" I said.

Cheryl looked over at Darius, then back to me. "We're spending Christmas with them. We'll look for a place then." She tucked a curl behind her ear. "Dad invited us to stay with him until we got settled, but I wanted to give you enough notice to find someone to rent my room…"

I listened as everyone talked at once. Darius and Cheryl making plans to move away. Liz and Zack making plans for the future. Cheryl placed her hand on Liz's tummy and talked to the baby. Zack and Darius fist bumped again. When Jack came up behind me and rubbed my shoulders, I sighed.

Everyone was moving forward, yet I was still in the same place. Stuck with an inheritance I didn't want. A challenge I didn't ask for. I'd lost my cat, my friend Russell, and what was left of my sanity over the whole mess. One of my best friends was moving away. I needed a stranger to help me find another stranger—who could be anywhere in the world. Or, right here in San Diego.

While their lives were coming together, mine was unraveling by the minute. My entire world seemed out of control. There was nothing I could do to fix it. Cheryl drove me places without judgement when I was too anxious to drive. We shared a bond of trusting each other. A bond Liz and I only recently discovered because of the *Gifts*.

The worst part was that I never had a chance to share the best part of the whole weekend with them. During the drive home I'd planned my big reveal. While the guys hung out, the three of us would sit around the table. I'd grab a bottle of chilled white wine, then uncork it in a showy fashion. I'd pour us drinks. Raise my glass. Then ask, "Guess who finally slept together?"

We'd giggle over the sordid details. Cheryl would ask intimate questions. I'd blush. Liz would gross out. We'd ask Liz if she and Zack "reacquainted" in proper fashion. Then Cheryl would share one of her and Darius' sex stories. We'd laugh 'til Cheryl peed her pants. Finally, I was part of the group who'd "done it." But I never got a chance to tell them.

Why couldn't things be like they were three months ago?

I wished I'd never met Russell.

And, as terrible as it sounds, I wished Cheryl had never found her father.

69

RONALD

D*amn it's cold out here.* I stomped my feet, then pulled a silver flask from my pocket and unscrewed the lid. Swigging my whiskey, I waited for the thick liquid to warm my insides. It burned going down but felt so good.

I'd been stopping by their apartment each night, watching and waiting. Tonight, someone was home. *Finally.* I could've walked in and taken my stuff, but I dropped my damned lock pick kit last week. I thought about forcing my way in, but what fun would that have been with no one around to scare?

Now, it's more than Steven's inheritance. It's time for them girls to pay. They made it hard on me and my idiot kid. What's mine is mine. By the time I'm done, someone—maybe even all of them—will understand no one screws with Ronald Garanski and lives to tell about it.

Been waiting by this rusty dumpster for the fat boyfriend. Stinks so bad, I can taste the sour milk and rotten turkey stench coming from the bin. They had pizza delivered a few hours ago. He should be out any time.

How do I know the boyfriend will show? Because he comes down here about midnight, dumps the trash, then smokes his weed. All because the girly girls don't like the smell. *Wimps*. Once he blazes up, he won't shut up. Tells me everything about everybody. After all, I'm just the friendly, downstairs neighbor.

Heavy footsteps on the stairs. I shoved my flask back in my pockets, then walked around to the other side of the dumpster. Sure enough. Right on time.

"Downstairs Dude." He tossed a kitchen trash bag and several pizza boxes into the bin, then held out his fist.

I forced myself to fist-bump back. "Upstairs Dude. What's been going on?" *The crap I have to deal with.*

"Not much." Reaching into his pocket, he pulled out a joint and offered it to me. "Just finished celebrating everyone's news."

I lit it and took two hits, then gave it back. "That so? What were you celebratin'?"

"All kinds of stuff. Lizzy and her boyfriend. Oh, wait. I think he's now a finance… financer… anyway, they're having a kid and getting married."

The skinny one's pregnant? That just made my revenge even better. After he finished his joint, I pulled out my flask and offered it to him. A little booze. A little weed. A lot more high. "You mean fiancé?"

"Yeah, Dude. That's it, a financer… And then me and Cheryl, we're moving."

"Is that so?" I said. *Hmmm, less chickadees in the nest.* "When?"

"Don't know. We're headed back before Christmas. When she tells me, I guess. You know how that is, right?"

Feeling a good buzz myself, I nodded. "Anything to please the little woman, right? *Dumbutt*. "Any other news?"

He took another sip from the flask. "Alli and Jack just got back from Flagstaff. That's in Arizona." He flashed a toothy grin.

My head cleared at the mention of that city. "So, it is. Visiting family for Thanksgiving?"

"Don't think so. She said something about finding a missing friend…"

My heart pounded. "You didn't happen to hear the name of her friend? I might be able to help… since I know a lot of people."

"I can't remember right now."

I grabbed his jacket. "Think hard. I have to know the name."

"Hey, Downstairs Dude. What's with the angry voice?" As he pulled away, he giggled. "You wanna comeback upwithme and ask her hisself? Herself?"

I backed off. "No, it's okay. Sorry." *Dammit. I had to know.*

He smiled at me. "Justin."

"What was that?"

He held up his hand. "She was looking for Justin. Or was it... Jasmin? No, that's a flower." He ran his thick fingers through his unruly hair. "It was like someone's kid... Joe's son? John's son...?"

Oh, my freaking... It would be next year before this jerk remembers anything. *Wait. Joes son... John's son...* "Do you mean Jason?"

"Yeah, that's it. Jay's son. I knew it was some guy's son." He turned and headed toward the stairs.

"Wait, um, Dude. One more question."

"Sure, Downstairs Dumpster Dude. Ask me what you want me to ask a question about." He turned, scratched his beard then picked his nose.

Holy crap. "You said she was looking for a Jason. Do you know if she found him?" I gripped the edge of the dumpster to avoid strangling the idiot.

"Well... I remember she said something about looking for Jay's son, but couldn't find him..."

I let out a breath as my body relaxed.

"But, I think she found his mom," he said, then turned.

I grabbed the back of his jacket.

He jerked around. "What the...?"

I held up hands, palms facing him. "Sorry, Dude, you were gonna step on a rat."

He looked down at his feet, then up at me.

Drumming my fingers on the edge of the dumpster, I glared at him. "Are you sure? Did you actually hear her say she found the mom?"

"When I went in the kitchen, I heard her whimper... um, whisper to Lizzy, that they found someone's mom. Her name was... It was like the son's. I dunno. I'm really buzzed."

"Was it Jennifer? Tell me yes or no. Then you can go sleep it off."

He stood silent for a while, then looked at me with half-closed eyes. "Yeah, Dude. It was Jennifer. How'd you know?"

"Lucky guess." I clenched my fists. "Forget we talked about this, okay?"

He rubbed his eyes. "Only if you promise to come up and have a beer with us sometime."

I smirked. "Wouldn't miss that for anything."

As he stumbled up the stairs, my mind raced. Jennifer and Jason were supposed to be dead. But, if she was alive… was he also alive?

70

ZACK

Funny how life changes. A week ago, I left my place a single guy with no girlfriend. Now I was engaged, with a kid on the way. Just before we announced our big news to everyone last night, I received a call but declined it. Figured it'd be better to wait until this next morning as I headed to work. Then we could talk in private.

"Hey, Mom… Getting in my car… Let me get buckled and I'll put you on speaker." I pulled away from the curb and headed toward the freeway. "So, what's up? You don't call me too often. Everything okay?"

"Zackary, I need to talk to you about something. It's important. But I'd rather wait until you're not driving."

Her voice sounded different. Like she'd been crying or something. "Mom, you're kinda freaking me out. What's going on?"

"Sweetie, we need to talk. But…"

I pulled off the road into a fast food parking lot and turned off the car. "Mom, what's going on? I'm not driving anymore."

"I wish I was there in person, Zackary. I hate to tell you this over the phone."

"We can video chat if you want. Would that be better?"

She went silent.

"Mom, are you still there?"

"Yes. Video is fine."

I swiped the chat icon and Mom's face materialized on the screen. Her eyes were puffy and swollen.

She cleared her throat. "Hon, I need to tell you something, but I'm not sure how to start. You might hate me…"

"I won't hate you. I promise. Please, just tell me what's going on."

She wiped her eyes and sighed. "I need… I need to tell you the truth. About who you really are."

Oh man. Mom never knew why I really left. All those years of searching. Seems we've both been hiding secrets from each other.

She coughed, then continued. "Do you remember your father? Or your grandfather?"

"A little bit. I remember Gran-Dad telling me stories. About magical things. And I remember you being sad… It was a long time ago."

"Twenty-five years ago. Your dad and I, I couldn't stay…" She stopped talking and looked away. "He was so mean. I couldn't take it anymore."

"I remember you crying," I said. "You woke me up. I was in my pajamas. I wanted Steven to come with us…" *Man, I hadn't thought about that in a long time.*

"You're right. Even though it broke my heart, I had to leave one of you with your grandpa, Russell… He promised to look after Steven… I drove us to my sister's house in Flagstaff. After we got there, your dad kept calling. And threatening. It was terrible…" She wiped her eyes and paused. "He wanted you… he wanted both of us… out of his way."

I wanted to hug her. My heart ached to see her so upset. "Mom, it's okay. You did what you had to do. You don't have to explain…"

"There's more I have to tell you. I've been holding onto a secret for all these years. I didn't want you to know. I wanted to keep you safe. But you need to make the decision, not me."

"What decision? What are you talking about?"

She took in a sharp breath. "You're not who you think you are."

I kept silent.

"Your name is not Zackary. That was your cousin's name..." She blew her nose and paused. "Your real name is... Jason. Jason Garanski. You have an inheritance. Your grandfather saved it for you. Now he's dead. Someone came looking for you and I didn't know what to do and I told them I'd tell you and that's what I'm doing and I'm so, so sorry I lied..." She talked so fast, I couldn't understand her. Then she broke down and bawled.

While it was a lot to process, it all made sense. "Mom, I need to ask you about the inheritance. Is that why my father wanted me...?"

"Yes. And it's why I had to hide you. But he knew where we were. He sent someone... there was an accident. My sister, her son... We became them so your father would leave us alone... only another month. You would have been safe."

"Mom, what are you talking about? What accident? What's in another month?"

"The accident... it's a long story." She wiped her eyes. "Your birthday... next month."

"But my birthday isn't until March."

"Honey, Zackary's birthday was in March. Your birthday is January second."

This was some freaky stuff. "So, hold on a minute. My birthday is next month? But what does that have to do with the inheritance?"

"Your grandfather held some artifacts in a box for you. It was such a weird story I didn't know if I should believe it. You were supposed to inherit them before you turned thirty... because of some family guardianship or something."

"The *Gifts*."

"How did you know?"

"I remember him telling me the story... the Guardians of the *Gifts*. He said it was up to me to make a difference. I was only five. I had no idea what he was talking about. But now, somehow it all makes sense..."

"Zackary, there's more. You're grandfather... he ..."

"Passed away. I know."

"What? How did you find out?"

I took a deep breath. "Okay, my turn to come clean."

"I don't understand," she said.

"Four years ago, I found a bunch of paperwork in your desk. I'm sorry I snooped. But, something wasn't right. I had to know the truth. When I left, I didn't really go to Fresno to attend college. I hired a private detective. I wanted to find my grandfather—something inside told me I needed to talk to him."

"Oh, Zackary. Where are you right now?"

"San Diego."

She clamped her hand over her mouth.

"I found Gran-Dad about three months ago. But, I never dared to talk to him. Until, well, one night. I went to his house. But then… he got really sick. And died."

"Zackary, that's crazy. Your dad also lives in San Diego… You can't let him find you."

"He doesn't know I'm here or what I look like. It's all good."

"He might have killed your grandfather. He'll kill you if he finds…"

"Son of a b—. Damn. I had no idea." My head ached. I grabbed the steering wheel to steady myself. "Mom. You said something about the inheritance—the *Gifts*. So it's not just a made-up story?"

"It's not. I promise you they're real. Someone came looking for you this last weekend. She has them and wants to make sure you get them."

"I don't understand…" I stared at her image on the screen.

"She said your grandfather wanted you to have them. After talking with her, I realize you deserve the chance to make your own decision."

"Who are you talking about… who came to see you?"

"She lives in San Diego. She knew your grandfather and wants you to have the *Gifts*, that is, if you want them." Mom leaned her head back and closed her eyes.

"She's here? In San Diego? What's her contact info?"

"Sweetie, please be careful. Your father will do anything to get them."

"Mom, I can take care of myself. Give me a sec to pull up my contacts, I'll add her in… Okay, what's her name?"

"Alli… Harper."

I typed in the first letter. My fingers froze. "Could you repeat that?"

"Alli. Harper. Her number is 619–509…"

Holy crap. Is that why Alli and Cheryl were at the hospital? And the cemetery? Did she know my gran-dad, Russell?

"Zackary? Did you get the number? You want me to repeat it?"

"No. Thanks. I have it." Now, to figure out what to do with it.

71

ALLI

The Monday after we arrived home from Flagstaff, I contacted my investigator Geoff again. I explained the name mix-up and rehired him to start a search for a "Zackary Freison."

Two long weeks have passed and it's almost mid-December. Not hearing a thing from Geoff, I figured he'd been unsuccessful. After all, it took months to locate Debora. Now, with only three weeks to go, I'd have to decide whether to keep the *Gifts* or…

There was no second choice. I had to keep them. But, without Russell's guidance, I didn't know what to do with them. Or, what it meant to be a Guardian. With my brain kicking around all the thoughts, my heart raced. Deep breath in. Breath out. In… Out...

Every night I was in panic mode. *Why can't something good happen? Is it too much to ask for Jason to show up and claim the stupid box?* Sure. And if I bought a lottery ticket, I'd be the next big winner.

For the first time in a week, I made my bed, even though it was almost time to sleep again. Gathering an armload of laundry, I tromped down the hall to our tiny washer/dryer combo. I tossed in the whites. And the colors. Might as well get them all done in one load. I turned and saw Liz head into the front room. Although she's still off work, the doctor said she could get up and do a little more since the bleeding had stopped.

Bending down, I picked up a stray sock on the carpet and tossed it back into my room. I walked over to Cheryl's room and poked my head in. Darius was snoring on the bed as Cheryl packed. After shoving a wad of clothes into her backpack, she pulled up the zippers, leaving them off-center and to the right.

My right eye twitched. *Darn my OCD.* "When are you guys leaving?" I asked.

"Tomorrow morning. Supposed to be a break in the weather. We want to get up there before the roads close." Cheryl turned and grabbed a pair of mittens, then pushed them down inside a side pocket. "Forgot these last time. 'Bout froze my fingers off."

"You pack extra socks? And blankets, just in case there's traffic issues?"

"No, on the socks. Thanks for the reminder. And yes, on the blankets. Already in the car." She grabbed two pair of socks from a dresser drawer and stuck them in the space reserved for the water bottle. "Did I tell you we're coming back before Christmas?"

"No. I thought you were spending it with your dad and the new family."

"Dad wanted me to be back here with you guys. He said we'd have plenty of time after we moved."

Now I felt really crappy about wishing she'd never found him. Guess he wasn't such a bad guy after all. "That's great. So, does that mean we can plan on celebrating Christmas together?"

"What's this about Christmas?" My senses picked up the sweet scent of Old Spice. As memories of Russell flooded my mind, I turned. Liz and Zack stood behind me in the hallway.

I cleared my head and swallowed hard. "Yes, let's plan on a big dinner."

Liz grasped Zack's hand and smiled.

He nodded and locked eyes with me. "Sure. Sounds great."

His tone reminded me of Russell's. It happened every time I caught the scent of his cologne. *My imagination playing tricks.* "We'll figure out the details when Cheryl and Darius get back," I said, turning away to break his gaze. As they continued to discuss menu options, I glanced down at my phone. Already after nine. Jack was supposed to stop by after work so we could decorate our five foot, purple Christmas tree.

I paced around our tiny front room, stopping only to check the street for his car. Him being late didn't help. Plus, after Zack eyed me, I couldn't shake my anxiety. Though my mind kept going back to the *Gifts*, I told myself they didn't exist. Because if they didn't, then neither did my problems. My will to forget them was so strong, I hadn't gone near the box since Flagstaff.

As each vehicle passed, I stopped and looked out the window again. Just a truck. Then a car. But not Jack's car. A man tossed a bag in the dumpster by the street. He stopped, lit a cigarette, then glanced up at our window. It was too dark to see who it was. I turned so he wouldn't think I was watching him.

As I stared out the window again, I spotted Jack's car. Probably looking for a parking space. If you're not here by six, you have to park a block or more away. I walked over to the door, unlatched and cracked it open. *Brrr.* The crisp air took me back to our Arizona trip. *Glad we don't have snow and that dreadful black ice to deal with.* I opened the door wider when I heard footsteps on the stairs.

"Hiya, Princess." Jack leaned down and kissed me. "Sorry I'm late. Paperwork. It's the bane of my existence."

Everyone gathered in the front room. Zack and Jack set up the tree, while Darius found some sappy Hallmark Christmas show on TV. For once, Liz didn't scoff. Even the guys didn't complain. Falling snow and roaring fireplaces on the screen created the perfect ambiance for the evening. Although we had our own fireplace, it hadn't been used since I'd moved in. We decided it was smarter to enjoy the one in the show, than risk a chimney fire and ruin our perfect evening.

As Liz made hot chocolate, Cheryl and I retrieved several large, dusty boxes from the attic. Cheryl took the ornament box into the front room where Liz organized our tiny treasures on the coffee table for hanging. I lugged the box with my mom's Christmas dishes into the kitchen and unpacked the set for a thorough cleaning.

As I walked into the front room, I noticed Darius staring out the window. I tapped him on the shoulder. "Everything okay?"

He sighed. "Just noticed my friend down by the dumpster."

I peeked out the window. "That guy taking out the trash?"

"Yeah. Downstairs Dude." He took a sip of his hot chocolate. "Just moved in. We talk sometimes."

Cheryl patted his arm. "Hon, that's so nice to make friends with our neighbors."

Darius looked back at me. "Since he's all by himself, you think we could invite him to our Christmas dinner? You don't have to, but he's got no family and…"

Glancing around the room, I took in the thick chocolate aroma. The white and multicolored lights twinkled on the tree. Liz and Zack snuggled on the couch digging into a box filled with red, glittery stockings. Cheryl and Darius picked through ornaments, pointing and reminiscing as they hung each one. Jack gazed at me and smiled. I knew what it was like to be lonely during the holidays. I empathized with the guy by the dumpster, all by himself on Christmas.

I stepped back and looked up at Jack. "Should you check him out first?"

He shrugged his shoulders. "Do you really think it's…?"

"Guess I'm too suspicious," I said. "No, it's fine. One more at dinner won't be a big deal."

Darius clapped as everyone nodded in agreement.

I turned to Darius. "Go ahead, ask your, um, what did you say his name was?"

He scratched his head. "Dunno. We call each other Upstairs Dude and Downstairs Dude. You know I never call people by their real names."

Must be a guy thing. "Next time you see him, invite the… um, downstairs guy to our dinner."

"Thanks, Dudette Alli. You're the best." Darius jumped off the couch, high-fived me, and headed out the door.

72

RONALD

Standing by the dumpster, I 'bout coughed myself into a frenzy. "Christmas dinner? You don't say?" An actual invite from the gals downstairs. I couldn't believe my friggin' frigid ears.

"Yeah, Dude," said Darius. "They all felt bad about you being all alone on the holiday and all."

I flicked a smoldering butt on the ground and crushed it with the toe of my boot. "Well, that was mighty nice of your friends. I do get sad this time of the year." I faked a sniff and wiped the corner of my eye for extra effect.

"You don't have to do that." Reaching into his pocket, he offered a mustard-stained paper towel. "Sorry, Downstairs Dude. Guess I don't have anything else."

Lord. I'd be glad when I didn't have to kiss the idiot's behind anymore. Not only had I 'bout caught pneumonia, but I'd also put up with his good Samaritan bullcrap. I waved the used towel away. "Don't worry, Dude. I'm good. So, you're leaving tomorrow?"

"Yeah. Me and Cheryl are headed to Reno. We'll be back before Friday. That's when Alli wants to have dinner, but I can't remember the date."

"Friday's the twenty-second."

"You're good at math," he said, pulling out a joint from his pocket. Lighting it, he continued, "I always had problems with numbers."

Obviously. "Friday dinner works for me. What about everyone else? Are they going to be home while you're gone?"

Idiot offered me a hit. "You mean in case you get lonely or something?"

"Yeah… That's it. In case I get lonely and need to talk to someone."

He thought for a while.

Probably clearing the weed-cobwebs from his tiny, little brain.

He scratched his beard, then tapped his finger on his fat, stubbly cheek. "Let's see… Lizzy and Alli will be there—Lizzy can't do stuff because of the baby. She's supposed to stay in bed or something."

I gripped the edge of the dumpster. "What about the other one?"

After taking another hit, he looked at me with half-glazed eyes. "You mean Alli? She works during the day. But she's home at dinnertime. So, if you need to stop by, someone will be there all the time. Just make sure you don't drink out of the milk carton or eat Lizzy's cereal. That makes her cranky. Although she's better now Zack's back."

"Is that so?" I rubbed my chin. "If I wanted to hang out with Zack… when would be the best time… so I wouldn't bother Liz?"

"He and Jack work late… During the week, they only catch the last half of the game. But on the weekends…"

Even better than what I'd hoped for. One gal couldn't leave. The other arrived home after dark. And, the guys ain't home 'til late. I shoved my hands in my pockets and nodded. "Hey, I need to get going. Thanks for the invite. Tell 'em I'll be there."

"No problem, Dude. See ya later." He turned and stomped back up the stairs.

I gave a half-wave and trudged two blocks up the street to my truck. As I waited for the cab to warm up, I considered my options. *Should I take my stuff back when the dumb boyfriend and his fat girlfriend were gone? Or... Should I use the knocked-up one to get even and get my stuff back?* I glanced at myself in the rearview mirror and smirked. *While them gals will find coal in their stockings this year, Santa will be fillin' my boy's stocking with his damn birthright.*

73

ALLI

After we all decorated the tree and finished the hot chocolate, Jack offered to help me with the last of the holiday tasks. Climbing on a chair, I reached up into the cabinet, took out our everyday plates, and handed them to him. "You notice anything different about Zack?" I asked.

"No, not really. But I've only really known him a few weeks." Jack laid the everyday plates on the counter. Picking up one of my mom's Christmas plates, he pointed to the gold bow atop the painted Victorian Christmas tree. "Very cheerful."

I motioned to the oval serving platter and three graduated serving bowls. "I love using her dishes during the holidays. Usually, I put them out right after Thanksgiving but this year's been a bit weird." I took care as I set stacks of cereal and soup bowls on the shelf. The fruit bowls were the smallest. My favorites for a late night ice cream snack. Nothing like a special bowl of yum when life gets crazy.

"That should be all of it," he said, handing me a stack of coffee cups. As I turned, he reached up and offered his hand. I grasped it and stepped down from the chair.

"Thanks," I said. "With Cheryl and Darius focused on their trip and Liz not able to lift more than a pencil, it would have taken me all night to exchange the regular dishes for the festive ones." I held his warm, strong hand as he kissed my cheek. "Something to eat, before you go?"

He slipped his arm around my waist. "I was thinking, maybe I could spend the night... If it's okay with you."

All my parts got tingly at the thought of being with Jack. All. Night. Long. But, since I still hadn't spilled my big secret, I wasn't sure if I should give anyone a head's up or just have him show up for breakfast. I smiled as he pushed my hair aside and kissed my neck. "You make it hard to resist," I said. As the edges of his mustache tickled my cheek, my legs went weak.

Jack winked. "That's my plan, Princess."

I leaned in and whispered, "I haven't told anyone we, you know, have been together."

He whispered back, "Makes it even more exciting." Taking my hand, he led me out of the kitchen.

"Not hungry?"

"Not for food."

I giggled. "Well, this time you'll have to be quieter. It's not like we're in a hotel next to strangers."

Jack nodded, then patted my butt. "If memory serves, you weren't too discreet either."

I ROLLED over and checked my phone, almost seven-thirty. Nothing like a night of uninhibited passion to help cure my chronic insomnia. Come to think of it, the nights Jack and I spent together I'd never taken my sleeping pills. One great reason for him to spend the night... along with lots of other reasons. As he stirred, he slid his hand past my waist then cupped my breast. His breath fell into a regular rhythm and he was asleep again. I really needed to pee, but I heard voices in the hallway. I figured I'd wait until everything quieted, or until I couldn't hold it anymore. Both options gave me more snuggle-time with Jack.

Soon the commotion died down. As soon as I heard the front door slam, I scooted out from under Jack's arm and slipped out of bed.

He yawned and ran his fingers through his gorgeous curly black hair.

"So sorry," I said. "Didn't mean to wake you. But…" I slipped on my pajama bottoms while crossing my legs—not an easy task. *Shouldn't have waited so long.*

"I don't suppose you would like to give me a kiss good morning?" He crinkled his eyes and smiled.

"No. Not. Yet. Be Right Back." I rushed out of the bedroom, closing the door behind me.

"Who you talking to?" said Liz.

"Out of my way. Gotta pee." I ran in the bathroom, barely making it in time. I let out an audible moan of relief as my bladder relaxed. After I finished, I opened the door and found Liz waiting, tapping her fingers on the door frame.

"Spent the night, didn't he?" She spoke in a loud whisper. "And in your room."

I shrugged my shoulders. "Interesting question. Why do you ask?"

She opened her mouth to speak as my bedroom door opened. Jack stood there, wearing a smile and my floral bathrobe.

"Um, morning Liz. Didn't think anyone else was up." He walked past us like it was something he did every day. Then he went into the bathroom and took the longest pee I'd ever heard anyone take in my entire life.

The whole time Liz stared at me, wide-eyed. Her lip twitched, but she didn't talk or move.

I gave her a toothy grin, then turned and went back into my room. After closing the door, I let out a groan. *Awkward.* Then I giggled. I couldn't believe it. Of all the people to see Jack, then hear him pee. I looked up when the bedroom door opened.

Jack came in, closed the door, and plopped on the bed. "Morning."

"Better?" I said.

"I'm always better when I'm with you." He leaned over kissing me on the lips.

"Not exactly what I was referring to, but aww, thanks. Morning to you, too. Hungry?"

"I could nibble on a few things right now." His fingers traced along my cheekbone, then down my neck toward my chest.

"I meant for breakfast." I pointed at the door. "Everyone's awake."

He moved in closer.

I pushed him away, giggling.

His mustache crinkled as he smiled. "Just hoping for something special before the day starts."

I winked. "How about if I promise we end the day with something special?"

He looked at me and cocked his head. "Can I get that in writing?"

I pushed him back down on the bed.

He pulled me on top of him.

Let's just say, we ended up starting the day with something special.

74

LIZ

The sweet scent of vanilla enveloped the kitchen. With errands to do before an early shift at the restaurant, Zack had already left. After I poured myself a cup of flavored coffee, I sat at the table, waiting for Alli and Jack. I hoped I'd have some time to chat with her before she left for work.

Ah, the lovebirds arrived. "Morning. Coffee's ready." I said as I took a sip in an attempt to hide my snickering.

Jack waved off the cup. "Thanks, but I'm in a hurry." He kissed Alli on the cheek and walked out the door, closing it behind him. Alli turned and strolled into the kitchen.

I stared at her. "Coffee? Or do we need something to build back our strength after a busy night? And morning?" I added a little cough for emphasis.

"Oh, shush." She poured herself a cup of coffee, then set it on the table as she gathered eggs and milk from the refrigerator. "You want breakfast?" she asked as she cracked the eggs in the skillet.

"Sure." I stirred my coffee. "So, when did you and Jack, you know…"

Alli turned and rolled her eyes. "Fine. It happened in Flagstaff. I was going to tell you and Cheryl when we got back. Then everyone had news to share, and the guys were always around…" She added salt and scrambled the mixture together with a spatula.

I got up and grabbed two plates from the cabinet. "Congrats. It's about damn time."

Using a red potholder, Alli brought the skillet over from the stove and scraped a pile of steaming eggs onto my plate.

"Thanks," I said.

After emptying the rest of the eggs on her plate, she sat down. "Sorry. But it's been kinda weird since we got back."

"In what way?" I asked as I spread grape jelly on an untoasted English muffin.

"You notice anything different about Zack?"

"Well, he is getting used to being around again. And being a daddy. That's enough to make anyone a bit off."

Alli poked at her eggs. "True. But there's something else. You know we talked to Jason's mom, right?"

I nodded taking a bite of eggs.

"She said Jason's still alive but didn't know where he lived."

"What are you getting at?"

"Well, Jack told me Zack said he was from Flagstaff. And Jennifer – Jason's mom, said her son went by the name of Zackary, for his safety. Do you think…?"

I stopped eating and stared at Alli. "Are you saying that my Zack might be your Jason?"

She looked at me, then down at her plate. "I know it's a longshot. But, think about it. He wears Old Spice like Russell. Coincidence?"

"Probably," I said. "A lot of guys wear that cologne.

"He was at the cemetery when we were holding Russell's memorial service. Coincidence?"

"He had been following me. We both know that."

Alli placed her fork on her plate. "Every time he talks, he reminds me of Russell. The other night, when he got a call, he put his phone away without answering it. The next time he came over he kept staring at me, watching me like… like, I don't know. But, I have a feeling."

I gripped my fork. "He better not be talking to her again."

Alli sipped her coffee. "Her who?"

I pounded my fist on the table. "The one he left me for when we broke up." My heart raced. *Why was Zack taking phone calls in secret?* "Heaven help me if he's cheating on me again, I'll…"

Alli placed her hand on my arm. "Liz, he's not cheating on you. He loves you."

"I'm so afraid he's going to leave me again." I stood and threw my fork in the sink.

"He told you he didn't cheat," said Alli gathering the plates. "Don't you believe him?"

"I don't know what to believe. I want to, but… There is something different, though I can't put my finger on it."

She leaned against the counter. "Is there something I can do to help? Maybe I can talk to him, you know, for you."

I thought for a moment, then snapped my fingers. "The glasses."

"The what?" said Alli.

I stood up. "Those truth glasses. You know, the ones you put on when you knew I was pregnant. The ones from the auction."

She shuddered. "I can't do that to Zack."

"He said he was working doubles the next two days but promised to be here Thursday. He always sits on the couch with his back to the hallway. Wait until he's watching TV, then stand behind him. Put on the glasses and do whatever you do. If I keep him distracted, he won't even realize you are reading his thoughts."

"Are you sure?" Alli swallowed and sighed. "Maybe we should just ask. I hate using those glasses. They always give me a weird headache."

I looked at her. "Don't you want to know if he's the Zackary from Flagstaff?"

"Well, yes. But…"

"And I want to know who he's been talking to. It's a win-win for both of us."

Alli glanced at the coffee pot clock. "Oh crap. I need to go catch the bus or I'll be late for work." She got up and rushed down the hall.

I stood and yelled after her. "At least promise me you'll think about it."

She came back buttoning up her sweater. "Fine. I'll think about it. Now, stop stressing and get some rest. I'll see you tonight."

After Alli left, I walked into the front room and sat on the couch. I'd better rest up. Things might get hectic in a few days.

75

ZACK

After Mom called and told me my name was really Jason, it's been hard to be around Alli. Questions raced through my mind. I wanted to ask about my gran-dad, Russell. I wanted to know more about my inheritance. I wondered about my twin brother, Steven. Did we look alike? I guess we didn't or Alli would have figured out who I was by now.

As much as I hated to admit it, I also wanted to know more about my dad. It freaked me out realizing if I passed him or my brother on the street, I wouldn't recognize them. Of course, they probably wouldn't remember me either—a good thing, the way everyone talked about my dad.

Mom called the other night again when we were all decorating the tree at Liz's apartment. When I didn't take the call, it made Liz upset. She said she trusted me and didn't want to know anything about the past three months. Deep down inside I knew she suspected something. And with a baby on the way, she's extra sensitive.

Christ. A baby. That's the last thing I expected when Liz invited me over. I was excited and happy we're back together. But now, the secret is making me crazy.

The more Alli stresses about finding Jason, the worse I feel. The more I hide the truth, Liz becomes more suspicious. Then I feel guilty for making everyone upset. I get heart palpitations just thinking about it.

Like this morning—Cheryl and Darius left for Reno again. Liz wanted me to stick around, but I bugged out early. I needed time to think. About what's best for me and Liz, and Alli. *Do I tell Liz? Or Alli? Or both?* And if, or when I do, then what? I sat in the car for an hour with that crap buzzing around my head. Instead of answers, I got a tension headache.

Now, I was on my way to work. At least there I'd be so busy I wouldn't have time to think about questions and answers and hurting anyone else. I was concentrating on the road and listening to my tunes when I got a call.

"Hey, Mom. Let me adjust the volume so I can hear you better."

"Zackary, have you told anyone yet? I haven't slept well since we last talked."

"Not yet. Still trying to figure it all out."

"Honey, I just worry… about, you know."

"My dad, you mean? Mom, I know. I've really been thinking about it all. I feel so bad that Alli's stressed out because she can't find Jason. And Liz, she knows I'm hiding something…"

"At this point, maybe telling them would be best. I'd hate to see you and Liz have problems again."

"I agree, Mom. I just wish things were easier… I wish Gran-dad were still around. He'd know what to do." I turned into the parking lot at work and found a spot away from the entrance. I unbuckled my seatbelt and leaned back, rubbing my eyes.

"Sweetie, he saved the inheritance for you. A long time ago, when you were just a toddler, he told me about the box in the storage place. I'm sorry I didn't tell you earlier. Maybe he'd still be alive…"

I sat up and stretched my neck. "Then it's settled. If he really wanted me to have that inheritance and he died keeping it from my dad, then I have to tell Alli. I have to claim what's supposed to be mine."

She stayed silent.

"Mom? You still there?"

She coughed, then cleared her throat. “Yes. I am. So, when will you tell her?”

“One of the servers took time off so I’ve got double shifts the next few days…” I scrolled through my schedule on my phone. “Thursday, I’m off at six. I’ll tell Liz and Alli that night, after work. With both of them there, it might be easier.”

She let out a nervous chuckle. “Might seem that way, but in reality, they’re both going to be in shock.”

“Yeah. At least I’ve had some time to process everything. But, I can’t keep putting off the inevitable. I’ve got to do it next time I’m there. No matter what.”

“I love you, Sweetie.”

“Love you too, Mom. Please don’t worry.” I ended the call. Tears rolled down my cheeks. As much as I hoped the next two days would speed up, not knowing how it would end, I also hoped they’d slow down.

76

RONALD

Ed and Betty Shears would be in the office today and Thursday. That would give me two days. I rummaged through the tool shed under the parking area next to the office. *Crowbar, duct tape, zip ties, rope... what else did I need?* My hand hovered over a half-empty box of rat poison. *Naw, she needed to stay alive until I was done with her.*

"Hey, Pops. Watcha doing out here?"

I grabbed the crowbar and turned to see Steven behind me, buttoning up a ragged jacket. "What are you doing? I warned you not to show up without knockin.' I 'bout cracked your skull wide open."

"Sorry, Pops. Dinner's ready. Didn't mean to scare you."

"Gonna have to tie a bell around your neck so I knows you're behind me." Damn. I turned around and dropped my "tools" in a frayed, army-green backpack. "You run along upstairs. I'll be there in a bit."

"You going somewhere?" Steven edged closer. "Can I come too?"

"What did I tell you about minding your own business? Just putting stuff in my bag to fix something, then having a smoke before dinner." I waved him back. "Stop breathin' down my neck like my old man. You get upstairs or I'll take a belt to you."

Steven backed up, then turned. He mumbled something under his breath, but I couldn't hear it. Might as well take the belt to him anyway, just to keep him in line. *Stupid fool.*

Grabbing the pack, I slung it over my shoulder. Then, I patted the bulging pocket of my flannel shirt. *My new lock pick kit.* Arrived just in time.

I climbed in the golf cart and dropped my pack on the floorboard. As I made my way over to a broken-down motorhome stored in the back lot, the whirring motor of the golf cart sent rats running. I flicked ashes at them as I passed by. *Damn rodents.*

I pulled up alongside a paint-flecked Minnie-Winnie, jumped out, and put my new kit to use. I opened the door like I owned the thing. The metal steps creaked as I climbed in and took one last look inside. After all, I wanted to make sure my "guest" would be comfortable. Bed, blanket, and piss room. And on the peeled countertop, a large box of granola bars and a case of water. *I'm not a total bastard.* Figured that was more than enough since she wouldn't be around long enough to use it all.

With the tiny motorhome locked up again, I tossed a half-smoked cigarette on the gritty pavement and headed back to my dinner. *Probably cold by now.* One more reason to take a belt to the boy. *Wait…* On second thought, we should celebrate. Tomorrow, after breakfast, I'd be heading out. Waiting for one chick to catch the bus for work leaving the knocked-up one home. All alone. All day.

77

ALLI

Less than two weeks until Christmas. Now shoppers want custom frames? I can't even begin to say how many times I've had to explain. "Custom framing, especially this time of the year, won't be delivered mid-January."

First, they stomp around. Then, they plead, "Will paying extra speed up the order?" Finally, after realizing it's fruitless, they ask me to help find something to make grandma's, or the grandkid's, or the family dog's photographs look extra special. I do my best with what's left in stock, but I'm no miracle worker. And the finished result, although stunning, is nothing like it could have been with more planning on their part.

An hour before closing, I called Liz for pizza topping suggestions. After standing all day I wanted to go home, sit on the couch, and enjoy something someone else had prepared. Although she'd been doing more around the house, I'd rather she rested as much as possible. Plus, pepperoni, pineapple, and mushrooms on a thick crust, topped with layers of gooey cheese sounded amazing. I called her twice. Each time it went to voice mail. *Probably sleeping*. I left messages.

At closing time, I turned on the night-time lights, locked the safe, then armed the alarm. I stood outside and called Liz one last time before heading to the bus stop. Still no answer. Maybe her battery died and she forgot to charge it? No, then it'd go straight to voice mail without ringing. *I hope she's okay*.

Arriving home, I tossed my keys on the table and placed a steaming pizza box on the kitchen counter. Living a block away from The Pizza Parlour had its advantages. I kicked off my shoes and grabbed two plates. So good to be home after dealing with customers all day. I'd be relieved when the holidays were over. Yet, stressed as my time to find Jason would almost be up. *Sigh.*

"Liz, you here?" She wasn't in the kitchen or front room. I rushed down the hall and peeked in her room. Strange. I hurried back to the front room and looked out the window. Her car was still parked in its space. I grabbed my phone out of my pocket and called again. Hearing her ringtone, I followed the sound to her bedroom. *Crap*. Her phone lay on the nightstand. *Odd. She never goes anywhere without it.*

My heart thumped harder. *Okay, stay calm*. There had to be a perfectly reasonable explanation. Maybe Zack picked her up for dinner. *Yeah, that's it*. She left with Zack and forgot her phone. I let out a long breath and walked back into the kitchen, then opened the box and grabbed a few pieces of pizza and a decaffeinated soda from the fridge. With my dinner on the coffee table, I flopped down on the couch and grabbed the remote. I browsed through the channels until I found an old Christmas movie. Might as well watch what I want if no one else was going to be here.

I picked a thick piece of pepperoni off a slice and popped it in my mouth. The unlit tree caught my eye. I got up, found the tree remote, and turned on the lights. They twinkled white, then multi-color, then back to white again. I preferred white and chose that mode, mesmerized by all tiny, glowing orbs hiding among the branches. I stepped back and admired our group effort.

I realized this would be the first holiday all of us had someone special in our lives. Despite losing Tippy Toes and Russell, I was thankful to be surrounded by my favorite people in the whole world. Walking over to the fireplace, I straightened the stockings, including the tiny, red and silver sequined one at the end for Tippy Toes. I hung it up because, in my mind, she was still here, just hiding under something, sleeping.

I headed back to the couch to finish my food and movie. Hopefully, Liz and Zack would be back soon. If they'd already eaten, leftover pizza for breakfast was always a plus. I picked up my phone to call Liz. As I readied my finger to swipe and start the call, my phone rang.

"Zack, so happy you called. I brought home pizza, when will you guys be… What…? Liz with me? No… I thought she was with you. Yeah, her phone is here so it keeps going to voice mail… When was the last time you talked to her? This morning… before lunch?" *Crap*.

My throat tightened. As I listened to Zack, I pulled an anti-anxiety pill from my metal pillbox and swallowed it before answering him. "Yes, her car is here. I checked…" I walked around the apartment again. Maybe she fell asleep in Cheryl's room. *Nope*. "Maybe she went downstairs…" I rushed to the front door, held the phone away from my mouth, and yelled. "Liz… you outside?"

I closed my eyes to clear my head. "Zack, I can't find her anywhere. She's not upstairs. Or outside. Her phone's here… That's a good idea. See you in a few minutes." While I was waiting, I looked through each room again. *What was I looking for? A clue? But to what?* I hoped she'd gone for a walk and forgot her phone. Maybe she'd be back any minute. It was getting darker and colder.

A loud knock on the door made me jump. I peeked through the peephole. Zack was outside, pacing in front of the door. I unlocked and opened it for him.

"Hey," I said.

"Have you heard anything?" He rushed back to her room, then into the kitchen, his eyes wide.

"No. I'm just as shocked as you are. When I left for work this morning, she'd settled on the couch with a blanket and cup of coffee. I never called during the day; it was too hectic."

He held up Liz's phone. "I can't believe she didn't take this."

"If we could just call her…" I walked into the kitchen to get something. Forgot what it was. And came back and stood by the couch.

Zack stared at me. "She thought I was cheating on her. I planned to tell her everything tonight. I hope she didn't do something stupid." He held her phone close to his chest and turned away.

"I'm sure she didn't. Especially with the baby. She loves you, more than you'll ever know." I walked over to him, placing my hand on his shoulder.

Zack turned back and faced me. "Alli, I need to talk to you."

My eyes widened. *Oh crap*. "About what?"

"So much has been going on the last few months. I didn't cheat. I tried to tell her the truth, but she wouldn't listen." He took in a deep breath and let it out. "There's something I need to tell you, but I'm not quite sure how to say it…"

I walked behind the couch, grasping the rough fabric for support. "Usually just blurting it all out is the best. Kinda like ripping off a bandage…"

He winced. "That always hurt like heck. Whoever came up with that analogy should be slapped."

I laughed a little. "Just tell me. I'm so stressed about Liz, nothing you could say could be worse… Or could it?"

"Alli," he cleared his throat. "I hope you understand. I'm not who you think I am… you see…"

My phone rang. I held up my hand to stop him. Though the number showed "unlisted," I picked it up. "Hello. Who is this?"

"Alli, it's me. Liz." She was crying.

"Oh no, Liz. Where are you? What's going on?"

Her crying became muffled. A male voice came on the phone. One that sent chills up my spine.

"Hello, Darlin.' Guess who?"

My entire body trembled. My head became fuzzy. "Where's Liz? What have you done with her?" I hit the speakerphone icon motioning to Zack to stay quiet.

Zack stared at my phone with wide eyes.

The voice began again, so smooth, yet so repulsive. "Well, seems like you might want to talk a little nicer, 'specially if we're going to do business together."

My stomach lurched. "I have nothing to say to you."

I heard Liz whimper as he raised his voice. "I disagree. You see, taking your stupid cat didn't seem to be a big deal. And when ol' Pop keeled over, you didn't blink an eye. But now..." He paused and coughed several times. "Now, I've got some special things you might want. And, if I remember, you have some special things I want..."

My whole body trembled. I could barely hold my phone. "Ronald, if you do anything to Liz, so help me..."

"Aww, the little friend is so worried about her knocked-up friend. My heart's just aching over how much you care."

Zack kicked the back of the couch. "What does he want?"

Ronald coughed. "And the punk boyfriend is there too. How quaint."

"I don't believe you," Alli cried out. "You're a monster."

He cleared his throat. "Actually, I'm not. But I'll keep them alive until we exchange... Christmas gifts." He laughed so hard he began coughing again. "And just in case you get any ideas this Santa ain't no fool. Don't send your cop boyfriend to save the day. You'll just make things worse. And, if you follow my instructions, you might just get them back in one piece." He ended the call.

I dropped my phone on the rug and curled into a fetal position. I felt Zack plop down beside me, sobbing. Ronald left me no choice. I had to give back the *Gifts*.

78

LIZ

When I heard honking, I looked out the apartment door. An old man in a small, beat-up RV was attempting to back out of our parking area but couldn't navigate into the street. He leaned out the motorhome door and shouted, asking for help. I nodded, pulled on a sweater, and went downstairs.

As I approached, the old guy jumped out, shoved a gun in my stomach, and forced me inside. He bound my hands and feet with zip ties, then pushed me onto a foul-smelling mattress and pulled a curtain, cutting most of the light.

"Who are you?" I yelled. "Where are you taking me?"

He didn't say anything.

"Where are we going? My friend's boyfriend is a cop. He'll find you." I patted my pocket for a phone. *Oh crap. I left it in my room.*

When my eyes adjusted, I realized I was locked inside a claustrophobic, gutted-out, spider-infested RV reeking of urine. Covering my mouth and nose, I noticed an overflowing cat box on the dilapidated flooring. A weak *Meow* startled me. To my shock, and relief, I found a very thin, matted Tippy Toes cowering on a makeshift mattress on top of what should have been a table. There was no stove. No cabinets. No rug or curtains. Just a counter with a tiny metal sink. A box of chocolate chip granola bars and a dozen or more empty cans of cat food lay in the sink. Three unopened cans of cat food, plus a case of off-brand grocery store water sat on the counter. Twenty-four bottles. *Where am I? Is it daytime? Or night?*

I reached out and held the now-purring cat. "Tippy Toes, I'm so… so happy to see you." I buried my face in her fur and held her tiny body up to me. Placing her back on the mattress, I maneuvered into the little bathroom to pee. Dim light came from behind a toaster-sized window. I picked at the wood, only to discover the window was boarded—inside and out.

When I came back Tippy Toes brushed against me and licked my hand. I winced. The ends of my nails were shredded. The tips of my fingers were bleeding.

HE DROVE FOR A WHILE, making a lot of turns. I rolled one way, then the other. I braced my foot against the wall for leverage, but it didn't help. I almost fell off the bed several times. Then we stopped. After he shut off the motor, I listened. Birds, like mourning doves, cooed outside. And a faint ding, ding, ding. The trolley?

I heard cars pass on what sounded like a road, but there wasn't enough traffic to be on a busy street. *The trolley. The birds. We must be in Balboa Park.* I tried to get his attention again. "Hey. You going to tell me what this is all about? Or do I have to come up there and kick your butt?"

I heard wood scraping on something, then the old man ripped open the curtain. He sneered at me and yanked off a white wig and dark glasses. My heart caught in my throat. "Oh no. You're that Ronald guy." I pressed my body against the rough plywood behind me.

"Don't you ever speak to me like that again." Ronald moved closer raising his hand as if to hit me. "Keep quiet. Or I'll…"

As he pulled back his jacket, my eyes were drawn to the butt of a small handgun tucked in his pocket.

"What do you want?" I asked, keeping the cat next to me.

He brought his hand level with my head

I clenched my jaw and turned away. The foul stench of nicotine on his clothes sickened me.

Ronald sat down on the edge of my makeshift bed. "Let's just say you're going to help me get what's mine." His raspy laugh shook the motorhome.

"If you're talking about your stupid stuff, I don't have it." I tried hiding my trembling hands, but it wasn't easy with him sitting only a few feet from me. It was the first time I'd seen him up close. Round face with sallow skin. Dark, ragged hair. Silver rimmed glasses. Narrow, watery-brown eyes. Pointed nose. Salt and pepper stubble. Thin, pale lips. And nicotine breath that could stop traffic.

"Of course, you don't have my stuff. But your selfish friend does. Let's hope she's willing to trade, now that I have two things to bargain with..." He cleared his throat and spit a wad of something in the corner. "Hopefully, before you both run out of food and water. Because when that's gone, so are you." He patted his pocket with the gun.

"So, no poison this time?" *What did I just say?*

He stood and glared at me. I braced for his wrath, but instead, he laughed. Hearty, gut-busting laughs until tears ran down his face. "That's a good one. You know, I thought about it with the cat. But, I'm no monster. And, I figured with you being knocked up and all, a bullet to the belly would be much more satisfying."

"You're making that up. You know nothing about me." *He knows I'm pregnant. But how?*

Laughing, he pulled up his flannel shirt and scratched his fuzzy, beer belly. "Actually. I do. Your fat roommate's bearded boyfriend was kind enough to share intimate details about all of you. Amazing how he loves to talk when he's buzzed."

"Darius?"

"He's got the brains of a baseball bat. You can thank him for your little vacation. After all, if it wasn't for him, I'd never had known you were expecting. And home. Alone. All day. By yourself." Ronald slapped the top of the sink and dust floated down through the cracks. He squared his shoulders and pulled out a phone. "Time to call your friend and let her know you're in my care. Oh, and let me put it on speakerphone so we can both enjoy the conversation, together."

I couldn't believe this. I closed my eyes and took a deep breath. *Think. What could I say to let Alli know I was at the park? With her cat? In an RV?*

Ronald dialed the number and placed the phone on the bed between us.

"Hello. Who is this?" Alli said.

I gritted my teeth. "Alli. It's me, Liz."

"Oh, Liz. Where are you? What's going on?"

"Hello, Darlin.' Guess who?"

Alli began shouting.

Ronald picked up the phone and held it closer to himself. "Well, seems like you might want to talk a little nicer, 'specially if we're going to do business together."

Whimpering, I tried to say something but Ronald raised his hand to hit me. I backed up into the corner again and held the cat close to my chest.

"I disagree," he said, glaring at me. "You see, taking your stupid cat didn't seem to be a big deal. And when ol' Pop keeled over; you didn't blink an eye. But now…" He paused and coughed several times, "Now, I've got some special things you might want. And, if I remember, you have some special things I want…"

"Ronald?" Alli cried. "What are you talking about?"

"Where are they?" shouted Zack. "What does he want?"

Ronald grinned and chided. "And the punk boyfriend is there too. How quaint."

"I don't believe you," Alli cried out. "You're a monster."

Ronald winked at me. "Actually, I'm not. But, Honey, if I don't get what's mine, you'll be searching for pieces of your friend and your cat all over San Diego County."

My stomach lurched. I knew he didn't make idle threats. I had to escape.

"You wouldn't…" cried Alli. "You already hurt me enough when you killed Tippy Toes."

I watched as a slow smile inched over Ronald's face. His eyes tightened into slits. "Here's the thing, I'll keep them alive until we exchange… Christmas gifts." He laughed so hard he began coughing again. "But, just in case you get any ideas…"

What can I say so they'll know where to find me? I opened my mouth, but it was too late.

Ronald swiped the end button and scowled. "And don't you get any bright ideas either." He pointed his finger in my face. "It don't matter to me if you two live or die. This time I'm doing whatever it takes to get what's mine… no matter who gets hurt." He turned and walked toward the front of the RV.

"Wait," I said. "How do I eat all tied up like this? Can't you…"

"You're the smart aleck broad. Figure it out." He took a few more steps, then pulled the curtain leaving me and Tippy Toes in the dark. I heard the RV door open and slam. Then, fumbling sounds and the heavy clicks of two padlocks.

Damn. For now, I was trapped inside my temporary prison.

79

ALLI

Ronald was holding Liz hostage in exchange for the *Gifts*. He threatened to hurt her, or worse if I contacted Jack. I looked over at Zack and whispered. "I'm so sorry."

He leaned his head against the back of the couch and looked over at me. "I feel so helpless."

"I'm confused. He referred to having two things… Oh no, do you think he knows Liz is pregnant?"

"He's just messing with your mind," said Zack.

I stood, walked into the kitchen, and sat at the table. I wasn't hungry, but I opened a bag of foil-wrapped chocolate trees, peeled one open, and popped the sweet, creamy treat in my mouth. Before I knew it, there was a pile of foil wrappings in front of me. I swiped my phone. "To heck with Ronald. I'm calling Jack. He needs to know."

"No." Zack rushed into the kitchen. "He'll call in half of the San Diego PD. You'll put Liz in danger."

"Then what are we supposed to do?" I slapped the table. "We're no match for Ronald. He's evil."

"I don't want Jack involved, at least for now." He paced in front of me, then stopped. "Promise me you won't tell Jack anything until we know more."

"Fine. But what about tomorrow? We can't make the exchange by ourselves."

Zack sat down next to me. "He seems to know a lot about us. He might even be watching right now, just to make sure Jack's not involved."

I turned and gazed at the front window. "You might be right. Especially if he knows Liz is pregnant." I pushed the half-empty bag of chocolate his way.

He waved me off. "My stomach is so upset, I don't think…" Before long, he had picked through the chocolates which resulted in his own pile of wrappers.

As I twisted the pieces of foil together, my phone beeped. I checked my phone. "A text from Jack… 'Working on a case. Won't be by tonight. Call U in AM. Hugs'."

Zack pointed to my phone. "That simplified things."

"Now what should we do?"

Zack leaned back and rubbed his temples. "Since Ronald will call back on your phone, make sure you keep it charged. And turn up the volume, so we don't miss it." He leaned his head from side to side, cracking his neck. "In the meantime, we should try to get some sleep."

I groaned. "Doubt that's gonna happen."

Zack nodded. "But we need to try. We can't help Liz if we're exhausted. I'll stay out here on the couch. If I can't sleep, at least I'll be able to watch the street."

"You really think Ronald's close by?" I asked.

"From what you've said, he has a knack for knowing what goes on up here. For him to stay in control, he's going to keep the odds in his favor."

I looked at Zack. "Meaning?"

"We should assume he's watching us."

My eyes widened. I ran my fingers through my hair. "That's crazy…"

Zack picked up the last piece of chocolate and unwrapped it. "We'll get through this. I promise it will be okay."

I nodded, then wiped a tear from my cheek. I waved goodnight and headed to my room. My body trembled from all the stress and chocolate. There was no way I'd sleep tonight.

80

JACK

I'd planned on going over to Alli's but changed my mind when I received a strange call on my cell. The number on the caller ID showed the Store-More, piquing my curiosity. "Hastings. How may I help you?"

Loud breathing on the other end.

"Hello? Is someone there?" I was ready to end the call when someone cleared their throat. Instead, I switched it to speaker and grabbed a pen to take notes.

"My pops didn't come home."

"Excuse me?" I said. "Who is this?"

"I'm not supposed to use the phone… I'll get in trouble."

I tapped my pen on my notebook. "I promise not to tell. Who is this? How did you get my number?"

"I have your card. You gave it to my pops when you came by that time."

"Can you give me a little more information? Have I met you?"

"No. Not really. Pops had me work while he talked to you. He called me his right-hand man."

I thought for a moment as I flipped back through my notebook. "Are you Garanski's son?" It had been a while since I'd been out there to speak with the father. I vaguely remembered the son. I reread my notes on him—tall, gangly kid. Late 20s, tousled brown hair, jeans, t-shirt, and red tennis shoes. Quiet. Great smile.

"I'm not supposed to be on the phone."

"I won't tell your dad. What's your name son?"

Silence.

"My name's Jack. What's your name?"

"Steven."

"Nice to meet you, Steven... You said your dad was missing?"

"I made breakfast for him. Eggs, bacon... he was busy and I went to find him. He got really mad at me and said I was spying on him. He chased me out of the shed and said he'd take his belt to me..."

"Are you okay?" *Poor kid.* His voice was shaky. I could barely hear him. Must be terrified of the bastard.

"Yes. I'm good. Well, I try to be good. But he always yells at me. He calls me bad names. He doesn't think I understand, but I do."

"I'm sorry to hear that, Steven. Why did you call me?"

"My pops went somewhere after breakfast. I made lunch for him, but he never came home to eat it. After I made dinner, I looked around and he was still gone."

"Did he take his truck?"

"No. He drove that big vacation home. I saw him leave. Can you keep another secret?"

Vacation home? "Yes, of course. I promise."

"He didn't know, but I followed him a couple of times when he checked on the storage units... when he found stuff to keep."

"And what was he doing, when you followed him?"

"He used a hammer... to fix a vacation home."

"Excuse me? What did you say?" I looked down at my phone and turned up the volume. "It's hard to hear you."

He cleared his throat and repeated himself. "A vacation home. You know, one of those big homes on wheels people take when they go on vacation."

"You mean a motorhome?"

"Yeah, a motor home. I watched him when he didn't know I was there. He was putting wood on the broken windows."

"Steven, when did you say he left?"

He hesitated for a bit. "Today, before lunch. I thought he was coming back to get me, but he didn't. Do you want me to check again? I don't have a flashlight."

"No, Steven. Don't go outside without a flashlight. Besides, it's too cold. I could use your help though."

"Like being your right-hand man?"

"Yes, Steven. I'd like you to be my right-hand man. I need you to remember things for me."

"Pops says I'm stupid and I don't remember stuff good. Sometimes he slaps me if I forget things."

Lord, what a jerk for a dad. "Steven, I know you are really smart."

"You really think so, Mr. Hastings?"

"You can call me Jack. Look, Steven, I believe in you. Now listen carefully. I need to you tell me a few things. What does the motorhome look like?"

"It's white… with brown marks on it … It's little. Not like the big one next to it."

I made lots of notes as he stuttered through the details. "Great. Now, tell me about your dad. What kinds of things were out in his shed?"

"I dunno. He had a bunch of tools and stuff. Um… a hammer, a big roll of sticky tape… Um, and some plastic things. I don't know what they're called. Sometimes we use them to tie stuff together."

"You're doing great. Anything else?"

"When he was at the vacation—I mean, motor home, he had water and some stuff to eat. Granola bars. I like those. Especially the ones with chocolate in them. That's why I thought he was going to take me too. Since he got stuff I like."

"Look how much you remembered. You're awesome, Steven."

"Thanks. Nobody ever says stuff like that about me. Well, except for my grandpa. But, I haven't seen him in a long time. Pops said he was sick and didn't want to visit me anymore."

For chrissake. "Steven, you've been more than helpful. If there's anything else you remember, will you promise to call me?"

"You mean I can still be your right-hand man?"

"Of course."

"Mr. Jack? I do remember one more thing."

"What's that Steven."

"When I saw my pops working on the motor thing, he bent over, and something was in his back pocket that scared me."

"And what was that?"

"Mr. Jack. Pops had a gun."

My fists clenched. "Thanks, Steven. You've been very helpful. Are you going to be okay by yourself tonight? Do you want someone to come and stay with you?"

"No, I'm fine. I'm old enough to stay by myself. My pops leaves me home every night when he goes places… Did you know I'm going to have a birthday soon? Right after Christmas."

"That's exciting. And it's good you can stay by yourself. But if you need to call me again—I'll keep my phone with me. Okay?"

"Thank you. Bye, Mr. Jack."

After I ended the call with Steven, I texted Alli to let her know I was working on a case and wouldn't be coming over. I tapped my pen on the desk and sipped my cold coffee.

What was Ronald planning to do? Fixing up an old motorhome. Left without telling his kid. He took food. And water. And a gun. What was that piece-of-crap-for-a-dad up to now?

81

ZACK

I rubbed the sleep from my eyes, though I didn't sleep much at all. That had to be one of the longest nights I've had in a long time. My thoughts focused on Liz. And my jerk father. I couldn't believe he'd taken her.

I sat up, then stood and stretched. I wasn't used to sleeping on a couch, especially in this apartment. Man, when I think back on all the fun times with Liz and her friends… this wasn't one of them. The click of the bathroom door interrupted my thoughts. *Guess Alli's up, too.* Hope she slept more than I did.

I headed down the hall to throw water on my face. On my way back to the kitchen, the sweet aroma of fresh-brewed coffee greeted me.

"Morning." Alli poured a steaming cup of the morning blend and set it in front of me. "Sleep at all?"

I added sugar to my cup and stirred. "Not much. You?"

"Who knows? I had weird dreams about Ronald and Liz and Tippy Toes." She grabbed bowls and spoons and two kinds of cereal, frosted oat and some kinds of bran flakes, and placed them on the table. She stopped for a moment and stared at me. "Even my friend Russell was in one of my dreams. He passed away a few months ago. I really wish he was here to help us." She took the milk from the refrigerator and sat down.

"You mind telling me more about your friend Russell?" I asked.

She looked up and smiled. "No, I don't mind." She filled her bowl with a mixture from both boxes, then added milk, and sugar. "He was a special guy. We used to talk a lot. He always had good advice."

"What was so special about him?" I sipped my coffee as I waited for her to continue.

"He was always a gentleman. Tipped his hat. Treated me like a lady. He never raised his voice or got upset when I was afraid. He gave me a big job, though I don't suppose you'd want to know about that. When I first met him, I didn't believe in myself. But, he helped me understand I was special. Someone he could trust with this, um, job until his other grandson was located."

"If you don't mind me asking—what happened to his other grandson?" I poured myself a bowl of the plain oat cereal, added milk and a bit of sugar.

"Been missing. For a long time." She shook her head. "I was supposed to find him… After all the dumb stuff Ronald did, I don't blame him for not coming back." She sighed and checked her phone. "Man, I wish he'd call. This waiting is making me crazy."

I wanted to tell her the truth, but this wasn't the time. Or the place. With Liz's life in jeopardy, my confession of being Jason, the missing grandson, could really screw things up. I'd have to wait a little longer to explain.

Alli chased the last of the cereal with her spoon and was about to take a bite when her phone buzzed. "It's him." She dropped the spoon, spilling milk on the table.

I stood and pointed at the phone. "Answer it before he hangs up."

She swiped her phone and pushed the speaker icon. "Hello? Liz, are you okay? Hello?"

"Good morning," said Ronald. "Sleep well?"

Alli cleared her throat. "I want to talk to Liz."

"Well, well. Making demands already? That's not very polite." He chuckled, then coughed.

I watched Alli's face. She forced a smile through gritted teeth. "Good. Morning. Ronald."

"Why yes, it is. Now, that wasn't too difficult, was it?" He hacked and spit again.

"Please, I'd like to talk to Liz."

"And manners now, too. Well, since you used the magic word …"

"Alli…" Liz's voice was hoarse.

Alli touched her phone. "Liz, are you okay?"

There were muffled voices and then Ronald's became louder. "She's fine. Enough of this catty chit-chat. Let's get down to business. Here's what's going to happen. Better take out some paper and a pencil so you don't miss nothin'. I ain't gonna say it twice. I'll even give you a whole minute… starting now. One… two… three…"

Damn his raspy voice counting off the seconds. I wanted to grab the phone and throw it across the room. My heart ached for Liz, and my fists clenched tighter and tighter as he kept up the annoying counting.

"Thirty-five… thirty-six…"

Alli grabbed paper and two pens and sat back down. "All right. I'm ready…"

"You are going to drive to meet me all by yourself. Got that?"

Alli interrupted. "Ronald, I don't drive. Please, I need Zack to bring me…"

"Hmmm… let me think about that for a minute." The longer he waited to respond the faster my heart thumped inside my chest. "Girlfriend and the boyfriend… yeah, that might work." He paused again, then continued. "Okay. Fine. Have him drive you out to Mt. Hope Cemetery. You know where that is?"

Alli and I looked at each other and nodded. She made a note, then spoke. "Yes, we do."

"There's a large palm tree near the trolley crossing. You'll park there and wait for my next phone call. Remember, I'll be able to see anyone coming or going, so if I notice anyone following you, or any cops, she's dead. You both got that?"

"Yes," we said together.

"You have one hour," said Ronald. "And, don't forget to bring my kid's inheritance."

I heard scuffling, then Liz yelled out. "Alli, I hid the stuff the other night…"

Ronald's tone changed. "I told you to shut up."

Liz continued as her voice got weaker, "…the green box in my closet…"

I heard something tearing. *Duct tape?* Then nothing else from Liz.

"Stupid gal. Didn't know when to shut up." Russell cleared his throat again. "Like I said, I'll call with the next set of instructions as soon as I see one car by the palm tree. You have until eleven o'clock." The call ended.

I looked at my phone to check the time, then over at Alli. "We need to get going. It's going to take the full hour to get out to Mt. Hope."

82

ALLI

Zack waited as I went back and I grabbed the green box of *Gifts* from Liz's closet. We had an hour to get to the cemetery. Barely enough time. Once there, Ronald would call us with the next step. As I got into Zack's Firebird, my heart became lighter. Though Liz was still in danger, I believed we had a chance to get her back.

As we were leaving, Jack called, but I didn't answer. I had no idea if Ronald was watching and I couldn't risk telling Jack. At least not yet. I stared out the rain-sprinkled passenger window and studied the trucks and cars on the freeway. I wondered if the one next to us held my friend. Watching through the mirror on my side of the car, I also searched for Ronald's truck.

I refocused and looked at Zack's phone's GPS map. "Looks like we're almost there."

"We made good time," he said. "About fifteen more minutes… Friggin' traffic is slowing down though. Not much I can do at this point. But, a bit of delay shouldn't make a difference." He focused on the road and was quiet.

I checked my phone. 10:40. We'd be cutting it close. I took in a deep breath. Zack didn't know about my anxiety. I really didn't want to tell him. I'd taken my anti-anxiety pills when I got up and was feeling okay. But, when it came down to facing Ronald… I had no idea what to expect. *Stay positive. Stay positive. This will be all over soon.* Without warning, gravity pulled me forward as Zack slammed on the brakes.

"Damn." He pounded his fist on the steering wheel.

"What happened?" I strained my neck to look up ahead. All I saw were red taillights.

Zack checked his phone. "Accident. Big rig jackknifed. All the left lanes are blocked, and they're only letting traffic through the far-right lane. We're stuck."

"What are we going to do?" I checked my phone. It was 10:45.

As Zack rolled down his window, exhaust fumes caught in my throat. He craned his neck to get a better view of the road. "Dammit." He pointed to a sign. "The next exit is over a mile away. Even if I could get over, there's no way we're going to make it in the next fifteen minutes."

My heart raced. I couldn't call Ronald. We only had until eleven. "Zack, do something."

He looked at me, his eyes wild. "What do you want me to do? We're stuck. I can't even change lanes." He flipped on his blinker and pounded on the steering wheel again.

We inched forward, then stopped. I looked over at him. "It's 10:50." I pulled at the shoulder strap of my seat belt. I couldn't breathe. My hands tingled.

Zack honked the horn. Drivers flipped him off. He returned the gesture as he merged into the next lane. There were two more before the shoulder. And no exit in sight.

My phone showed 10:55.

Zack honked again, then forced us over one more lane to the right. The sign on the side of the road showed the next exit was still a half-mile away.

"Do you think we'll make it?" I asked.

He looked at me and shook his head.

My hands trembled. My mouth was dry. I looked down at my phone. 11:00 exactly. The screen flashed with an incoming call. I answered it and put it on speaker.

"I'm sorry," I said. "But we're stuck in traffic… An accident… If you could give us just a little more time…"

"Sorry. Your time, and hers is up." The phone went silent.

As the icon faded and my phone screen went dark, I covered my face and sobbed.

83

LIZ

The ding, ding, ding of the trolley stirred me from a fitful sleep. Every part of my body ached. I opened my eyes and closed them again. Tippy Toes rubbed against me and purred. *Still in this nightmare.* I petted the cat, waiting for my head to clear, then hopped to the small bathroom, which was more like a stink hole filled with sewage and who-knows-what. Holding my breath, I peed then I pulled up my pants and closed the flimsy door. *Hope the stench didn't follow me.*

I opened a can of food for the cat and laid it on the mattress. My stomach ached from hunger. So far, I'd only eaten three granola bars. Without knowing how long I'd be stuck in here, I wanted them to last as long as possible. At the sound of rattling keys, I braced myself for the jerk. *If I live through this, I'm going kick him so hard he won't sit for a month.* I unclenched my fists and waited, refusing to let him get the best of me.

Ronald pulled back the curtain and stepped inside my makeshift dungeon. "Good morning. Sleep well?" He laughed and pointed to the box of granola bars. "I see you and your roommate are enjoying your meals."

I blinked several times as my eyes adjusted to the light. "Yes. Thanks so much." I tried to hold my sarcasm, but it just came out.

"You'll be happy to know your friends are on their way. Supposed to be here soon with my stuff. Isn't that exciting?"

I nodded.

"Aww, not much in the mood for chit chat?"

I shook my head.

"Makes no difference to me." He pulled out a cigarette and lit it, then took a deep drag. Exhaling, he filled the room with hazy, acrid smoke, burning my eyes and lungs. He looked me up and down, then leaned closer. "You said you hid them things in a box? Tell me, what should be in there… in case she leaves somethin' out?"

I coughed and wiped my eyes with the back of my dust-streaked hand. Glaring at him, I clenched my jaw and stroked the cat's mangy fur. "A feather pen. A paintbrush. Glasses. A hat… And a book."

He stuck his thick finger in his ear, picked at something, then brought his finger out, staring at the tip. "Book? What kind of book?"

"Instructions or something. I don't know. I never read it."

He wiped his finger on the mattress and stared at me. "That it?"

Coughing again, I nodded.

He removed his phone from his jacket and grinned revealing crooked, yellow teeth. "Almost meetin' time. I'll go check and see if our guests are here yet. Don't go anywhere." He flicked his cigarette on the rotted floor, crushed it with the heel of his boot, and disappeared behind the curtain.

I leaned close to the boarded-up window and listened for familiar noises. The trolley passed by us again. More birds. A few cars…

Ronald flung back the curtain and slapped the countertop, making the RV shudder. "Damn. She's not out there." He marched over to me and held up his phone. "11:00… Where are they?" He swiped the screen holding it up to his ear while his other hand fingered the gun handle in his jeans pocket. "Sorry. Your time, and hers is up." He glared at me and threw his phone on the bed.

"No," I said. "Please give them more time. I'm sure they will be here any minute…"

He narrowed his eyes and leaned against the wall. He drew the gun and aimed it at me. "They let me down… just like everyone else. Why should I give them another chance?"

I held up my hands. "Please, Ronald. You want those things for your son, right? Alli said she'd bring them to you. She always tells the truth."

While pointing the gun at me, he came over and sat on the bed. "She said there'd been an accident. She made it up."

"Wait." I pointed to his phone. "There's a way to look it up. I'll show you… If she's telling the truth, will you give them more time?"

His eyes widened as he shoved the gun in his front jacket pocket. He picked up his phone and pointed to the screen. "How do you do that?"

I walked him through the steps of going to the California road information page and typing 805 for the freeway. Within seconds it showed a timetable of the accident along with updated road info. He held the phone up for me to see.

"They were telling the truth," I said. "Looks like the roads are clearing a bit. But it might take them a while. I told you Alli wouldn't lie."

Ronald stared at his phone for a while, scrolling through the information. He looked up at me. "Well, that's a first. Damned near everyone in my life gave me grief. My Pop took away my inheritance. Tried to take Steven, too. Mama said she'd always be there for me. She also lied…"

"Sorry about your mom." *Maybe I could make a connection. Anything to keep him talking.* "My dad died when I was young," I said.

"Oh yeah? How'd that happen?"

"Neighbor shot him."

He looked down at his phone again. "Bastard."

I reached over to the counter and grabbed two bottles of water, offering one to him. He glanced at me, nodded, and took it. *One small step. Come on, Alli. Hurry up…*

Eyeing his phone again, he showed me the screen. "11:15. I'll give 'em another fifteen minutes. That's it."

With my hands still bound, I struggled with my water bottle.

Ronald reached over and took it from me. He unscrewed the lid and handed it back.

"Thank you." I took a sip, holding it between my trembling hands. The cat settled in my lap and purred, which helped calm me.

He let out a deep sigh. "Look, this was never about you." His shoulders slumped. His eyes turned dark. "This was about proving something to my pop. Mama died when I was five. I made up stories about why she wasn't around. My friends made fun of me. I got into fights…

"Pop said I wasn't fit to be his next Guardian. He took away my birthright and gave it to Jason. Then, Jennifer took Jason from me. I kept Steven, hoping he'd inherit it…

"Then your friend showed up and ruined everything. I offered her twice what she paid. But she refused. What was I supposed to do?" Running his thick fingers through his greasy hair, he glared at me. "For as long as I remember, everyone took from me… Heaven took my mama. Pop took my birthright. Wife took my son."

He stood and punched the brittle wall, leaving a fist-sized hole. His nostrils flared. His eyes flashed. "All I ever wanted was a damn chance to prove to him that I was good enough." Gasping for breath, he rushed to the other side of the curtain.

If I hadn't hated him so much, I might have felt sorry for the poor jerk.

84

JACK

I spent a restless night cramped in my car a block away from Alli's apartment. After I saw Zack arrive and head upstairs, I stayed where I was, watching for the motorhome Steven described. Poor kid. So much to give. And a big heart broken by his piss-poor excuse for a father. I had no idea what Ronald might do. I didn't tell Alli anything. The last thing she needed was more stress.

My stomach reminded me I hadn't eaten since last night's fast food burrito blowout. It was just after nine, so I drove to the closest Starbucks. Though the line was long, I stopped in, relieved myself, then picked up some treats to surprise everyone with breakfast. I even remembered to get one of those giant blueberry muffins with the sugar sprinkles for Alli.

It was past ten when I got back to their apartment. Rushing up the stairs with the sugary, caffeinated treats, I rapped on the door. No one answered. Turning, I scanned the parking lot. Liz's car was there, but Zack's was gone. *Damn.* With the dark, grey clouds hanging low in the sky, I figured he and Liz must have taken Alli to work.

Heading downstairs, I got back into my car, hoping to catch Alli before her shift. I drove over to the frame shop. Needed few things for an office gift exchange… might as well get my shopping done at the same time.

When I arrived at *Framed,* Alli wasn't at the counter. A thin, tanned gal, with long, straight auburn hair stocking shelves said she never showed up. No phone call or anything. *Damn.* I set the coffee and bag of muffins on the counter and checked my phone. Almost eleven.

I turned to a woman with bright red hair and dangly, lighted earrings standing behind the register. "Excuse me. What time is Alli supposed to be here?"

She walked back into the office, then poked her head around the corner. Her earrings reflecting off the wall as she moved her head. "Looks like ten-thirty. Got no idea why she's not here. Always lets us know if she's running late or not coming in. Good I got here early; it's been crazy busy lately with…"

I thanked her for her time, grabbed my coffee and bag, and rushed out to my car. I sipped my coffee, hoping it would help me think. Zack's car was there before I went to get the coffee, so everything was okay then. But, thirty minutes later they'd left. It was only a ten-minute trip to *Framed.* So where did they go? I checked the traffic alerts. The only major accident was a jackknifed big-rig, but that was twenty minutes in the opposite direction.

It was after eleven. My gut told me something was wrong. I called Alli's phone again. This time she answered.

"Jack, something terrible's happened…"

"What, Alli? Where are you?"

"I can't tell you… he'll hurt Liz." There was panic in her voice.

"Who will hurt Liz? Isn't she with you and Zack?"

"How did you know I was with Zack?" Her voice rose higher as we spoke.

"Alli, I went by the apartment. No one was home… Look, that doesn't make any difference. Where are you?"

"Ronald's got Liz. We were supposed to be there at eleven, but there was an accident…"

"You were in an accident…"

"No, the road's blocked. We're stuck. Ronald called. He said we were out of time..."

I struggled to understand her over honking in the background. "Hon, listen to me... Where are you? Where are you supposed to meet Ronald?"

"He said if you showed up, he'd kill her. Jack, I want to tell you but I can't. I just can't..." said Alli.

I heard Zack mention something about traffic moving and they could take the next exit, then the backroads. I started my car but didn't know which way to drive. I couldn't help her if she wouldn't... wait, she said they were stuck behind an accident. I put my phone on speaker to keep talking, then scrolled back to the accident report. A big rig jackknifed, right near the 13B exit on the 805. "Alli, are you on the 805?"

"What makes you think...?"

"Alli, answer yes or no. Are you on the 805?"

Zack responded. "Yes."

Alli muffled the phone, though I still heard her yell. "Why did you say that?"

"Ronald said *you* couldn't tell Jack," he said. "But that doesn't mean I can't answer his questions."

"Zack, are you on the 805, near that accident?"

"Yes," said Zack.

I started my car and proceeded towards the freeway, though I had no idea where I was going. "Alli, Zack, ya gotta help me out here."

Zack cleared his throat. "Ronald called last night. He had Liz. He said he'd give her back if we brought him his things. We're on our way now."

I dug my fingernails into the palms of my hands. "Where are you meeting him? Can you give me a damned hint?"

Zack coughed. "We're supposed to park by the Trolley crossing..."

"Jack, we're almost there," said Alli. "I have to go." The call ended.

Though I had a few answers, now I had more questions. *Where were they? And where were they meeting?*

85

ALLI

I glared at Zack. "Why did you tell him?"

He checked the mirrors, exited the highway, and took the back road to the cemetery. "Alli, we're not prepared to fight Ronald. Did you consider not calling Jack might get Liz killed?"

No, I hadn't. I only knew that giving Ronald the box might save her life, otherwise none of us could save her. Not Zack. Or I. Or Jack. I scanned the streets surrounding the cemetery. Still no sign of Ronald's old pickup. "He just better not have done anything stupid. It's not our fault we couldn't get there on time…"

Zack let out a long breath. "We should be there in less than five minutes. Don't give up." He looked in the rear-view mirror and brushed a stray hair behind his ear. "I can't figure why he's so bent on getting that stuff back. Why is it so important?"

Glancing at Zack, I realized he had no clue. The significance of the *Gifts*. The stories of the Guardians. Why Ronald killed to get his hands on them. *At this point, would it really make a difference to let him in on the big secret?* His fiancé was in grave danger because of my decisions.

"You really don't know do you?" I said.

He shrugged.

"It's a long story, and I don't have time to explain it all. Just know that stuff is powerful."

"Powerful? Like how?" He pointed to a sign indicating Mt. Hope's entrance was about a block away.

I let out a long sigh. "There's a pair of glasses and whoever wears them can see people's thoughts... You probably think I've been into Darius' stash, but I'm telling the truth. That's how I knew Liz was pregnant."

"Seriously?" He looked over at me as we drove through the front gates.

"Yes, and if Ronald were to get the *Gifts*, um, that's what Russell called them... if Ronald had them, he would know everything about everyone. Do you realize the havoc he'd create if he had that much power?"

Zack focused on the road. "Where's that trolley crossing? I'd seen it before when—"

"When you followed Liz out here the day of Russell's service. As much as you wanted to talk to her, that wasn't cool."

"Alli, I wasn't following her. I was out here to pay respects to someone that had just passed away..."

"Sorry. I didn't know..." I cleared my throat. "Look, there's the sign. Head over that way." My heart pounded. I wiped my sweaty palms on my pants. Taking a deep breath, I held it, then exhaled. My hands trembled as I held up my phone and talked to the screen. "Please call back. Please. Please."

We parked near a large palm tree about twenty feet from the tracks. I looked around and noticed a few people riding bicycles. A car driving the opposite direction. An old dilapidated motorhome. But no sign of Ronald's truck.

"Do you see him?" said Zack unbuckling his seat belt.

"Maybe they're not here yet." Jumping when my phone signaled a call coming in, I answered and pushed the speaker icon.

A gravelly voice chuckled. "See you finally made it."

"Ronald, we got here as fast as we could. The traffic... An accident... Please, please can I talk to Liz?"

"Wow, two pleases. You learned some manners since we last spoke." He cleared his throat. "Where's my stuff?"

My voice broke. "Is Liz still okay?"

"You don't get to ask the questions." He paused for what seemed to be forever, then continued. "See the motorhome up ahead? We're both inside getting to know each other a little better."

Zack punched himself in the thigh and gritted his teeth. As he opened his mouth, I put my finger over my lips and whispered. "Don't let him get to you. We're so close."

Ronald coughed and spit. "Here's what's gonna happen. You're going to get out of your car with my stuff. I'm going to get out of my vehicle with your friend."

I motioned to Zack and we both exited his car. As he went back to open the trunk and remove the box, I glanced around praying I wouldn't see Jack or any police cars. A few moments later, Zack joined me in front of his Firebird. My head pounded and got fuzzy. I leaned against the car for support, then stared at the motorhome.

The door creaked open. Ronald appeared in the doorway. Stepping down onto the first step, he looked around. He continued talking to me by phone. "Making sure we're still alone." He proceeded down the steps one-at-a-time, then waited.

I saw Liz and gasped. Her hands were bound. A strip of grey duct tape covered her mouth. She was walking on her own next to Ronald holding something. Except for her hair being all wonky, she seemed okay.

He stopped again and scanned the cemetery. "So far. So good. You two bring me my stuff. We'll meet on your side."

Just as I agreed, my voice was drowned out from the dinging of the approaching trolley. Everyone froze, waiting for the crossing arms to come down. After what seemed several minutes, the two-car trolley whooshed by. Zack and I continued walking, then stopped about fifteen feet from the tracks.

Ronald and Liz stood on the other side. I still couldn't tell what she was holding. Maybe a stuffed animal? When we came within talking distance, he hung up and shoved his phone in his back pocket, then reached into his jacket and pulled out a small gun. "Now don't none of you get any weird ideas or do something stupid. I came to get my stuff. But until I do…" He held the gun against Liz's rounded belly. As he shoved her forward with his other hand, she whimpered and opened her arms.

I gulped. *Tippy Toes?*

Liz's eyes were wild. She was trembling.

I stared at the cat wanting to believe it was really her, but it was so tiny and thin.

Ronald kept the gun tight against Liz they walked across the tracks. He motioned to a spot on the freshly-mowed grass and glared at Zack. "Set it right there."

"Be careful," I said. "Please just do what he says."

"Good advice." Ronald scoffed. "After all, we wouldn't want someone to get hurt now, would we?"

Zack carried the box to the designated spot. After setting it down, he stepped back a few feet.

With the gun still pressed to her stomach, Ronald nudged Liz closer to the box. Staring at Zack, he scowled, "Open it. Show me what's inside." He motioned at me. "I wanna make sure she didn't leave nothin' out."

Zack inched up to the box, crouched down, and opened the lid. He pulled back the flaps. Holding up each item, he called them off. "Hat… Glasses… Paintbrush… Pen… Book…" Placing them back in the box, he stood. "You have what you came for. Now let her go."

Ronald stiffened. "You little piss ant of a boyfriend. Who are you to be telling me what to do? I should just shoot her right now."

Liz flinched as he jabbed the gun deeper into her side.

Zack balled up his fists and lunged at Ronald. "You jerk. If you kill Liz, you'll kill your grandchild."

86

ZACK

Ronald shoved Liz at me countering my advance. "What did you just say?"

Grasping her around the waist before she fell on the hard, gritty pavement, I brought her in close to my chest. The cat kept out of her arms and took off. I turned back to Ronald. "I said, if you shoot Liz, you'll kill your own grandkid." Lowering her to the grass, I winced as I yanked the duct tape from the skin around her mouth. "I'm so sorry," I whispered to her.

Ronald gasped. "My grandkid?" He pointed the gun at my face. "Jason? You're supposed to be dead."

I shrugged my shoulders and stared him down. "According to my mom, so were you."

Ronald kicked the box toward the tracks and glared at me. "You got some nerve showing up after all this time."

Crouching down next to Liz, I stroked her face. Her wrists were raw from the zip ties. Her face was blotchy pink from where the tape had been. I wanted to stay and comfort her, but I knew I needed to refocus on Ronald and that gun. I turned and looked up at him. "I only came back to find my gran-dad."

She looked up at me, her eyes wide. "Why didn't you tell me…?"

"Hon, I just found out. I wanted to, but I didn't know how. I'm so, so sorry."

Ronald cleared his throat. "Aww. Lookie at you two. A lover's spat. Boo-friggin' hoo." He paced in front of us, pointing the gun at me, then Liz, then back to me. "Maybe I should just take care of the whole family at the same time."

Liz whimpered. "You have what you want. Just leave us alone."

I stood in Ronald's direct line of sight to her. "Just take your stuff. That's what you came for."

Ronald stopped. Then coughed hard and spit a wad of something in the gutter. "I came to take what was mine." Then he motioned to Alli. "And to take what was hers." Alli stood about fifteen feet away, crouched down holding the cat. She kept looking at me, shaking her head, and muttering something to herself. I could only imagine what she must be thinking.

Ronald cleared his throat and stared at me with dark eyes. "I thought I already took care of you and that backstabbing mother of yours. Doing it a second time… won't bother me in the least."

I braced myself as he raised the handgun and aimed it at my face.

Liz turned and flinched.

"Click," he yelled.

Alli screamed.

He let out a loud, guttural belly laugh. From his actions, I knew he enjoyed taunting us with his sadistic humor. From what he said, I realized he wanted to hurt Alli the most—emotionally, not physically. At some point, he'd stop pretending, and Liz and I would bear the brunt of his deadly games.

I needed to come up with another angle. Something that would take his mind off us for a while. *Since he hated not having that inheritance, would not knowing how to use it be worse?*

I squared my shoulders and crossed my arms. "Well, if you're going to kill us, don't you want to at least know how your stuff works?" I talked loud enough for Alli to hear. "If we're all dead before you learn the secrets it has no power." I looked back at her. "Right, Alli?"

She frowned at me.

Ronald stomped his boot on the pavement. "You're lying. How would you know?"

I motioned to Alli. "On the way over she told me unless you know how to use it, the stuff is useless." I hoped Alli bought into my plan. At least until Ronald lowered his guard or his gun.

He shouted to Alli. "That true?"

I nodded at her.

She mimicked me and nodded. "Yes, Ronald," she shouted. "It's true."

Ronald narrowed his eyes and frowned at me. "Not sure about this… But, since you volunteered to be the helpful boyfriend." He took a step closer to the box and craned his neck to peek in. Then, he looked over at Liz, motioning at her with his gun. "Boy, you better not do nothin' stupid… or she dies."

I repositioned myself to block his view of Liz while moving in closer to him. "Start with the glasses," I said.

He walked up to the box, stooped down, and dug through it. Holding the glasses in the air, he stood. "These?"

Liz whispered. "I hope you know what you're doing."

I looked back at her and winked. Then I turned back to Ronald. "Yes. Those."

"What now?" He turned them over in one hand, letting the gun droop in his other hand.

"There are a few steps to make them work. First, take off your own glasses. Once you put on the glasses, you'll need to hold the top of the frames—one side in each hand… because one is broken…" I coughed as my voice became strained from shouting, but I wanted to make sure Alli heard me.

He leaned to the side and glared at Alli. "He's making that up."

"It's the truth, Ronald." She raised her voice. "The energy needs to flow through your body. If you only use one hand, the power is broken."

I reached behind my back and gave Alli a thumbs-up. *Smart lady. That actually sounded pretty convincing.*

Ronald hesitated, then removed his own glasses, shoving them into his jacket pocket. He looked at us, then down at the "magic" glasses, as Alli called them. He turned them over and inspected them, then he looked back at me.

I detected the faint sound of the trolley bell. Damn. I didn't want any distractions, especially right now. "Put them on," I said, hoping to nudge him. "Then I'll explain how to use them so you'll know what we're thinking."

"Fine." He shoved the gun in the back pocket of his jeans and took his time adjusting the glasses on his face, making sure the unbroken side hooked behind his ear. Narrowing his eyes, he turned to me. "I can't see nothin'."

As he reached for his gun again, I shouted. "No, you have to keep your fingers on the rims, it takes a while when someone new wears them." *Man, I was never good at improv, but after this, I might go try out at one of the comedy clubs*. "It can take anywhere from three to five minutes. Be patient or you'll have to start the process all over again."

I inched backwards toward Liz and waved my hand behind me hoping she'd understand and scoot away. I looked back at Alli. She stepped behind a large oak tree. With the girls safe and Ronald without his gun, I hoped I could take tackle him before he knew what hit him. The dinging was louder. I had to keep his attention on me.

Ronald looked back at me, squinting. "How much more time? I ain't got all day." Something caught his attention and he jerked to the side. He yanked off the *Gifts* glasses and threw them into the box. While fumbling to put back on his own glasses, he dropped them on the street. "Crap." He reached into his back pocket and pulled out the gun, aiming toward me.

The crossing arms lowered. The dinging changed to clanging. The ground rumbled below me.

It was now, or never. I rushed forward.

The gun discharged.

Someone screamed.

I felt a sharp, searing pain near my hip.

Ronald grabbed the box and darted toward the tracks.

My head grew woozy.
Red flashed in front of me.
Brakes screeched.
Someone shouted.
I lost consciousness.

87

ALLI

D*id Zack just say his kid was Ronald's grandchild?* My ears rang and became numb. *Zack is Ronald's son? He's Jason?* I tried to sort out the details as the thin cat came up to me and meowed. "Tippy Toes?" I crouched down, picked her up, and held her close to me. Tears stung my eyes. Tippy Toes was still alive and Zack was Jason? Jennifer had said Jason was alive. We knew his name was Zackary. *How could he be Liz's Zack?* My brain couldn't deal with all of it right now. Ronald had a gun. That was more important.

I watched in horror as Ronald pointed the gun at Zack, then Liz. When he aimed and yelled "Click" I screamed. I couldn't help myself. *He's going to hurt someone.* I was powerless against him and that gun.

Zack stood up to his father and shouted. "Well, if you're going to kill us, don't you want to at least know how your stuff works?" He looked back at me. "Right, Alli?"

What is he talking about? Zack doesn't know anything about the *Gifts*.

Ronald kicked at something on the street. "You're lying to me…"

Zack motioned back toward me. "On the way over she told me unless you know how to use it, the stuff is useless."

Ronald shouted to me. "That true?"

Looking back at me, Zack flashed a quick smile. *He did have a plan.*

"Yes, Ronald," I said. "It's true." My heart pounded as I watched them interact. Zack convinced Ronald to take off his glasses and put the gun away. Then Zack motioned for Liz and me to get somewhere safe. I clutched my purring Tippy Toes and backed away.

As Zack took another step forward, Ronald jerked around. He yanked off the *Gifts* glasses and fumbled for his own. Zack moved closer as Ronald pulled out the gun, pointing it toward every sound.

"Zack," I screamed. "Watch out." *Did he even hear me?*

The crossing arms dropped. Ronald grabbed the box with one hand. He darted toward the tracks while waving the gun with his other hand.

As Zack jumped at Ronald, I heard a gunshot. My heart almost stopped. The scent of gunpowder burned my nostrils. Zack stopped, then hesitated as Ronald raced across the tracks. As Zack collapsed on the ground, I screamed again. Brakes screeched. The trolley slowed and came to a stop about a hundred feet from the crossing.

Although Zack lay in the middle of the road bleeding, I ran to Liz first. Still holding Tippy Toes in one hand, I patted my back pocket for my phone. *Crap. Still in Zack's car.* I needed to call for help, but I didn't want to leave Liz.

As I held her hand, tires crunched on the pavement behind me. Red and blue lights reflected off the marble statues. A car door opened, then slammed. I turned and stared as a man ran toward us.

My eyes filled with tears. "Jack…"

"Your cat?"

I nodded.

He glanced around, then focused on me. "Why didn't you tell me where you were going? You could have been killed." Squatting next to Liz, he pulled out a pocketknife. After he cut her zip ties, he reached for my hand. "You okay?"

Still trying to process what had just happened, I nodded, then pointed to Zack.

Jack rushed over to Zack. Crouching down, he touched his arm then made a call. He looked back at us. "Whatever you do, don't move him. Ambulance on the way." Then he stood and sprinted down the tracks. A female trolley operator stood near the first car.

I rubbed Liz's shoulder. "I'm so sorry. Are you okay?"

She massaged her wrists, then her stomach. "Just a bad headache. What about Zack?"

I held my cat out to her. "Do you mind?" She shook her head and took Tippy Toes from me, holding her close while I scrambling over to where Zack lay sprawled on his side, moaning.

"You're going to be okay. Jack called for an ambulance." I touched his arm, realizing this was really Jason—the person I'd searched for, for months. Right now though, all that mattered was that he and Liz were okay and Tippy Toes was alive. As I sat on the road with Zack, I heard sirens in the distance. I took a deep breath and closed my eyes, resting my chin on my chest.

Jack ran back to me as the ambulance pulled up. "Do you need medical care?"

"I'm fine. Just really shaken up. Liz doesn't look so good. I'm worried about her and the baby. And Zack…"

Jack pulled me up into his arms, then held me. "I can't believe you all did this."

I looked up into his green eyes as a gentle breeze tousled his dark hair. I swallowed hard. Tears streamed down my cheeks. "He said he would kill her. I didn't know what else to do…" I buried my head in Jack's warm chest and sobbed.

"I'm just relieved you're okay…" Jack rubbed my back. "And that it's finally over."

"What do you mean? Ronald took the box of *Gifts*…" I stepped back and looked around.

Jack touched my cheek and turned my face toward him. "Ronald's body is wedged underneath the first car. The trolley dragged him after impact. Whatever he had was destroyed…" He sighed and wrapped his arms around me.

Ronald's dead? The Gifts destroyed? But Liz was okay. Tippy Toes was alive. Waves of relief and remorse washed over me. Though Jason had been located, now his inheritance was gone, just like Russell. While I grieved the losses, I also realized for the first time in months, I was safe.

88

ALLI

I grabbed two red and green, chunky potholders from the cabinet drawer, removed the sizzling turkey from the oven, and set it on the counter. Poking the meat thermometer in the thickest part of the breast, a little puff of steam escaped as I watched the temperature rise to 165. *Perfect.* I covered it with foil to let it rest.

I checked my list. Everything was ready but the rolls. Cheryl and Darius had made mashed potatoes, gravy, and cornbread stuffing. Liz had baked her famous Carrots Au Gratin. Zack, two pies—pumpkin and apple. He'd also bought two kinds of cranberry sauces—jellied and whole berry. Jack had made some almond, green bean dish that smelled and looked amazing, plus he insisted on bringing a glazed ham, a throwback to his childhood Christmas traditions.

From the kitchen, I listened as everyone talked at once. Just home from their trip, Cheryl and Darius were in awe of everything that had happened since they'd left. Darius savored over the details, pumping his fist each time Zack recounted the final moments before the trolley ended Ronald's life.

Zack looked over at me, then limped into the kitchen. "Smells amazing in here." He reached for a chunk of turkey. "When are we eating?"

I smacked his hand. "No samples. We're waiting on guests."

He glanced around the front room. "Looks like everyone is here... Just a small bite? I'll sacrifice myself for the good of the group."

Tippy Toes padded into the kitchen and meowed.

"Look what you started." I grabbed a tablespoon, dipped it into the bowl of creamy potatoes, and handed it to him along with a pinch of turkey for my cat. "That's all you two get until we eat. Now take Liz some water and get outta here so I can finish up."

He hobbled back into the front room. The bullet from Ronald's gun had lodged in his butt cheek. Thankfully, it didn't cause muscle damage, but it would leave a good-sized scar. Plus, he wouldn't be sitting much for a while.

"Zack, I'm fine. Really." Liz pushed Zack's hand away as he handed her the water. "Please, use your cane. It'll be much easier to get around."

He grimaced as he lowered himself on the couch cushion next to her. "Just taking care of you and our baby."

It was good to see them happy again. As much as I was shocked to learn Zack was Jason, I understood his hesitancy to say anything on the way to the cemetery. I would have freaked out. And messed up his plan to save Liz. Fortunately, after granola bars and water for twenty-four hours, her doctor said she and the baby were fine, except for mild dehydration. The doctor ordered an IV to get her fluids back to normal and released her the same night. Now, Zack takes water to her at least once an hour—much to her dismay, and delight.

Tippy Toes was also dehydrated and malnourished after being locked in the RV for six weeks. The vet suggested extra-rich cat food until she gained back the lost weight. And with all of us doting over her, she was already looking like her old self again.

"Everything smells so good... I'm starving..." Jack stumbled into the kitchen and held onto the table for support.

"Seriously?" I said. "You're as bad as Zack and Tippy Toes. And after that huge breakfast of bacon and eggs?"

Jack slipped his arms around my waist and kissed the back of my neck. "But you wore me out last night... and this morning."

I nudged him away, laughing. "Drink some water or have a beer."

He looked at me and pouted. "Zack got potatoes… Tippy Toes got turkey. I want potatoes and turkey, too."

I picked up my wooden spoon ready to swat his backside when several loud knocks on the front door stopped me. I put down my "swatting" spoon and rushed into the front room with Jack following close behind.

"Downstairs Dude?" Darius shouted as he stood.

Oh man. I never had the heart to explain Ronald and his dumpster friend were the same person. I looked back at him and shook my head.

I opened the door and squeezed outside. "I didn't tell him you were coming. It's going to be a total surprise."

I came back inside and nodded to Jack, his cue to grab the remote and mute the sound. "Excuse me, everyone…" I said. I opened the door and watched Zack's face.

Zack looked at me, then the doorway. "Oh my gosh." He tottered over to the door. "Mom. I didn't know… I…"

The room fell silent as they hugged. I grabbed a tissue from my pocket and wiped my eyes. My heart swelled watching the joy on their faces.

Jennifer stepped back and smiled at Zack. "Hon, I have another surprise for you." She tugged on the arm of a tall, lanky young man. "Zachary, this is your brother. Steven." She brushed tears from her cheeks as her sons stared at each other, then hugged.

Zack looked back at me. "I don't know what to say…"

"Jack and I made arrangements for her to be here and with Steven," I said. "We wanted your entire family to be part of our Christmas dinner."

With his mom on one side and his brother on the other, he nodded and mouthed, "Thank you."

I raised my hand and pointed to the kitchen. "Now we can eat." Jack and I headed back into the kitchen. He carved the turkey and ham as I put the rolls in the oven and set the timer. After I uncovered the hot food, I set both cranberry sauces and a veggie tray on the table.

Everyone, including the cat, gathered in the kitchen ready to pounce on the nearest dish. "Wait," said Liz. A collective groan went up.

"What now?" asked Darius.

Zack leaned on the table and pulled something from his pocket. "We have an announcement."

Together they said, "We're having a boy." Zack held up a fuzzy picture of their little one, pointing to one area. "See, there's his manly parts." Everyone laughed and offered high fives, pats on the back, and hugs. One by one, they filled their plates and settled on the couch and living room floor.

After Zack filled his plate, Jennifer came up to me and gave me a big hug. "Thank you for bringing my family together again."

I blinked back tears. "I'm just glad it all worked out."

She leaned in close to me. "A few minutes ago, I heard someone mention the box was destroyed. Does that mean the inheritance is gone?"

I turned and smiled. "Actually… the box was destroyed. The inheritance wasn't."

Jennifer placed her hand to her mouth. "I don't understand."

"When Ronald had Liz, she told me she'd hidden the box in her room, so that's the one I took to the cemetery." I paused and removed the rolls from the oven, then faced her again. "After Ronald was killed I realized we'd lost the inheritance."

"Oh no," she said. "That must have been terrible."

"Yes, I couldn't believe it after all we'd gone through. Later that night, after Liz felt better, she reminded me about the box of fake items we'd put together when Ronald took my cat, Tippy Toes. We planned to use them to get her back…"

"So, without knowing, you took the fake box to get Liz?"

"It really was a genius plan." I handed her an empty plate and motioned toward the food. "Zack didn't know. He had his own plan to save Liz."

Jennifer plopped a spoonful of potatoes on her plate, along with two slices of ham. "The box that was destroyed… the fake items?"

"Yes, thank goodness. The real ones were safe here at the apartment." I walked behind her filling my plate with mashed potatoes, gravy, and turkey.

Jennifer stopped and looked back at me. "Did Zackary ever decide what he was going to do with his inheritance?"

As she spoke, Zack hobbled into the kitchen. "Someone mention my name?"

Jennifer smiled. "I was just asking Alli if you'd decided to accept your inheritance."

Zack looked down, then at his mom and at me.

Jennifer's eyes widened. "And…?"

Zack cleared his throat. "I searched for Gran-dad because I felt I was supposed to do something for him. I even changed my last name to Thomas so no one would find me.

"Finding him wasn't a coincidence. I just wish I'd been able to talk to him before he died. Though, a part of me thinks he knew I was there because the few times we made eye contact, there was a special feeling, like a bond, between us." He looked over at me again. "After Alli explained what it meant to be a Guardian, and everything she'd gone through to protect the *Gifts*, I had to accept my birthright."

Jennifer placed her hand on her heart. "Oh, Zackary…"

He limped over to her and placed his hand on her shoulder. "It's what I'm supposed to do, Mom. I hope you understand."

She nodded and looked at me.

I smiled at Jennifer. "I told Zack I'd do whatever I could to help him. Especially, since the journal is hard to decipher and there's no "*Gifts* for Dummies" book."

We laughed as Jennifer dished up a second plate and helped Steven get settled in the front room with Cheryl, Liz, and Darius.

Zack smiled at me. "Thanks for being strong and refusing to give back the *Gifts* to my father. If it wasn't for you, who knows what could have happened…"

I twirled my spoon in my mashed potatoes. "I'm not strong at all. If you only knew…"

Zack touched my arm and looked me in the eyes. "Alli, you are the strongest, bravest person I know. You stood up to Ronald. You used the *Gifts* to find my mother. And you saved my fiancé and our baby. Maybe you don't believe it, but you are an amazing person. That's why Gran-dad chose you to be the Guardian."

I shook my head. "I just did what Russell always told me to do."

"And what was that?" asked Zack.

"Follow my heart." I turned and joined my friends in the front room. After I was settled on the floor, I picked up a small piece of turkey and was about to feed it to the cat when Jack jumped up. I cocked my head as he rushed down the hallway. "What the…"

"Hold on, Alli," he said. "I have something for you." He came back and handed me a bag.

"What's this?"

"I saw it and thought it would make a good addition to your tree. Kinda like an ornament to celebrate… us."

Peeking into the bag, I grinned and pulled out small box—an ornament from the Disney store. Snow White and Prince Charming embracing with little sparkly twinkles around them. "This is great. I love it." I reached up and hugged him, relaxing in his strong arms. At that moment, nothing else mattered. I was safe. "My hero."

He closed his eyes, then pumped his fist. "Yes. She called me her hero." Sitting down next to me, he whispered in my ear. "Anything for you, Princess."

ACKNOWLEDGMENTS

I am fortunate to have had so many people support me while I wrote this book.

Thanks to my family. To my husband, David, thank you for putting up with my moments of crazy when words eluded me. To my daughter, Michelle, thanks for answering my questions and providing me with updated lingo when I needed help. To my son Brian, I appreciate your support and all the bestseller books as Christmas gifts each year. Each one helped me believe in myself. To my son Matt, thanks for understanding when I needed quiet to write and rescheduled band practice. And also for your help with terminology for dialogue passages.

Thanks to my critique partners. My Monday night and Wednesday morning critique group members: Sue, Donnee, Jennifer, Larry, and Tabi; along with Jenny, Cynthia, Annis, Sandy, Brian, Michelle; and all the others who read countless versions of my manuscript. Through complete rewrites, to changes in point of view, your comments and suggestions made me a better writer. Your encouragement kept me going and helped me realize I wasn't wasting my time.

Thanks to those who helped with the specialized stuff. For the information about police procedure and terminology, thanks to my long-time friend Jeff Santos, who shared his expertise and knowledge, along with answering all of my technical questions. Many thanks to B. Adam Richardson with The Writer's Detective for answering my questions, offering help, and responding so quickly to my email questions. Any mistakes with police procedure are my responsibility.

I'm grateful for my friend, Sandy Moffett, who generously shared her knowledge about funerals, cemeteries, and burial procedures. Again, any mistakes in these areas are mine alone.

Many thanks to my sports expert extraordinaire friend, Bruce McDavid, for answering my football-related questions. Any sports-related mistakes are my responsibility.

Thank you to Cathy Walker of Cathy's Covers for the amazing cover design. I'm also very grateful to Todd Sturgell for designing the Red Knot logo. You both created what I had envisioned from the beginning.

And to all of my readers, thank you so much for reading *Guardian of the Gifts*. It would mean a lot to me if you would take a moment to leave a review on Goodreads or your favorite online retailer.

I welcome contact from my readers. Find me at joanraymondwriting.com to sign up for my newsletter to be notified of new releases, read my blog, and find me on social networking.

BOOKS BY JOAN RAYMOND

For Adults

WOMEN'S FICTION

Guardian of the Gifts (2019)

BEE'S KNEES MYSTERY SERIES

Crafty Alibis: Book One (2021)

Crafty Motives: Book Two (Spring 2022)

For Kids

METAMORPHOSIS SERIES

Fly on the Wall: Book One (2020)

Spaghetti and Meatball: Book Two (Spring 2022)

Made in United States
North Haven, CT
16 March 2023

34121773R00193